Contents

Gutter
Editorial

What a difference a year makes. Unemployment soaring, stratospheric national debt, England crashing out of the World Cup, a Tory prime minister prising open the door to Number 10 with his yellow-tinged fingernails, festival goers partying in the summer fields, and a sharp, relevant literary magazine leading Scottish writing into a new decade. Why, it's like 1970 all over again. Except that magazine is *Gutter*.

We are one, happy birthday to us. Over that first, tentative year we have read much, learned more and received encouragement and criticism in pleasantly unequal measure. We hope, however, to have listened carefully to both. If one thing has become increasingly clear to us, it is that what we hoped a year ago holds true: there is an indisputable need for this magazine, for a well-founded home for the best new Scottish writing.

Our belief that good writing deserves good presentation was rewarded in May when *Gutter* won Best Publication and also the coveted Chairman's Award at the Scottish Design Awards 2010 (and was Commended for its typography). Credit for this achievement goes in no small measure to our designer, Stephen Kelman, who has made real our brief for a simple, stylish layout that is entirely subservient to the written word.

*

But *Gutter* doesn't simply exist between the covers you are now holding. In contemporary culture, any magazine that does not reach out to new readers – and listenerships – will quickly find itself irrelevant. This year has seen *Gutter* on the road (if you'll pardon the allusion) to events in Wigtown, Glasgow, St Andrews and Edinburgh. We have held three highly popular reading and music nights, including our *Night in the Gutter* strand at the National Library of Scotland and, this August, we are delighted to be hosting *McSex* – a rare celebration of Scottish erotic literature – as part of the Edinburgh International Book Festival's *Unbound* programme on Sunday August 15th. We consider this work as vital to the literary health of the nation as the printed magazine.

*

This issue, it so happens, is dominated by the excellent new work being produced by Scotland's women writers. We start with a wonderful piece from Glasgow-based Canadian writer Michaela Maftei. Then we have a new short story from the queen of Scottish noir, Louise Welsh. Recent debut novelists Kirsten McKenzie and Elaine diRollo provide a short story and second novel extract respectively. Zoë Strachan also shares an extract from her much anticipated third novel. We have a sneak preview of acclaimed short story specialist Colette Paul's contribution to *The Year of Open Doors*, a new anthology of Scottish writing from Cargo.

Macallan winner, Dorothy Alexander, hits home with a sequence of hospital-based flash fictions and there is new poetry from former StAnza Festival director, Brian Johnstone, Hazel Frew and Bridget Kursheed, while Sally Evans, editor of *Poetry Scotland*, closes the verse section with a piece about that 'infuriating lesbian', the muse. Among writers likely to be new to you is Jenni Fagan, with a magic realist *tour de force* and new work from Marion McCready, whose first collection is currently in incubation.

From the gentlemen, we have new prose from Ewan Gault, who makes it a hat-trick, already having appeared in *Gutter* 01 and 02, and a Carnbeg story by one of our favourite writers, Ronald Frame. Carl MacDougall, novelist, short story writer, editor and great literary educator, provides a new story, and you get two for the price of one from Ewan's Morrison's new story collection, *Tales from the Mall*. Stuart Finlayson's bitterly funny (and in moments highly charged) *More Death in Venice* is another wonderful contribution. The poets are represented by Graham Fulton,

Andrew C Ferguson (and his spot on poem, *Scotland as an Xbox game*), a damning piece by Rob A. Mackenzie and *Poetry Scotland* regular Jim Ferguson.

*

'Why do we write?' a question with such a multiplicity of extant answers that to ask it seems quite banal. To quote Kenneth Goldsmith's paraphrasing of conceptual artist Douglas Huebler's sentiment, 'the world is full of texts, more or less interesting; I do not wish to add any more.' A strange comment for the editorial column of a new writing magazine, you might think. But the response is more complex. In a world saturated with unparalleled quantities of existing 'text', what is the virtue of adding more? For us, as editors, the joy is in the transcription, the collation of others' work, and its communication to a thinking readership that, we imagine, appreciates the gesture. Believe it or not, we take pleasure in reading everything we receive (no, it's true), no matter the stage of development of the submitting writer. There is value and integrity in every piece. However, we make no apology for being driven by the desire to discover the work that genuinely deserves as wide an audience as possible. We have high standards, and aim to maintain them at all costs. But we all – readers, writers, editors – must learn to navigate through the sea of writing that already surrounds us, and it is this point that we wish to convey to prospective *Gutter* submitters: before you get creative, get uncreative, then recreate. Read and rewrite the work of people you admire, type out The Bible, do anything that teaches you more about the physical properties of good writing. Push away what Tom Leonard calls 'the suffocating weight of a static, supposedly integral cultural past'.

Where are all the experimenters? As you might expect, much of the work we are sent as editors is derivative. A scarily larger portion is competent but anaesthetised. Although it may be well-written, possibly in the style of someone else, it does not get under the skin. It is stage two writing. To reach stage three, rip it up and start again. Take risks, send us the risks, take risks again. We are in a Depression, where new movements should blossom. So read this, get thriving, and send us the good stuff.

Melissa
Micaela Maftei

WE DROVE ACROSS the country when I was twelve. It was summer vacation; we had a lot to get away from. I was bored with the trappings of childhood and wondered why everyone around me seemed to think they were in any way still relevant to me. When we got to Pennsylvania we rented a small boat and paddled it around a lake. Only one person was allowed to steer the boat at a time and it couldn't be my father because he was busy videotaping the whole thing. My brother and I ducked violently out of the way of the camera; we found my father's insistence on videotaping tedious and embarrassing, even when there was no one else around to witness it.

My time controlling the boat was unfairly short. When it was my brother's turn I gave up the job unwillingly, ungracefully. He was too brash and energetic. Didn't he know boat trips were supposed to be lazy, slow affairs? He didn't know anything about boats. I was the person for the job. I asked to take over again and my father said no. I assumed a cold, silent indifference.

I saw the video again ten years later, when my father was going through his things in preparation for moving out of the house and into a condo. I was appalled. Every ten second a disembodied little girl's voice could be heard off-camera, a whining, high-pitched complainer. The voice interrupted the person talking and managed to jostle the boat constantly, as though talking was a whole-body experience. 'Now can I do it, Dad?' it asked. After every answer it said, 'come on, *now* can I?'

Watching the evidence, I pretended that I still lacked any interest whatsoever in the record of the trip, to spare myself the image that contradicted everything I remembered. Maybe if the grizzly bear we had seen had been caught on film it would not have been the behemoth I remember, maybe it would have been the size of a river rat. Maybe the time my father spilled tea in the tent and burned his leg would have been a legitimate accident and not just our dad always trying to make something interesting happen, pretty pathetic, actually, were all immigrants like this?

This became one of the million things I tell and re-tell to Robert in bed, the place where we talk best. The boat story was one of the first I returned to when it started looking more and more certain that Melissa wasn't coming back.

'This is a story about your childhood,' Robert reminded me. 'There's no reason it has to have anything to do with Melissa.'

'Everything has to do with Melissa,' I told him. How could he not know this? Even things that had happened years before she was born. Robert and I had never taken any videos. The memory of those endless tapes, carefully labeled, had never stopped making me shudder. Who wants to recall the painful awkwardness of their childhood? Melissa would grow up without being prodded into a frame, sunburnt and sullen. We'd been firm on that.

Another thing I remind him of is the story of my mother turning white as a sheet and passing out when I had meningitis at age six. I don't remember this story actually happening, but it was told to me often enough that I might as well.

'A headache isn't meningitis,' Robert said, 'you didn't actually have meningitis.'

'You're right. A headache is a headache and meningitis is meningitis.' I tell him, 'but the story is about my mother and how she didn't know that at the time.'

'Your poor mother.'

'Poor nothing. That was her life. Old Country.' She'd had her coffee grounds read once and been told her first child would die young. Enough to make anyone turn white and pass out.

'She hadn't even taken you to the doctor!'

'Jesus, Robert, you don't argue with coffee grounds. It's like the weather report. You don't argue with it, you just listen to it and you plan.'

'That's why she came to America? To fulfill the coffee grounds?'

'No. She came to America because of the communists. But not even communists have power over the coffee grounds. You're out of your league here, honey.'

He shook his head. 'You don't have to reinterpret your whole life to try and make sense of what's happening,' he said.

In the end it was my mother herself who died young. Maybe she'd been holding her own mother's coffee cup, I always thought, even though it wasn't possible, someone would have noticed a thing like that. It was just an honest mistake. In the end the oldest child of the oldest child gave birth to an oldest child who ran away from home when she was fifteen. I had a rough idea of where Melissa was spending most of her time, a gutted house whose lawn was filled with empty beer bottles and deflated packs of cigarettes. At the start I would leave bags of groceries on the steps, picking my way though the rotten boards and trying not to look through the windows. We never changed our own locks. It was terrifying but deeply satisfying to come home and see that she had pilfered some small comforts while the house was empty – a bag of pasta, a pillow, some nail polish. When she started taking jewelry I had to lock it up, and that made her presence slowly withdraw from our bedroom.

'Maybe she never wanted to move to Oregon,' Robert offered one night, talking into the pillow.

'Who ever wants to move to Oregon?' I asked, mildly. We were over Oregon. Oregon was just the word we used for all the things that maybe we shouldn't have done. Oregon was the word we used for the life that happens even though you'd really prefer something different. Oregon was the whipping boy. When we couldn't find a parking spot in town, it was because we'd moved to Oregon. When the convenience store closed five minutes before one of us remembered we needed something, it was because we lived in Oregon. When it rained – well, that actually was because we lived in Oregon.

It was in bed, of course, when Robert had first introduced the idea.

'And they would give me a pretty handsome relocation amount.'

'Since when do you use the word handsome?'

'Well, I don't. I guess Ted did.'

'God, he has that awful drawl.'

'You're not getting the point.'

'Of course I'm getting the point. They want you to go to Oregon and you have to say no.'

'It's a lot of money.'

'For Oregon, I bet it is. I could sell bananas and make money in Oregon.'

'What are you talking about? It's not the end of the world. Oregon is nice.'

'Honey, we live in California. Why would we want to go to Oregon?'

'Neither of us has been there.'

'Well neither of us has been to Sudan, but let's not move there either, ok?'

In the end I was the one who made us move to Oregon. When I was pregnant with Melissa, Robert repulsed me. The way he smelled, the feeling of his body anywhere near mine. I made him sleep in another room. Seeing hairs in the sink after he shaved was enough to make me retch. He had to do his own laundry. He eventually treated me like a leper, leaving out food and clearing the room. One evening I

➤

picked up the house phone in the middle of the night.

'What is it?' I snapped, 'who is this?'

'I miss you so much,' said Robert.

'Where are you? Hello?' I struggled to sit up and inside my body Melissa kicked up a fuss.

'I'm right here,' he said. I suddenly heard his voice from the spare bedroom.

'Are you using your cell phone? Honey, I was sleeping.'

'I can't sleep without you. I really miss you.'

I hoisted both of us out of bed and waddled down the hall. The smell of him was sunken into the carpets. He wiggled over, making room in the too-small bed. I had brought one of my own old t-shirts and held it close to my face like a damp rag against smoke.

'Soon she'll be born. Soon things will be normal.' My doctor had told me this when I begged for a cure. I was sure she only half-believed my claims that the smell and sight of my husband nauseated me.

'I hate this.'

'Don't say that. She can hear you. She can hear us.'

Robert buried his head in my arms.

'No, no, don't. God, I'm so sorry. I have to go. Here, take this.' I left him the t-shirt and staggered back to the bedroom.

But Robert was the only man who repulsed me. No one else did, and one in particular did not at all. I couldn't tell him until after Melissa was born and it was all safely over.

'It was a crazy thing, Robert, remember how crazy it was?'

'No, I don't remember. I didn't know anything about it.'

'I mean the whole time. The whole time was crazy, honey.'

'What do you mean by crazy? Are you fifteen? Things just got, like, you know, crazy and all?'

'It was just a... crazy thing,' I faltered, 'it doesn't matter. It never mattered.'

'Who has an affair with a pregnant woman?'

'What does that have to do with it? I mean, lots of people. I don't know. People do. But it doesn't matter.'

Melissa was sleeping under the table. She could sleep through anything. Still I hated the idea that the words were entering her mind, curling up and waiting to activate when she was grown, when she wouldn't know what to do with them.

'Don't you tell me this doesn't matter. Look at me. Look at this mattering to me.'

'I know, I mean, it does matter. But it also doesn't matter.'

'You always want it both ways.'

'Please let's not drag anything else into this.'

'I guess that would make it inconvenient for you.'

'Please Robert, please. I told you so that this could go away.'

'Go away where? This is how you make things go away?'

'No, but, you know. To somehow. I don't know. Deal with it.'

'Oh yeah, sure, maybe you know a gypsy spell or something?'

'That's so rude.'

'I spent fucking months in exile in my own fucking house. I spent months waiting for the chance that maybe you would take pity on me and give me, oh, I don't know, a cup of coffee? Maybe ask me about my day? Months.'

'And what, you're jealous? Of a lay? You're my husband. My *husband*.'

'Maybe you should have remembered that. Do not interrupt me. I spent months while you treated me like a fucking parasite and spent your time hauling your pregnant ass all over town.'

'Robert, please. These are the kinds of words you are going to remember saying to me forever. Until the day you die.'

'You think I don't know that?'

We did that for weeks, until one night he came home and watched me nursing Melissa and told me that either all three of us moved or he moved. That was the last argument.

'Robert, I don't think you should take a job in a crappy place because I did something stupid.'

'You think it's a crappy place. I don't think that. You're just so fucking deaf to anyone else's opinion.'

'It's *outside of* Portland. Since when do you want to live outside of anywhere? This is our home. This is our city.'

'I can't stand walking around anymore. I can't stand looking at everyone's face.' I had never told him who it was. It was someone we both knew, who I still saw regularly around the neighborhood.

'My god Robert, you want to blame everyone you see? I wasn't lying when I said it was over. I don't care if I see this person every day for the rest of my life.'

'Well, I do. I do. I care a lot.'

'So what if we see each other in the grocery store?' I yelled, exasperated. 'How many times do you want me to say it? I choose you I choose you I choose you!' I screamed dementedly. Melissa woke up and started to scream too. *This is how you destroy something*, I thought, as I started rocking her stupidly, shushing her.

'What does it matter? What does it matter! The grocery... don't give me this John Updike shit. Why don't you guys have coffee every Saturday morning and you can tell him all about how you chose me while he goes down on you.'

'Don't be coarse.'

'*Coarse* you fucking harlot, that's rich.'

So we moved to Oregon.

The first time she stayed out all night I came home with a bad feeling in my bones. Robert was already lying in the bed, still wearing all his clothes, when I got home. He heard me come into the room but didn't bother lifting his head out of the pillows.

'I don't like the way this is going.'

I took my socks off slowly. Until then it had been limited to broken curfews and screaming matches over short skirts and makeup and rolling papers found in jean pockets.

'I really don't.'

I lay down beside him. 'It's only seven.'

'She's not coming home.'

'I've told you a hundred times. If you say it it comes true.' My mother had taught me that.

'The problem is she has no fear.'

'I thought we were trying to raise her not to have fear?'

'Don't you think a fifteen year old girl should have some fear? Of something?'

'It's only seven. Let's make something to eat. Let's not get ahead of ourselves.'

But he was right. That was the first night.

We tried everything. These are some of the things we tried: notes, phone messages, screaming, bribery, coaxing, crying, begging, threatening, ordering, pretending we were getting high blood pressure (which we probably were), calling the police, taking turns driving around in the car with the lights on, sweeping up and down deserted streets. On her sixteenth birthday Robert and I sat alone at the kitchen table, shell-shocked, speaking in half-sentences, distracted by the images of her we were having.

I saw her once on the street, torn jeans and biting her fingernails, and tailed her. That was the first time I saw the house. When she took a key out of the mailbox and unlocked the door I closed my eyes and leaned my head against the steering wheel. After half an hour she came outside with a boy and another girl about her age and they smoked a cigarette on the porch, kicking an empty beer can back and forth. When she went back inside I drove home and went straight to bed.

'What did he look like? Who is this kid?'

'Robert, he's just some boy. It has nothing to do with him. He's not the first, I'm sure.'

'I want to kill this boy.'

'It's not the boy's fault, Robert.'

'I want to kill this boy with my hands. With one hand. I could kill this boy with one finger. Just by looking at him.'

'She has a roof over her head. She's not sleeping on the street.'

'I want you to tell me where it is.'

'Not until you promise you won't go there.'

I stopped going to work. I took whatever leave they would give me and after that I just started

➡

calling in sick.

'You're going to get fired.'

'Who cares?'

'You need to eat. We need to eat.'

'Do you not have this guilt that sits on you? That just sits and waits?'

'Of course I do.'

'So what the hell are you telling me about eating for? What the fuck are you talking about?'

Finally I took him to the house; one night we both went. We circled the blocks, drove past Melissa's old school, changed radio stations nervously, peered through the black night at every person walking on the street. When I parked in front of the house Robert said, 'what?'

'Here it is.'

'This?'

'You wanted to see it.'

Robert opened the car door.

'Don't. Don't don't don't.'

He ran across the street without looking and pounded on the door. The skinny boy from before opened it. He tried to close the door and Robert held it open. They talked for a few minutes. When Robert shoved the boy backwards into the house I screamed and got out of the car.

'Come back here!' I shouted across the street. 'Both of you, come back here.' I was too scared to follow him and when a police cruiser drove by I flagged it down madly.

'Please help me. Please will you get them please?'

One of them led me back to the driver's seat and stood by the car with me. She had called the police on us. It was no crime to run away once you were 16. The second officer led Robert back to the car calmly and told him he was lucky the boy hadn't wanted to press assault charges.

'Didn't she look sad to you?' he pleaded with the officer. 'Couldn't you see how sad she was?'

'Is she allowed to do this?' I kept asking, 'is she really allowed?'

From then on we started having the kind of tearful, half-spoken conversations that people in movies have.

'I never meant-'

'Of course not.'

'But I feel-'

'There was nothing you could have-'

'If only-'

'She was so small.'

'This is all my fault.'

'Don't say that.'

We would fall asleep that way, in the middle of sentences, still wearing our clothing, exhausted from the pressure of hating everything we had done for sixteen years in case that was what had done it.

Eventually I went back to work. Eventually Robert and I went out for dinner and paid parking tickets and returned library books and forgot to pick things up at the grocery store. Eventually I could drive home from work past the house without crying. *Eventually* has become *now*. Last week I drove home one day and suddenly there was a For Sale sign posted on the lawn. I nearly lost control of the car. She had been coming by the house less and less. The next day I left her a massive note on the kitchen counter – SAW HOUSE FOR SALE PLEASE TELL ME WHERE YOU'RE LIVING. I pinned twenty bucks to the paper. I considered leaving fifty. When I came home I saw she had left a mark on the page, in heavy black lipstick. I picked it up to kiss it back and looked closer at the shape of the lips. It did not look like a kiss. It looked like a sneer.

A Simple Life

Louise Welsh

DAVID PRESTON STILL felt his wife Michelle's presence, though he could no longer remember her name or what she looked like. She was represented by a sense of anxiety, ownership and resentment which they had called love, though it might as easily been described as duty, co-dependency and shared interests.

Their shared interests were also there in the small side ward which David had been removed to the night before. Lauren and young Davie, aged thirty-five and forty-three respectively. David Preston no longer had any awareness of his son and daughter's existence, though concern for their wellbeing had been the mainstay of his life ever since he quit the drink thirty years ago, and had filled a large portion of his thoughts even before then.

David Preston had all but gone now. His obituary notice would be the same as his own father's, *Died after a long struggle*. Reading it back in 1973 David had thought, 'Aye, that'd be life'. But David had no real thoughts now, just dreams and half filtered memories, colours and shapes drifting through the morphine swim he was floating in. The pain had been awful. Hard on everyone. But now it was over. Everything was almost over.

David Preston didn't hear young Davie ask Lauren if she wanted to take their mum for a cup of tea, or Michelle's, 'I want to stay with your Dad', the flurry of jagged words formed in his family's attempt to express their love for each other. It would have irritated him. Always nip, nip, bicker, bicker. But David Preston perceived none of it, not even Michelle's sobbing or the click of the door as his son left the room. He was somewhere else, a world of vague and swirling ambers.

In life David had been a smartly dressed man, though never a dandy; more inclined to Marks & Spenser than Pringle. Now his skin had taken on a pale, scrofulous look, his chin was unshaved, the bristles coming through grey and scraggy; strange that they should still grow while the rest of him was closing down. He resembled one of the tramps that had been a regular feature of Glasgow in his youth, or maybe an aged earthquake victim glimpsed on a news report being pulled from the wreckage of a collapsed building. 'Poor old soul,' David would have said. 'He's not going to make it. They shouldn't show that on the TV.'

David smacked his flaking lips and muttered, 'Drink'.

'What's that Dad?'

His daughter put her ear close to his mouth and perhaps he heard her because he muttered again. 'Drink.'

Lauren moistened her father's mouth. It was all that she could do. The doctors had cut all other nutrients and now it was a slow race between starvation and the cancer.

'Drink.' The dry lips smacked again. 'Whisky.'

David had first tasted spirits around the age of five. A sip stolen from an uncle's almost empty glass left overnight on the coffee table after some family celebration or other. His uncle hadn't been a particularly suave man and David, or young Davie as he'd been while his father was alive, had fished a drowned dout from the bottom of the glass before raising the magic liquid to his lips. It tasted like poison. He coughed and felt a familiar pain in his head caused, not by the whisky, but the back of his mother's hand connecting with his ear. Sometimes he thought it was a wonder he could hear anything at all.

Alcohol had left David Preston's life for many years after that first adventure. That is, the taste of alcohol left his life, but 'the drink', as his mother called it, was all around him. It scented the breath of his father and uncles on days when they came back cheery. It gave a swing to his granddad's stagger as he made his way home in late afternoon. Drink was magical. It transformed sober adults into singers. Even his mother would take a shandy or two and give them 'Danny Boy'. But it was there too in the bruises on their neighbour Mrs Mitchell's face. And more than once David was woken by voices blurred of edges shouting words he'd been told not even to whisper. Somehow he knew that was drink too.

In their teens David and his pals would spend Friday nights loitering outside one or other of the neighbourhood's corner pubs, hoping that one of the men reeling out from the mysterious depths would be moved to generosity and tip them enough for a poke of chips. Or that some woman, too shy to go in herself, would commission them to find her husband and send him home for his tea. The boys would kick a ball around or play pitch and toss, but David always had one ear cocked for the swing of the saloon door, savouring the glimpse of warmth and manly camaraderie, the roar of laughter or snatch of well told story that drifted into the street. The corner bars had seemed like a heaven to David, somewhere marvellous that you would be admitted to in the sweet by-and-by. High expectations often lead to disappointment, but David's father had taken him to Gibson's on his eighteenth birthday for his first official pint.

Gibson's was a temple to alcohol. The pub's windows were made from stained glass, as elaborate as any church's. But instead of showing the lives of saints, or what might befall sinners who slipped from the path of righteousness, Gibson's windows were decorated with portraits of poets. Rabbie Burns curled his lips in a smile and lifted a rose, ready to exchange it for a kiss. Sir Walter Scott looked up from his manuscript, a hard working man, but still fond of a well-earned dram. Robert Louis Stevenson, hair long, moustache drooping, smiled dreamily, a cigarette crooked between his fingers. Above the door was inscribed the legend, *Freedom an whisky gang thegither*. All of these decorations were merely adjuncts to the bar itself, a large oak carved Victorian masterpiece, the capital of the little city that was Gibson's, Vatican to all the rest's Rome. Glass shone behind the gantry too. And standing before and beyond it, there in itself and in its reflection, transformed and transforming, were regiments of spirits lined straight as soldiers ready to die for their country.

The only woman in the room was the barmaid, her black skirt tight, white blouse frothed with frills. She pulled on the beer pump with lowered eyes that met David's when she placed the golden drink before him.

His father sucked the head off his pint. 'Thanks Mary, and one for yourself.'

David had been impressed by Gibson's, but it had been his father's generosity that amazed him. That this man who balked at even necessary expenses should bestow a drink on a virtual stranger was astounding. But drink, as he was to discover, had the power to alter folk.

'What did he say?' Young Davie stepped back into the hospital anteroom. It might have been the harsh fluorescent lights that gave his eyes a red tinge.

'I'm not sure.' Lauren flashed a look that said, *don't ask*. 'I think he's thirsty.'

'Whisky.' Michelle's voice was as grey and expressionless as her husband's face. 'He asked for whisky.'

'Are you sure?'

But there was no need for anyone to answer young Davie's question, because his father said it again, more clearly this time.

'A whisky.'

The dancing had been the place to go and meet girls. The dancehalls were unlicensed and you abandoned your bottles and your blades at the door with no hope of getting them back. The trick was to have a few beers before you went. Not a skin-full – that hampered the chances of a lumber – but enough to take the edge off and give you the courage to invite a girl to dance.

It was all jiving back then, rocking and a rolling, slipping and a sliding. David had been pretty good, though not as good as some. It was a manly kind of dancing. Not like the hip shaking and bum wiggling that came later. It required strength to fling a woman over your shoulder and make sure she touched the ground safely, especially some of the women that went to the Barralands. Back then David Preston had enjoyed a drink, but it was a Friday night, Saturday evening thing and no real hardship to go without one during the week. It was later that it seemed to take over.

Lauren moistened her father's lips.

Young Davie said, 'It's not water he's wanting.'

'I don't happen to have a bottle of Bells in my bag.' Lauren snapped.

'I won't have you arguing with each other across your father's deathbed.'

It was the first time that anyone had mentioned death out loud and Davie looked at his feet. 'Sorry.' He walked across the room and put a hand on his sister's shoulder just as their father spoke again.

'Whisky.'

'Shit,' it was a mark of his distress that young Davie didn't realise he'd sworn in front of his mother. 'Do you think I should go out and get him some?'

'Dad doesn't drink.'

David's breaths came hoarse and rattling from the bed. His family kept silent, each one locked in their own thoughts. Then the voice croaked again. 'Whisky.'

Lauren giggled. It was a high, nervous, unexpected sound, loud in the small room. 'Sorry.' She held her face in her hands and it was hard to tell if she was laughing or crying.

Davie looked at his mother. 'What will we do?'

They said that if your father was an alcoholic, odds were you'd be one too. David Preston's father had liked a drink, no doubt about that, but he knew when to stop. At first David had too. He was never sure when it had all got out of hand. Maybe it was the job. Working in kitchens was thirsty work and there was generally a bottle or two waiting at the end of the night to quench the thirst of the hotel's waiters, chefs and kitchen porters. They manned one of the busiest hotels in Scotland and it was a relief to sit back with a drink in your hand after the controlled madness that made up their evenings. It was a chance to laugh at their mistakes, smooth words said in the heat of the moment – heat of the ovens – for the waiters to relay what dishes had gone down well, for the chefs to mingle with the front of house. It was letting off steam time, and there was always easy company waiting if you wanted more. Who cared if the pubs had shut? There were pool halls, shabeens, private clubs, house parties and waitresses who liked to wind down before they went to bed. Hell, they were all unwinding, rocking and a rolling, slipping and a sliding.

It might have been the death of his parents, his father first, his mother six months later, that altered the quality of his drinking. It was certainly true that David got beyond drunk after his mother's funeral. Ever afterwards, the thought of her death was tied up with a cringing embarrassment at the unremembered night. The grief that needed to be drowned.

But perhaps it was merely some accident in his chemical makeup that made David Preston thirstier than all of his friends. He loved the flinging off of his conscious self, the elation the third drink brought, the hilarity that followed the fourth or fifth, the cleansing nature of a night on the batter, the blessed release of it. After a few drams David knew he was faster, wittier, cleverer than his sober self. His erudition was unconfined. He found himself an expert

→

on subjects workaday David Preston professed himself ignorant of. He was *passionate*. Could hold his own with anyone, be they lecturer, lawyer or lord. He could *astound*. And it had no effect on his work. No effect whatsoever. He could swear to it. Swear on the bible. Not that he was a religious man you understand. But after a half a bottle David Preston (Presto it should have been because surely to God he was a fucking wizard), David Preston was still able to run a busy kitchen better than any of these London fuckers and was still as fast with a chopping knife as any magician.

David had got drunk at his and Michelle's wedding, blind, reeling, legless. Eventually his best man and one of Michelle's brothers had hooked him under the oxters and hauled him senseless up to the honeymoon suite. The other men were three sheets to the wind, but sober as nuns compared to David. He had woken in the night, knocked over the bedside lamp and staggered to the unfamiliar bathroom, where he was gloriously, gut wrenchingly, jaw stretchingly sick. All the wedding meal, the vole au vents and titbits carefully deliberated over and painstakingly prepared by his staff, were consigned to the porcelain. It was a wonder Michelle didn't leave him right there and then. She didn't leave him though. Not then, not ever. Sometimes he thought she must be stupid. There were times when he told her so, times when he shouted at her to leave and times when he begged her not to.

When he had finally managed to quit for good David trained himself to think of his drinking days as a waste of a youth. He forced himself to remember the guarded looks his children had started to glance his way and exiled all memories of the soaring rightness he felt when the alcohol fused with the electrons in his brain. Because there had been good times, very good times, times when he had known the secret of living.

'There's an off-licence close to where I parked. I could go and get something if you want?' Young Davie, soon to become big Davie, looked at his mother.

Lauren's voice was small and frightened.

'Dad worked hard to get off the drink. I don't think we should sabotage his efforts when he's not well enough to know what's going on.'

The dry lips moved again and the almost-corpse whispered, 'Whisky.'

David looked at Michelle sitting drained and miserable by her husband's bed.

'Mum?'

What a lot of money David had spent on it over the years. He once sat down and tried to work it out, but it was too much to cope with: the holidays, the cars, perhaps even the houses they might have had. But at the time, when the drink was on him, the soaring greatness of it, all these things had never worried him. It was life he was celebrating. One day you would be dead and cars, holidays and houses all as nothing. Better to fill your veins with the water of life while you still could.

Of course it hadn't all been good times. There were the mornings. The agony of a 5am rise to get to the vegetable market. The crashing headache and sandpaper mouth, the body that felt as if it had fallen onto concrete from a speeding car.

There were nights too when it all went wrong. When an encounter shifted inexplicably from hale-fellow-well-met into fisticuffs or where the drink, instead of lifting him, sank him down into a mire of self-recrimination and words started muttering themselves unbidden from his lips. But the worst times were the mornings after lost nights when he hadn't made it home.

Coming to on a friend's or even a stranger's couch was manageable. He woke early – always early thank God – and dressed quickly in whatever he had been wearing the night before. More than once David emerged into an unfamiliar landscape, confused at where in the city he had landed. But sooner or later he would manage to hail a cab and get back to home territory. Waking up in strangers' beds was worse.

David never knew if Michelle realised how many times he'd awoken beside the naked, drink-scented form of a woman he didn't know. Sometimes he would manage to slide from between the sheets without waking them. He'd step out into the street, relief at his escape drenched in guilt. David would walk towards the nearest busy junction, unsure of what had taken place between them, wondering if the woman would remember him when she surfaced. But even worse were mornings when the woman was a light as sleeper as himself. Sometimes there would be tears and recriminations, others a silent resentment. Once a woman had somehow got hold of his telephone number and called Michelle. David had claimed she was a waitress, bitter at being fired, but he knew his wife didn't believe him and for a while he'd been afraid that this time she really would go.

Oh the whisky, the whisky. It hadn't felt like an illness. It was the fuel that moved his thoughts and without it he could feel as dull as an overcast morning.

David Preston stirred slightly in his hospital bed and his ratchet breath grew harsher. He was no longer aware of his wife, though she reached out a hand and placed it gently on his face. But instead of her touch David felt a lifting of his senses, a drifting as his consciousness began to loosen itself from his body. The light behind his eyes was burnished gold. Young Davie slipped into the room and Michelle held out her hand. 'Give it to me.'

There had been no sudden revelation, no Road to Damascus, no hit and run accident or car crash. No waking to a murder, no jail sentence of any kind. He had simply known he had to stop and so eventually, he had. It was a bereavement of sorts. A whole way of life gone and friends, drinking buddies, he had to cast aside. At first David hadn't known what to do with the free time. The kids got on his nerves; everything got on his nerves. He hated the TV, blathering on in the corner, couldn't stand mixing with people, was brilliantly, hypocritically censorious towards drunks. But slowly things got better.

David took up golf and found that he'd been right to despise it in his drinking days.

Michelle suggested he decorate the house and he found he liked that better. It wasn't so different from cooking. You saw the fruits of your labours, got to share them with others, witnessed the pleasure in their eyes and took pleasure in turn from that.

Eventually he and Michelle had bought a restaurant in one of the satellite towns that edged the city, renovated it and gone into business for themselves. It hadn't worked out, but David had been stalwart. The bottles were locked behind a grill out of opening hours and Michelle kept the keys. Not once had he searched for them, though he'd thought about it often. Very often.

He went back to working for someone else. But that had been fine too, a relief in a way. The kids were getting bigger and David and Michelle had more time to themselves. They discovered they still liked each other and began occasionally to go out together in the evenings, sometimes to a movie or a show, but more often to a restaurant, David driving and Michelle having the odd glass of wine, though she would have been happy to go without. He became proud of being teetotal. Had to be proud. There wasn't a day when he didn't feel like just the one. Just the bucketful.

Michelle unscrewed the cap from the bottle of malt her son had bought. She stopped the end with her finger then rubbed her husband's parched lips with whisky. The spirit should have burnt, but David Preston felt nothing. He had left his body behind and was speeding along a brilliant corridor of light. David would have felt sorrow at leaving Michelle, Lauren and young Davie had he remembered them, but his consciousness was fading and all that was left were the gold, browns and ambers that had washed through his mind in his final days. He was approaching the end of the corridor, the end of his journey. Up ahead David saw the colours coalesce into a wondrous shape. He experienced a brilliant lifting of the soul as he saw and knew the Holy Spirit's rightness. There was a moment of ecstasy then he was absorbed into the peat-scented bliss. And all the rest was Heaven.

Impilo
Jenni Fagan

I FALL BACKWARDS into the screech. The lawnmower blades whirr once, twice then gouge into flesh, muscles sever, bone cracks and splinters, the sky turns white. The motor snarls somewhere down there, its jagged steel teeth rip into sinews, tear at globules of fat, gnaw tissue ragged. Blood arcs up into the vast bleached-out airless nothing. The daffodils nod their heads quietly. I feel like I'm falling. The motor sputters to a metallic halt.

Silence.

The motor screeches, drags me back under the great white sky, in the kitchen I see Ama put her mug on the draining board, look up and cover her mouth. Between us, on the lawn, the blades of the mower still grind round spattered in blood and raw lumps of meat. My leg spurts out blood, the severed shin and foot; no longer attached. Ama is running down the small back hallway, her bare feet thud off the creaky old floorboards. My severed leg struggles upright, it lurches away toward the rosebush. The ankle is purple, flesh curls away at the calf: one clean shard of bone stabs out the top. The back door whacks open, Ama unwinds her headscarf frantically as she runs and skids down onto her knees.

The toes of the leg wriggle at me.

'It's going to do a tap-dance,' I moan.

'No the fuckin' day it's no,' Ama rapidly winds her scarf around the stump below my knee, tight, so tight I can feel it through the pain, singing at me, screeching up through my body, emptying me of blood. The leg hops away from us, it wavers on the edge of the decking before catching its balance and planking itself firmly down. It bleeds all over the decking Ama finished for me coming home. My heart hollers. The leg tap-dances across to an old cracked mirror behind the peonies, admires its reflection, turns this way and that to see every bloodied angle. Ama creeps up slowly behind it, she lunges but it leaps out of her reach and hops frantically through the wild garlic patch, by the bin, then it shuffles right underneath the rose bush. Just the toes stick out. Ama pretends to have lost interest and it doesn't move, she turns quick on her heel and throws herself at it grabbing it in both hands. It wriggles as she stands up holds it out before her and marches inside. Ama is brandishing the phone at the kitchen window but I shake my head furiously. She won't do it. She won't hand me over. We both know I can't take anymore time, I am not going back to jail. Ama comes back with a duvet. Then there is a pulling, thuds, my sweat slick and cold and the building roar of white noise. I see my dead dog with a leg in its mouth, it runs off through the gate, runs toward the cliffs, the sea.

Everything recedes.

Time leaves, it will have no part in this. I am laid out in the kitchen, on the linoleum. Ama grabs a rubber hose, snaps it round my arm and yanks hard. She lays out her beach towel, a bottle of gin, her needle kit, some brown, water, morphine she said she didn't have and a saw. She bubbles brown in a teaspoon like she never stopped. I thought she'd stopped.

'It's okay,' she whispers repeatedly as she flicks the needle, finds a vein and pushes the stopper all the way in. Warm floods through me. She lifts my thigh and leans it straight up against the fridge freezer to slow the bleeding. My other leg is folded up against me. I am a half lotus. She is beautiful – so we float. Ama strokes my hair. A black starless sky whorls through the kitchen door keyhole and drags its weight across me. Ama shrinks. Through a tiny pinprick of light I see her reach for the saw.

I am on the train, it is yesterday and the world is too wide. Ama, Ama, Ama, the train chugs. As the train crosses the border the windows rattle, way hey!

'Escape?' the tea lady asks me coffee pot poised. I look out the window at cliff tops where seven dead girls sway, just like they hung in their cells, each of them grins widely and waves me on my way.

'Thank you, yes,' I say to the tea lady.

In a morgue the seven suicides cell girls rub at the red marks around their necks. They snap vertebrae back into place, look at each other and nod.

'She wouldn't have survived much longer' they say.

'I couldn't do another two years' the youngest adds.

'You couldn't do another ten minutes,' her sister sniggers.

'Mercy mercy,' they murmur as the morgue man comes to drain their fluids away.

The train smells of beans. It smells of floor. It smells of smelly old man. It does not smell of metal, keys, doors, linoleum, bleach or despair. I will not go back. I won't make it if I do.

I get out at a train station I have not seen for ten years. The marble floor echoes, it seems to ripple like water. A raggedy pigeon hops by, it has one red eye and a slicked up grease of feathers like a mohawk. The red eye is oozin pus. It looks like one claw is gnarled back up, growing back into its leg.

I run up the back steps, air burning at my lungs, out the station, past some homeless guy, round the corner and she is there and she kisses me again and again. Her hair smells like coconut. I can't stop smiling, this is everything I want. The nine-hour drive to the cottage is me taking in her silhouette, her hand on the gear

stick - driving like it's so easy. Her laugh light and nervous, our words of mush rolling over each other, saying nothing, saying I love you – I am here, you are here, this is us again.

The cottage is sixty miles away from anywhere.

The forests are holy. The fields an gates an earth an skies an brooks an stiles an rabbits are holy. Tomorrow I will mow this holy lawn. I will love Ama every single day.

Bits of bone, cartilage drop into the bucket, towels soaked bloody, tissue. Clean gauze soaks in, yellow fluid seeps out. Another needle, more haze. I don't know how many days have passed when I wake. There is a knock knock knock from the porch. Knock, knock, knock, walking sticks getting rattled over, welly boots flung around. That limb was never so active on me. It's like having a puppy.

'What do ye want to do with it?' Ama asks.

'Build a bonfire.'

She takes it up to the bathroom. Bathes it in the sink. She reckons I have to say goodbye to it, that I have to take a wee look.

'Or it'll itch and ache ay,' she calls down the stair to me, 'I saw it in a documentary, these people sayin goodbye tae their limbs on a cushion in a chapel, it helped them accept what had happened eh?' She is sat on the chair at the top of the stairs patting the leg dry. She knows I'm watching, she sat there with her dressing gown open trying to catch my eye a million times before this all happened, before I went away.

'Chanel black' she offers, as she concentrates, paints each nail carefully. I miss my fucking cell. Ama says burning it should be a celebration.

'What is there tae celebrate Ama?'

'Celebrate ye ever had it in the first place!' she says slowly.

She is clearly insane. I can smell rotting on what's left of the meat around my kneecap but she's sewn it up neat I'll give her that. Ama says the smell is all in my brain. Toes dried, Ama wraps a silk scarf round the top of the

➤

limb. She cradles it carefully, pads down the stairs barefoot, bare-skinned, kimono flowing. She sits the leg down on a velvet cushion on the table. I wonder if that scarf is long enough to strangle her with. She would look beautiful strangled.

'Look,' she says as she lights candles. I sigh. I look. Despite the glitter an the Chanel nails an the velvet cushion an the candles an her sitting with her tits out like soon as I need some, she's there, despite all the ceremony, that leg looks queasy to me; it looks like it's in drag. Ama photographs the leg with her digital Nikon. I remember when she took Polaroids.

'It's not art,' I state.

'It's all art,' she replies 'every breath you inhale into yer cells all multiplyin an dying an recreating, it's all art.'

'Like shit in a tin it's art.'

She snorts and begins to laugh so hard she glows. I want to kiss her but first I'd have to punch her and I can't get up yet by myself. Ama's knocked me out some good ones. She trapped my head in the front door once, just trapped it in there, my eyes bulging, shouting, screaming, that was then, then is not now. Now I couldn't touch her wrong no matter how much I might feel like it.

I wake as Ama is lacing a daisy chain anklet round the leg.

'Your barometer of normal is fucked!'

'I never did do normal,' she says.

She's not lying. She never did do normal. She did other stuff, like the piercings through her lip an her chin an her clit an that, she did them by herself, sealed the wounds with almost boiling salty water. She's got amazing delicate ornate wee flower tattoos trailing down her belly, round her waist, ornate on her tiny feet. She's lived on a barge, in a shack, a cave and a commune. She's lived in the forest on a platform on stilts where bison ran below each night. A tepee for three years, until she was twenty-three and got left the cottage and it was here she brought me.

'This place is for us,' she said.

She lavished it with love and made everything grow wild and tall and beautiful, even me. I shouldn't have tried to cut the grass. I shouldn't have had a gin for breakfast. I shouldn't have let Ama meet my Mother in 83'. My Mother looked at her like she was some kind of disease made up by some kind of being no-one's even heard of. Ama took it like a real big compliment. Ama isn't keen on normal as an idea. She says that normal is just something they bludgeon you guilty with. She says we're raised to think that normal is a real thing so we police our thoughts and our actions for any aberrations that could outcast us. Ama says that's just how the system wants it, so people keep giving them their money and shut the fuck up. She made stew last night. Greens out the garden. Rabbit out the trap. She told me about her Uncle Willie's scars over pudding. He was stabbed in Glasgow, scars all over his back, stomach and part of his right ear was hacked off.

'An then there's the masterpiece,' she says 'this three inch scar eh, right round his wrist, I am tellin' ye he wears that scar like a Rolex, straight up! Like a Rolex he isnae ever takin' off, no until his dyin' day.'

I was twenty-nine when I met Ama an I'd felt numb my whole life. I never thought anyone could change that. But she did, she's like that, there's always a lot Ama can do. You need a room painted nice, she paints nice. You need someone help you with something makes most people sick, call her – nothing can make that girl vomit. You want to talk about them Greek weirdos with the big thoughts, she'll pontificate philosophy till the cows come home. You want to tell someone bout something bad and dirty and not feel dumb? Ama'll make you a cup of tea.

She only has one friend.

'One's all I need,' she says.

'What about when Mick dies?' I ask her.

'I just won't see him for a while,' she says. She reckons if she needs people again she'll go out and find some.

'Plenty of em out there,' she states. Ama says the trees are her friends. The ocean, the stars, the sand, the sky, the soup she cooks and the bread she bakes an the films she cries to with a big smile on her face. My love is enough she reckons.

'You're broke as fuck,' I tell her.

'Nah,' she says, 'I just got lucky that way.'

We wait until night. She gets the wheelbarrow. Puts a duvet in it. Two pillows. Lifts me under the arms. I've had my extra morphine. I feel pretty good all in all. Ama wheels me out the back. The night smells clean and sharp. The stars are so beautiful, so bright and cold looking it makes me feel breathless. I can smell grass and wild garlic and flowers, the scents are crisp, like the cold air is preserving them. Ama holds my hand, sits down on an old deckchair. I pull the duvet tight. She hands me a box of matches and I strike a big one, launch it at the bonfire. Whoosh. It purrs an pops right away, crackles little sparks out and up especially when the leg begins to sizzle, perched there on the top like a fucked bit of lamb an the foot, the foot does not look like it should be there, it's painted nails shining in the flames. I give it a hard bloody whack with a stick. Ama strokes my hand real gentle and I want to kiss her again. I only need what I need. What I need is all I need. I don't need that limb. I don't. What's weird is that piece of dead meat burning doesn't seem like anything to do with me. Mine feels like it's still here, but it's not. It's not and somehow I just don't care. It spits a huge bit of fat out and we both recoil startled for a second.

'Last time you help out in the garden,' Ama says slowly. I giggle, it begins with a shaking in my stomach, up my spine, I can feel Ama shaking too, her mouth open, silently helpless with laughter. The moon stares down in a silent O and the old willow tree at the bottom of the garden swishes to an fro, to an fro.

It sounds like waves.

In the Beginning
Jen Campbell

EVE IS BORED – extremely, superbly, emphatically; she shapes as many words on her tongue as will fit and tries them out for size. She likes to come up with her own, too, just to join in with the game. She doesn't like sitting around fanning herself with bracken unless she can string some of these together. It's something she uses to build her character.

'What about hupponening?' she suggests, raising an eyebrow with it too. 'It can mean dancing.'

'But I already named *dance*.'

'Well this can be a different kind.'

Adam stops scraping bark off a tree. 'What kind?'

'I don't know... with fruit or something.'

Adam rolls his eyes and doesn't answer. He prefers to name things on his own – he has a clipboard and stickers; it is very authoritarian. Secretly Eve thinks his beard is getting a little too long to be considered business-like. He writes letters down in a clumsy scrawl and then sticks them to whatever he's claiming. Eve has just spent a happy hour watching him try and catch a deer so he could put a sticker on its nose.

'And where are the clothes?'

'What are clothes?'

'You know... things to wear.'

'Never heard of them.'

'I just made them up.'

'Well you *can't*.'

'They have them over there,' Eve indicates the hedge just behind them. 'I've seen them; they exist.'

'Yeah, well...'

Adam isn't all that keen on 'out there.' It encompasses all the things he doesn't understand yet. You can see it when you climb to the top of the apple tree, all these different plots of land with extraordinary people. Each land has its own boundaries, each land has its own people, and they don't really seem to interact at all. Most are like Adam, and pretend the others are not there. Eve thinks that the hedges denote different religions, though she is unsure of this word. Religions and regions sound very similar, and she's still getting her head round the long list that Adam has made. At the other side of the next patch of land, she can sometimes see a man with many arms who appears to have blue skin. She tried to wave to him once, but she doesn't think he saw her.

Eve sighs. 'I'm bored.'

She blows air out of her nose and slides down onto the grass again, carefully, so as to avoid grass stains. She looks at the mud trapped underneath her fingernails, and twists strands of grass around her thumb.

Adam smiles: 'Do you want me to tell you a story?'

Eve doesn't like way he's titling his head to one side as though he's speaking to an idiot. She gets frustrated when he dismisses everything she says, just because he was here first.

'If it's the one where you say "Hey, I shall call her wo-man, as she was taken out of man," then, please, spare me.'

Adam scowls; he's rather fond of that pun, himself. 'I gave you part of my body, you know.'

Eve snorts. It's like he thinks she has penis

envy or something. She doesn't. She *really* doesn't.

Over the hedge, due West:

Medusa doesn't have any mirrors, so she never knows how she looks. She peers down at what she's wearing, plucks out all the creases. Occasionally she catches a glimpse of a cheekbone in a pool of water, and once saw a tongue in a wine glass, but otherwise she has to ask if she wants to know, but mostly she doesn't. Some people call her a monster; some say she is the most beautiful thing they have ever seen. The latter don't live long, and she isn't sure how much sense they are talking. She can seduce them; she knows that. The snakes around her head whisper into the air. She's seen the way their eyes glaze over. From the waist down, at least, she knows that she is stunning.

She has never looked at herself in a mirror. She doesn't trust her own reflection because she has seen what her eyes do to other people. She has wondered before whether it is easier being a woman with no face, and she has seen, from the side, the snakes that entangle her head, curling around like coat hangers, holding up her neck. She is not immortal; she feels guilt at killing others, and this in turn makes her feel weaker.

Sometimes the temptation to see her own beauty drives her insane. She has been known to cradle a mirror, hunched on a stairwell, wondering if she should look. Just this once, just to see. Those are dark hours, a dull hissing inside her brain. Only the dead can make her stop. They are her keepsakes to drag her back to common sense – to remind her who she is. They are sickening trophies that litter her house like ornaments picked up from a car boot sale. She kisses each one in the morning, her hair twisting around her ears. She paints lipstick on their marble faces whenever she gets bored.

The statues stand in chronological order, from the dining room to her bedroom. The first being her nursery nurse; she had never meant to do it. The last her latest conquest. She has a nasty habit of wanting to look at them, after sex, when they're asleep.

'It's your damn fault for waking!' She yells,

dragging half a tonne of marble off her sweat ridden sheets.

The sex. It saves her soul. It puts off the need to examine the contours of her nose. She used to do it for a living; she used to make videos with her head blurred out; they sold well; they paid for her house before her production manager froze because he chose to look too closely. She keeps his head on the mantelpiece and stores Brazil nuts between his teeth.

But now the foundations of her house are starting to crumble under the weight of three hundred bodies all made out of stone. Her kitchen tips at twenty degrees; her plates are in danger of smashing, so she grabs them all one morning and throws them to the floor. Through the window, she notices a face appearing over the hedge at the sound of the crash. It is a woman. She has seen this woman before, but has never spoken to her. She doesn't talk to people of the same sex; it unnerves her. This woman is currently sitting between two branches of a tree as though she's surveying her own kingdom. This woman is always naked. There is a man that lives with her. He is also always naked; she has seen him from the balcony upstairs. Medusa finds them strange beings, running around outside with no house and no clothes. She takes her clothes off for a specific purpose, but she's never seen them engage in that sort of activity. There is an aura of innocence surrounding them. It reminds her of childhood, a very early childhood before she knew that her eyes were what they are. It makes her hate them.

There is a knock at her front door, and then a scramble as the person who has knocked runs away again as fast as they can. Medusa sighs, picks her way across the kitchen floor. She wonders if there's anything there, whether it's Pan and his nymphs playing games again: knock, knock, run away. She strains her ears for the sound of hooves but can't hear anything.

There is no one outside the front door, but there is a parcel. It has a strand of seaweed draped across it, and has a faint smell of fish. She wrinkles her nose and takes off its lid, half expecting to find some strangled animal. But,

➡

instead, it is something beautiful. It is a dress. It glints in the sun. She bends down and gently lifts it out of its container, lets the fabric flow to the floor as though it's water, red water. It smells of apples. It is beautiful. There is a note, with her name on it. She cannot remember the last time anyone wrote her name down, and it takes her a while to register that someone has taken the time to write something for her. Men hate her and love her. It is a control that she has little say over. It both rules and saves her life. This parcel is from Poseidon – he is eternally curious. She looks up to see that the woman is still watching. Medusa wants to meet her and her strange unclothed husband. She decides to play on their intrigue. She smiles wickedly, revelling in the power.

Over the hedge, due East:

Eve has seen the dress from her vantage point, and it is the most beautiful thing she has ever seen. She imagines putting it on her own body, letting the material slide right down over her, pooling at her feet. She imagines that it is cool on the outside; she imagines that it sends shivers down her spine.

'What have you named that is red?' She calls down to Adam, needing to know at once. She has the strong urge to know what else is like that dress; she needs to know where she can find such things and to make one of her very own. She needs to see that colour.

'Well,' Adam gets ready to launch into a long speech. 'There are many things that are red in our garden right here, though it depends on what shade of red you mean. I've categorised them all here,' he flicks through his clipboard. 'They are on page four nine five. There is burgundy, maroon, cerise, auburn, et cetra,' and here he pauses for effect. 'But, generally speaking, there are berries, tomatoes... there are roses....'

'No, no, those are actual things,' Eve says, frowning. 'I don't think that's what I meant. I can touch those things; I can see them.'

Adam looks at her as though she's mad. 'Well, yes.' And he trails off, confused.

She turns back to look at the dress, frustrated that she can't express herself. She

does not have the words to do so; she has not learnt them yet. Eve instinctively knows she didn't mean red as in berries and blood and roses. She thinks she meant something inside of her instead. She thinks she meant love, and anger. Those two things at the same time.

That is red, she thinks, looking at that dress and the strange way that Medusa's hair is dancing around her head. Yes, the colour red is a feeling. It is desire.

The next day

Adam wakes up to find Eve trying to thread leaves onto a stick.

He yawns. 'What are you doing?'

She looks up, twigs in her mouth. 'I'm making a dress.'

'A what?'

She spits the twigs onto the floor. 'A dress.'

'What's a dress?'

'Oh for God's sake, come here,' and she grabs his hand, pushing him towards the apple tree. 'Go on, climb.'

She forces him up the trunk, his bare feet slipping on the bark.

He glances back over his shoulder: 'Is this really necessary?'

'Think of it as being at one with nature, or something. Now come *on.*'

It takes them a while to get there but, at the top of the tree, they can see everything. Adam has never come up here before because he likes to think that it doesn't exist. Also, he's not too great with heights. He pauses, licks his lips, looks nervously down towards the ground.

'I'm really not sure we should be up here, you know. Do we not have to get permission?'

She rolls her eyes. 'I thought you made all the rules around here?'

'Shh! Not so loud!'

'Look. Do you really think this tree would be here if we weren't supposed to climb it?'

It is an interesting question, and he knows it. Adam has always said that things happen here for a reason. That is his truth.

'That,' she points over the hedge to where Medusa is dancing around the garden. 'That, right there, that red thing, is a dress.'

She gives him a moment to take it in, watching the way his expression changes. Eve is fascinated by his eyes. At first she sees he is confused, indignant even that he is having to follow her instructions, but then the frown lines soften and curiosity sets in. Adam crouches so that he's sitting on the branch, legs dangling over. The height seems to be forgotten.

'Who is she?' and the way he says that is not a tone he has ever used when talking to her. Eve would be offended, if she cared. As it is, she feels as though she's just about hit the bull's eye.

'I don't know her name,' she admits, sitting down beside him. 'I just see her walking around sometimes.'

'Her hair moves?'

'Yes,' and Eve swears she hears a hiss from the other side of the fence. She knows she needs to use Adam to get that dress - she needs a reason for Medusa to take the dress off, which she does with men; Eve has seen it.

'Why does her hair move?'

'I don't know.'

'It's... it's beautiful,'

Over the fence, Medusa is spinning around the garden. She knows they are watching; she has seen them. She laughs, turning circles, the red hits the sun. They can smell the grass on her feet, the heat of her skin.

Eve smiles, sensing Adam weakening right there and then. 'We have to get me that dress. You need to help me.'

He nods. He can't say no. This dress, as Adam watches it, seems to mould itself to her figure in a way that makes him appreciate her body more. He's never really taken much notice of Eve's in this way; her body has always been there, on display, in front of him. God had said her body would give him children - her hands make shelter, his hands find food. Their bodies are practical things. This woman on the other side of the hedge is not anything to do with the word practicality, as Adam rolls the word around his tongue. She embodies a whole new type of word. She is beautiful because she is, and she appears to live in order to be it. It is powerful, he decides, that's what it is, and he can't help being drawn to that power. He looks

to his right, at Eve, at her brown knotted hair, mud stains down both of her cheeks. She is spindly and childlike. He promises to her that he will do anything he can do get hold of what she calls this dress, and secretly hopes that he will get to meet this other creature in the process. He has a feeling that he has something to say to this new woman, though for the life of him he can't work out what. He lets the air hit the base of his tongue and hang there.

There is one problem: they are not supposed to leave the garden.

'It's fine,' Eve shrugs, trying to hide her glee at how easily Adam has been persuaded. 'I'm sure He won't really notice.' She is starting to see why so many men knock on this woman's door – they can't help themselves. Eve wonders if, when she gets her hands on it, the dress will allow her to find a different man – one who doesn't insist on being so God damned authoritarian. She senses it will make her powerful. She has also noticed that men who enter this woman's house seldom come out of it again. She imagines leaving Adam there, walking off, pulling the straps over her shoulders, feeling the cool material on her skin. She imagines cutting holes through each of the fences and winding her way through all the land she can see. She imagines meeting people and telling them she is a woman from nowhere and everywhere – that she is as free as a bird.

Her own hair moves in front of her eyes in the breeze. She smiles to herself, pictures herself as a map with dotted lines, lets her fingers tip toe down the side of her leg.

'We can easily jump down from here, you know,' she indicates a branch hanging over the other side.

'You think so?' Adam says, not even looking in her direction.

'Sure. You first,' and Eve nudges him forward, a sour taste in her mouth, like venom.

The Bob Conn Experience
Jenni Fagan

He'd been places, sex parlours and Woodstock and driving bareback
on a Harley cross Canada in the 60s where the Indian girls would call

after him on the road, 'Why you call me honey in the bedroom and
squaw in the street?' and the men would fish barefoot off the rapids,

spears and salmon to glint in sun and his first armed robbery wasn't
really planned so, he found himself whistling, whistling in a cell

next to a native Indian wide as we was tall, eight years in Stoney
Mountain Penitentiary then kicked out of the country, sent on a plane

to a place where he couldn't get work or money and it was a matter
of months before he stole the shotguns (two from a farm) held up a

post office (got twenty-five grand) was grassed by his neighbour
and whilst digging up the guns saw a cop on the path and held the

long barrel up to the officer's head (another eight years) and then,
the day he got out of jail, they handed him jeans too big and trainers

with soles flapping away like loose tongues, they waggled all the way
to the halfway house, a basement dank as shit where he had to stay

for sixty days with three other prisoners just released, a paedophile,
a schizophrenic rapist, a murderer and Mr Conn, just your average

garden variety bank robber thief had seen worse and heard better
and the paedophile had questionable taste in shoes, ate everything

with ketchup, corn flakes and ketchup, burritos with ketchup, spam
and sweetcorn all covered in ketchup too and the schizophrenic

knew fifteen different ways to bring Satan through a crack in the wall,
like a great vagina of doom, portal of sorts, and while they sat and got

high and drunk, the murderer watched the lights of the buses streak by
the window like great electric eels in the night, their blue shimmering

the walls incandescent as his cigarette ash fell slowly to the floor.

Scotland as an Xbox Game
Andrew C Ferguson

You start on a dark screen, a void
(no Enlightenment for several levels)
groping towards a white x, dimly seen
with no sense of yourself.
Kill the English knight with your bare hands
and you're Wallace: green fields
and rivers of blood unroll in front of you.

Eventually, if you make it through the hack and slash
you're into the strategy game
the silicon chip on both shoulders
making you seem bigger than you are
to your enemies at court. Before you know it
you're making unlikely alliances
on the multiplayer function, sacrificing queens
and credibility points to get to London.

The next levels are disappointing:
the Enlightenment flares past like a firework;
then endless foreign wars, grim landscapes
games of football played in the rain
that looks like analogue interference.
Your dubious weapons of bitterness
and working class authenticity
only useful against Scottish opponents.

In the end, you have to re-terraform
but your Parliament's permanently over-budget
and you can never stick enough windfarms in the North Sea
to stop your populace moaning.
It may just be me
but there seems to be an inbuilt advantage
in using American English.

No one has yet made it
to the next level.

a sincere apology
Josh Byer

i'm not scottish
but my family was
a long, long time
ago

scottish jews
you heard me

500 years ago
those lost relations
were evicted
from your great nation
for stealing horses

it's true,
no joke

so
i'm sorry,
scotland

look
i even wrote a poem

Historic Scotland
Graham Fulton

The familiar path up
the face of Dunadd.

A stinging cloudburst hones my focus,
tests my resolve to squelch to the top.
The entrance that cleaves its way through
the stone.

A curve of outlines, a hawk on a branch.
A view of the Great uncoloured Moss.
Jura, The Sound, whatever's beyond.
The Ross of Mull? I'm not too sure.

My left foot matches
the print of the King,
especially without my shoe and sock.
One of these years it probably won't.
The further I go the faster
I shrink.

The line of Ogham
I've never found.

The shouts of cricket-playing-people
next to the car park, somewhere below.
Latest dialects, lost in the air.
English, Norse, Irish, Scots.
Time is always disguising its voice.

The sacred basin is full of rain.
I cup my hands, slosh it across
the back of a boar carved into the rock.
It makes what I can't see more
clearly defined.

At the Church of Scotland General Assembly
Rob A Mackenzie

Masks veil presbyters' faces. The church debates
gay ministers. Liberals present niceties,
prosaic and dutiful, truthful folk who fake it

when suited, that 'respect' for the opposition
a guise slipped on, slipped off for one audience
or another. Conservatives beguile themselves

with theological patois. If they just said it,
the idea of two men fucking fucking
disgusts me, and here are the verses

to prove it, I'd at least wake up, being no fan
of political correctness. Meanwhile, barefaced
wisdom erupts like no one talking to no one.

Ever fallen in love?

Extract from the novel *What I Was Going to Do*

Zoë Strachan

YOU KNOW WHERE I came from, I told Luke, you know the kind of place. Stunted, grey, the industry gone, black carcasses of pits on the outskirts of town where teenagers go to drink cheap, fortified wines with poignant names. Between fighting and fucking and sucking dirty heroin into their tarry, vitamin-deprived lungs. A shithole, we called it, and it was. Education the best way out, that and crime. Or, like Kenny Dodd, a swooping, swallow-like dive from the remains of the pithead to the rough, broken concrete below. Eldorado.

But Luke pressed me for the piquant details and flattered, I obliged. Though I called myself working class, and it was true, we were part of the elite in the 'Leck, in that both parents actually worked, in jobs they hoped to keep until death or retirement did them part. My father, whose father and his father before him had held their breaths as the cage took them deep down underground, now drove up the valley to a manufacturing plant. Plastics, I think it was. He didn't say much about it (and shame on me, I didn't ask). My mother was not a dentist's receptionist, she worked at the surgery in an administrative capacity (ditto). So no Thunderbird or smack for me. Strongbow in the swing park, rather, with those from my year who would tolerate me.

I should mention, though it seems rather ungrateful to do so only as an aside, that I did love my parents. They did their best, comforted me when I was bullied (though I wouldn't tell them why), gave me pocket money and no reason to cry. And yet, alone in my room night after night, fat, selfish tears would moisten my pillow. The huge, insurmountable wedge between us was of course my inversion, my deviancy, my never-to-be-confessed secret. Later I was fascinated by the tales my more out-coming contemporaries told of how their mother always knew. Well I'd been keeping my sexuality double-bagged, like a furtive bottle of sherry from the late shop, the sordid little weakness in the shopping of a spinster. So my mother didn't know, though of course it was to be revealed with a flourish – tada! – later on.

It might seem hard to believe, but all I dreamt of was a big double bed with a patchwork counterpane like the one my granny stitched by the gas fire; the coal, like her husband, long dead. Somewhere to indulge a gentle and romantic relationship, a pure love. But no one was gay, or if they were they kept it quiet, haunted by the memory of the man who was lynched in the town down the valley because he loved other men. This in the 1980's, mind.

There was television, there were books (not many, but some, and the interlibrary loan for that first tantalising Edmund White). I knew the lie of the land pretty early, all told. Even if, when my voice deepened and my penis developed a life of its own, there was no-one to receive the fire of my loins. The shame started then, I suppose. Oh, I harboured secret passions, for a boy in the sixth year nicknamed Coco, and Mr Martin the maths master, with his tight, teacherly trousers. But I knew they must stay secret, or else.

One day, just below and to the right of the ripely swelling breasts of Mandy, 18, 34-25-36

➤→

with her frozen lip-gloss smile and neon tanga briefs, an article in the newspaper caught my eye. A city scandal, resulting in the closure of public conveniences around Glasgow. The first time I'd heard the term cottaging. Instantly I thought of the roughcast, cream painted public bog down by the railway path. Imagined that inside the door, amid the metal urinals and shit-smeared walls, there might exist a dreamy gymnasium packed with lithe lads throwing discuses. Or the Scottish equivalent of such. Clones of the porridge oats man perhaps, in his pristine t-shirt and convenient kilt.

Knowing the mindset of some of the local lads – if any of them had seen the article, the punishment delivered upon anyone spied within a half mile radius of a public toilet would be swift and brutal – I waited until another winter evening a few weeks down the line before I casually went for a stroll. Which wasn't very casual. Both my mother and my father asked what I was doing, as I ran fingers through my hair and splashed on my aftershave (Hi Karate, can you imagine?). Walking without a dog was considered morally suspect somehow, so I made up a story about going to see someone. This was implausible given that I didn't have any friends, but it worked out for the best as my jumpy, forced bonhomie convinced my parents that there was some girl I fancied and hoped to glimpse. An involuntary, perfect ruse.

Of course, when I got there, there were no boys with bows and arrows, no gentle, thorough Greek teachers, never mind the porridge oats man. Not that night, nor the next time I went, nor the one after that. By my fourth visit, I'd given up hope. Dejected I sat in the only cubicle, reading the signs of my Armitage Shanks Sibyl. Kirsty McGill is a slag. Benny does dugs. For a good time call Stanesy's maw. More promisingly, down beside the broken toilet roll holder, smaller letters proclaimed, I need hard dick. Meet me here 7pm. Where are you now, Hard Dick? I pondered, and then I heard a phlegmy cough.

I leapt to my feet and lunged towards the urinal, whipping open my fly en route. It might have been thought poofy to bother going to a public convenience to piss when you could just expose yourself in the street, but it would have been even more unseemly to be caught in a public convenience not pissing at all.

In came a man, who nodded at me and with inebriated clumsiness, withdrew a whopping great dong from the depths of his trousers, groaning as he started a long, luxurious urination. I recognized him, the curious blue pock marks on his face. It was Mr Sim from the miner's cottages by the war memorial. I stopped peeing, but I didn't stop staring. The thing was immense. I had only seen, during unguarded moments in the PE changing room, the youthful, teenage specimen. This was positively Neanderthal. Homo He noticed I hadn't moved, and swiftly, with trembling hands, I did up my jeans. But I must have tuned in and activated my long-dormant gaydar, because he swivelled round, newly-relieved penis still out in the open, and met my eye. I backed against the wall, wanting nothing more than to run past him and away, along the railway path and home, to Red Dwarf on the telly and my mother nipping at my Stephie for being a little madam.

Well, whit are ye waitin fur?

And that was that. I sank to the ground. Mr Sim seized me by the ears to better adjust my position, and growled with pleasure as I got to work on his savoury, urine-tanged member. I soon realised the significance of the swallow or spit debate amongst the loucher girls in my year. Mr Sim unleashed such a torrent (of a consistency not unlike over-diluted Campbell's condensed mushroom soup) into my mouth that it didn't go down in the first swallow, but spilled out over my chin. He sighed, withdrew, hauled me to my feet. I hadn't even got as far as thinking that he might reciprocate when he slammed me against the wall and pinned one massive hand to my throat. With the other he seized my twitching testicles through my jeans and squeezed until tears came to my eyes.

If ye open yer gub aboot this, ah'll throttle ye, ye wee pervert. Comprende?

I nodded, he released me, and rapturous, my knees soaked through with what was probably piss, I ran home. I was in love. Not with unwashed, beer-addled Mr Sim, but with my future.

New Lovers Who Polish Their Stories Like Shoes
Tracey Emerson

NEW LOVERS.

New Lovers Who....

New Lovers Who What?

They do something she thinks. What is it?

She thinks this as she walks from the West End to the East, past Castle, Mound and Bridge, on the way to meet her lover.

Her new lover.

She thinks of what she has told him.

About the woman she loved and loves still, although they are no longer lovers and love in a different way now.

About the past. Childhood and school. Parental affairs, separations, reconciliations. The college years – her drug dealer next-door neighbour and their lost summers. Of leaving her last boyfriend in bed while she went to buy a newspaper and never going back.

All the stories are refined, honed. She recasts herself. Sinner to Saint. Victim to Victor.

As she walks, she drifts back to three days ago. He lay in her bed at five a.m. He spread out his stories, childhood regurgitated, and she laughed. Laughed as she had not done with a man for quite some time. He spun the stories around her - quirky, engaging tales from Australia's Blue Mountains, starring himself, his sister and his dog-breeding parents. The hours they'd spent in packed cars on the way to small-town dog shows. His anecdotes danced on a reel before her, all cult-indie comedy, and the picture that stayed with her was one of two sweating children on the backseat of a stifling car, an over-sized Esky towering between them, cutting them off from one another. Pathos. He

curled up on his side, foetal as he talked. As he polished his stories for her, polished them like...

What?

She passes the café where they ate lunch last week. They drank Rioja and he said he'd like to know her in the future, however their connection developed, and she'd thought, this is someone who knows how things evolve and she'd wanted to say - if the café was not so quiet she might have said it - did he not know what he had done already? Did he not know how much he'd mended in such a short time? Her entire body licked times over, wounds and all, fucking it all out of her and gently inserting something else, something green and alive that thrust through the cracks and made a garden out of the past. Did he not know that?

She crosses the road and takes a left. Soon she will reach his office and, as she reclines in his blue chair with his head between her legs, she will look at the bookcase that inspires his work and think once again how good the titles would look in a story about the two of them. *Sexual Fluidity – Understanding Women's Desires, Freud in the Bedroom, Psychology of a Prostitute.* She will decide, before losing reason to orgasm, that it is too perfect an image not to use.

Stories not yet formed. Chrysalis tales.

Stories not yet shared. Kept in reserve.

Like the one about her grandfather, the murderer. Jailed as a soldier in Calcutta during World War Two for throwing a military policeman from a train. Released on the

➤➤

condition he join the Chindits and fight behind Japanese lines in Burma. He was one of the few to survive. Minus an ear.

She would describe how she remembered him. Short and fit and frightening, pumping his arms with a Bullworker. Pulling out her loose teeth with a pair of pliers.

And every day cleaning his shoes, military-style. Sitting in his outhouse with three pairs lined up in front of him. Polishing and buffing.

New Lovers Who Polish Their Stories Like Shoes.

Yes, she thinks, as she turns the corner.

Yes, that's it.

After it was over she thought: Who will I tell myself to now?

Ex-Lovers Who Tell their Stories to Who?

She deleted his texts and e-mails, seven months worth, after saving them to a memory stick. She placed the stick full of memories in a box, along with his cards and letters.

She missed him in her body, cunt begging like a dog, but in her head it was worse. One-sided conversations, still telling him about her day, the fantasies she had of him at night and why she'd walked away.

All the stories he would have appreciated. Like the one about the photographs. Which photographs? The ones she'd taken of herself for him, the naked ones, black and white, the ones she'd given to him in their café, watching him blush as he looked at them. Those ones.

She'd taken her camera to a family dinner party, forgetting the images were stored there. Late at night, the adults all drunk, her five-year-old nephew got bored and borrowed the camera. He snapped away at everyone then pressed play to look at his handiwork. Confused by what he found, the nephew passed the camera to his Grandad.

'What's that?' he asked.

She'd only realised when her father, stony-faced, passed the camera back to her. Her sister found it hilarious. A cracking yarn.

The first person she'd wanted to tell was him.

With him gone, she had time to analyse, pick apart, pore over, rummage through. She replayed his narrative to herself, sifted the facts.

With hindsight, his chronology was skewed. Which dates he'd lived in which country, was married to which woman, screwed which lover. Not everything added up. She feared he was all fiction. I think, she thought, that New Lovers accept each other's stories blindly. Not accept, devour. She'd devoured his stories. They were extensions of his body, of the flesh that she kissed, licked and scratched.

He would have created an explanation for her leaving. A Myth of The End that depicted him as in control and longed for, her as weak and lovelorn. It angered her that he should be allowed to get it so wrong.

She'd spun her tales too, mind you. A selection to choose from. Most days she picked the version in which she came off best, and each time she did so she thought, how can we ever... what is the point... how can truth exist between two people when each of them carries a different story in their head?

Ex Lovers Who Use Their Stories To...

What?

Her city is no longer hers. It is theirs. Legends have attached themselves to parks and gardens, restaurants and galleries.

The instillation gallery where they often met. It had secluded rooms and dark spaces. They saw an exhibition there that focused on the close up – small things made big so one could see them with greater clarity. It was mid afternoon, quiet. Projections floated around a black walled room – a woman's body parts magnified. A nipple, a navel, an ear lobe. No one else in there. His fingers at her throat, the way he kissed her. She'd gone all eighteenth century, thought she might faint.

After a month without him, she visited a new exhibition with friends – a husband and wife and their two small boys. The kids bombed around the now white walls, poking at the award-winning piles of stones and flicking dangling ropes. Everyone laughed. She'd laughed hardest, as if the sound could cleanse, purify.

A few days later, she visited the hotel spa where she was a member. She'd meant to take him there but never had. She thought about that as she floated in the rooftop pool. Haunted by stories that hadn't even happened.

A voice next to her said, hello. A male voice. American. She looked at him and saw that he was younger than her, had eyes like a cat. They talked and he invited her to visit him that evening.

A chance to spawn fresh memories.

That night she squeezed into stilettos and took a taxi to the hotel. The American opened the door to his room and five minutes later they were naked. Between bouts they talked and drank wine. It was sad and funny and easy and strange.

The next morning she felt foolish, wobbling home through town in her heels. She couldn't wait to tell her friends though. He said I was 'awesome', really, not kidding, 'awesome'. Only twenty-four. I know, it's disgraceful.

Her friends would love it. You dog, they'd tell her, you lucky dog.

As she walked, she let this new story settle on top of the old ones. She saw herself as sediment, the history of lost loves running through her, layer upon layer.

She hoped she'd done enough to stop her Ex-Lover getting through. At least some of the time.

Ex Lovers Who...

They did something, what was it?

Forget it, she told herself as she turned a corner.

Forget it.

The Monday to Friday Routine
Mary Paulson-Ellis

Monday

They weigh his heart, then they slice it in two. Afterwards they peel away enough of his face to get at his brain. That goes on the scales as well. It's amazing what you can learn from the heaviness of things.

They squeeze his lungs. Not bad. But his liver is like paste. And huge. Nothing like the ones you buy in the shops tiny and sleek with blood, each in its own little membrane sac.

His pancreas delivers a verdict, as if it were in doubt. Six, seven pints a day. Special Brew, extra strong. He's drunk himself to death. Some medical terminology covers the form, but that's about the strength of it. He's sat down night after night and drunk and drunk and drunk 'til his wife's left him, his kids have moved out, his friends no longer call and his neighbours don't even know he exists. Then he's drunk some more.

We'll never know which was his last. He had two to hand: glass of whisky, empty; can of Special, spilt on the floor. They only found him because of the smell. Downstairs flat complained, went knocking on doors.

At first his neighbours thought it was the drains. Got some firm out to do rodding and sucking and plunging in the holes in the street outside. Two days and his neighbours watched from their individual kitchens, making their individual cups of tea as the men sweated and plunged and sweated and sucked and swore. Two days and they stood in the stairwell conscious of the smell seeping further into their lives, waiting to hear some news, laughing about how bad it might get, the sweetness of it

that isn't sweet at all. Two days until the men stood back, wiped their hands, pushed overalls down at the waist and insisted, 'There's nothing we can do.'

Still the smell lingered on until somebody finally rang his bell. And they'll have known the moment the doorjamb split that this man's flat was where it came from all along.

Two police constables in their bulky vests went in first, hands over nostrils and mouths. They found him in his chair, the remote still on the arm. They tried the light switches, but the electricity was off – the card machine by the front door ran through its excess way before. They looked around a bit then backed out as soon as they could, got on their radios, waited for people with white suits and proper masks to tell them nothing suspicious had gone on.

They used his bills to ID him in the end, so I'm told. 'His ex-wife refused,' the policeman said. 'Didn't think it was her job.' They looked at his wallet and his driver's licence, the gas bills piled up in a kitchen drawer. 'It was fairly easy to tell. Who else could it be?'

'He was a bastard on the drink.' That was what his ex-wife told the officers in charge. Hit the kids and her too. 'My new man's much nicer.' That was what she said, as they wrote it all down.

Later she must have felt bad. They were together eighteen years after all and perhaps she remembered his mother. She got some money together, stood by as the coffin wheeled out, one wreath and a wee notice in the paper in case anyone else out there wanted to see. Bu nobody tried to say anything nice. What was the point? He drank himself to death. Her kids didn't come. Hardly anyone came except her and her new man, holding hands, and me. On the steps outside, as I passed, they talked about their wedding. The food she had planned. The fact that all her children would be there for that do.

They cut him up nice and good. Then they stitched him up nice and good too. They laughed while they did it. Just another ordinary day.

I leave them outside his front door on my way home. It's a mixed bunch, fading a little at the edges. I know no one else will bother, but I think he deserves something. He was here once, after all, just like us. I prop the bunch against the wall by the broken door jamb where I know it will stay for a while, decaying gently just like him, until the cleaners are brought in. 'See if you can't do something about that smell, won't you,' his neighbours will say when they see the cleaners arrive with their latex gloves and their black plastic sacks. 'Don't want it hanging around forever.'

Tuesday

It's a drugs overdose. They don't say, but I know. They found her bent over, praying to the mattress; blood like a birth mark, like a dark tattoo, gathered from fingertips to elbow, hands blown up to half again their size. I'm sure she wouldn't like it if she could see.

I think she liked handbags and hair clips and nail varnish. I think she liked skirts and shoes with heels and lipstick. I think she liked playing with her little sister, watching the TV.

They didn't find her for a while but it wasn't like she was missing. There were no notices in the papers or appeals on the local news. She just failed to answer her phone. Her mum will have called her and so will her friends. But it's normal these days, isn't it, to have a life of one's own. To do your own thing. When you want. How you want. Independence. It's a good thing.

Her flatmate found her first. Came back from a trip, probably dropped her bag in the hall, shouted 'Hello!' or, 'I'm back'. Maybe even knocked at the bedroom door. But there won't have been any reply. Then the flatmate will have gone into the kitchen and switched on the kettle and the television, texted a few friends to let them know she was home before something made her raise her head and say it again, call it this time, 'Sarah? Sarah!'

They all loved her – her mum, her dad, her little sister. I could tell from the way they huddled in the corridor as I wheeled their daughter away. A small group, just the three. There wasn't anything dark or unexplored, nothing to explain. It's just, there's always a first time. And sometimes the first time's a last time too. Experimenting. That's what it's called.

I leave them outside by their hedge. Chrysanthemums – tiny faces bursting with colour. She deserves something pretty so that's what I've brought, though it's the little sister I feel sorry for now. Nothing will ever be the same for her. I go home on the bus and as I look out of the window I hope that even just for a moment, whatever empty space that dead girl had inside was filled in some kind of way.

Wednesday

And he had burned well, the old man inside the house. Three boys, a box of matches, a senior citizen and a house full of furniture made of foam. It wasn't much of a competition, was it? Oh, and a laugh. Don't forget the laugh. That's what they said it was for.

The door went up like a firework, so the police report said, before it fell over flat into the hall, varnish bubbling and squealing in the heat. Even the boys were amazed. 'Did you see that!' one of them shouted before they started to run.

The flames crept over the ceiling first, then down the light fitting and around the living room door. They burned up a picture of flowers hanging by the bottom of this old man's stairs. They burned up a pair of his black boots and a rain mac, dark blue with six buttons. They burned up an old carpet that needed replaced and a library book he was planning to return. They burned up wallpaper and skirting and gloss and plasterboard. This old man didn't stand a chance. One minute he was dozing,

➡

the next he was going like a chimney fire, the remains of his hair shrinking in the heat. It's amazing, really, what the experts can tell.

I go past on my lunch break to see: and the chair where the old man sat is just a ring of black; the windows where he watched the world pass by are scattered across his front grass; his curtains no longer exist. Nor does the granddaughter he was babysitting that night, found upstairs breathing smoke, her throat a furnace as she gasped in vain for air. It's one way to go.

I stand in the street as the neighbours come out to look. 'Oh my God,' one of them says as she wheels her buggy past, slow. The others bend close and hold their hands over their mouths. 'The poor wee soul,' they say. 'And the old man too - such a shame. Wouldn't hurt a fly.' Some of them cry.

It doesn't take long. They aren't savvy these three boys and they're only wee.

One says, 'He took my brother's ball.'

The other, 'He shouted at my sister.'

The third, 'We were bored.'

I tie them to the fence, just back from the broken glass and the newly boarded front door. There are lots. It's a shame. Men don't often get flowers so it seems a pity now they've arrived in abundance, that this old man won't get to see them at all.

Thursday

Is busy. The corridors are full. There are lots of people talking. I stand with my trolley and listen to the urgency of low voices, the quick bark of commands, the endless trill of phones. I listen and this is what they say.

The child's face was white.

Her hair was dirty.

Her green sweatshirt was gone.

A boy found her. Someone the same age. One minute he was wandering about, picking things up, tossing them down, the next he was looking at those fingers sticking out from underneath a mattress - so pale, so blue he thought perhaps they were a toy. Until he bent to touch. Then he knew.

The boy ran, stumbling, breathing heavy, told his dad. His dad ran - this boy had probably never seen his dad run so fast, not for years – and his dad was shouting as he was running, 'Call the police.' And somehow, because his dad was running, the boy was running and other people were running too and stumbling and calling, so when the boy got back there was a small crowd, a whole group of them.

They stood together and looked at the fingers. Then his dad bent down and lifted the mattress. The boy saw it. They all saw it.

Her wide-open eyes.

Her dirty hair.

Her parted lips, blue like her fingertips.

No one bothered to check for her pulse. About that, they all agree.

They said later, the people who were around in the house when it happened, that the mother collapsed, that she caved in. And as she caved in her husband held her on one side while a policewoman held her on the other. For a moment the mother hung there and everyone was silent. Then she began to moan.

They didn't tell her about the sprawl of her daughter's legs. She didn't need to know. About the buttons ripped from her daughter's shirt. She knew anyway.

Outside their gate, house number thirty-three, on the pavement, there are teddy bears and stuffed animals and cards with little hearts drawn by other children the same age. Everyone's put a message:

'darling',

'angel',

'princess'.

Everyone's got something to say.

I take mine somewhere else instead. As near as I can get to where she breathed her last. I think of her on my trolley, in my corridor with the strips for lights, taking up so little room. Then I lay them down amongst a pile of rubbish – broken bottles, crisp packets, dog shit, cardboard slashed and worn. They look lost, the daffodils, amongst all the debris. Still at least they are here, just like she used to be.

Friday

Afternoon and the end of the week at last. I finish early and make my way over to find someone else's funeral has just gone on.

Twenty-one and a wreath in white plastic and blue ribbon. Not very well made. SON. It's a shame.

He's lying there now in his earthy pit, little stones and worms and clumps of clay all piled on top, borrowed black tie, bright shoes and that suit he probably got for his first job interview, the one with the breast pocket and the lining in deepest grey. He'll have liked that suit, no doubt, but he probably only wore it twice - the job interview and now down there.

It's an ordinary row. Near the top end of the cemetery where they put in the extension ground a couple of years ago. There are no trees here, just one or two benches. There's a gravel path and most of the stones are really new. I walk along and watch as they un-scroll past my eyes – the James's and Evelyn's and 2007s and 2008s and 'lost are the' and 'suffer little' and 'in remembrance' and uncles and grandmas and wives. He's unusual, this boy. There aren't many sons up here.

I wonder then why it happened to him, instead of the rest. Perhaps he fell off a wall and crushed his head. Or into a river and swamped his lungs. Or maybe he just had an incurable disease. Got a headache and couldn't get out of bed and his mum thought he was kidding on because he could be lazy sometimes, always late for work so she said to him, 'What do you think you're doing wasting your life not making the most you never know people out there got to take life by the...' She'll feel bad about it now, no doubt, but what can she do.

My mother is three rows back and five along. Quite a few have filled up the spaces in between since I put her here, all with their best suits, their hair dos and their flesh slowly going black, a few last remnants sticking to their bones.

My mother's flesh was rotten before all that. Before wreaths and headstones and wooden boxes with brass handles. Before clay and worms and lumps of earth thrown down from on top. Her skin had already sloughed off, marked the carpet where she lay, soft tissue turned purple then grey before I had any idea that days had gone by since she had been out, weeks since she had used the phone, months since anyone had heard from her at all. My mother's flesh had well and truly rotted long before people began to complain about the smell.

I bring her carnations, pink with a white stripe. I've always hated carnations - the kind of thing you buy in petrol stations, suffocating under shiny plastic. I take them out of their cover and leave them propped up against the grey stone where it says 'beloved'. They look good actually and I'm glad. I stand there for a little, before I leave. That night I have macaroni cheese with sliced tomatoes on top for my tea.

Saturday
On Saturday I read the newspaper and consider my week ahead.

Sunday
On Sunday I watch Songs of Praise and sing along to all the tunes.

Extract from the novel *Guitar Man*

Lesley Wilson

I AM LEANING against a wall by the newsagents lighting a cigarette, when she passes. Beside me unwanted magazines wilt in the sea-mist.

She comes near, much nearer than you usually get to strangers. This, in itself, jars me from my dehydrated fugue. But it is her scent that really gets me going.

The coming and going of her fragrance kills my cigarette smoke, kills the sharp sea-rot in the air. I know it immediately – an amalgam of amber, woodsmoke, the last breath of summer flowers before they die. Cloying some would say. Too intense. Not for me though. Intense is good.

I watch the girl walk away, blind to everything but the curtain of her dark hair and her mesmerising movement. I throw down my cigarette and follow her. But she moves swiftly as though trying to escape me, the chill vapour colluding.

Her fragrance is lost in the smell of the sea as she increases her distance from me. I am aware of other people again, irritatingly in my way. My nerves are ragged. I am grubby inside my skin and my legs are heavy.

Of course it's not Elvira. It can't be. She is twenty years too young. Once more my whole situation strikes me as ridiculous. But still she gave me that feeling, this girl. And it's the *feéling* I need again; more than answers, more than any result.

The beat of my heart rises and I quicken my step. I follow her past the sea-front shops, towards the outskirts of town and the back streets.

The sun, fortuitous, knowing, begins to burn through the mist. Her lifting hair shines, her pale dress dazzles and floats. Other people are no longer there – just she and I, moving past the low worn-out buildings, not so far apart now.

She turns a corner into the street where the second-hand shop is, where I go to look at the books and old CDs. I will her to stop there. I follow her into the shadow.

If she raises her arm in its white linen to reach for the door I will take her for an angel.

And she does. I watch the soft turning of her body. Her hand, tiny for the rest of her frame, is flat against the dingy glass.

Her skin is the colour of caramel and she wears a star-shaped ring, heavy and dark on her little finger. It looks odd and cumbersome on her lovely hand and yet it is beautiful too, in its own way. But it's not for her. She wears it like a penance. I have a sense of the burden of that ring, the touch of that small hand, her name, even.

I feel I should know her name but I can't bring it to mind. She is not Elvira. But I know this girl just the same.

When I enter the shop there is a blast of warm air and the tiny bells clash like demons. The woman behind the counter looks up at me and smiles. Then *she,* who I don't immediately see, drifts from behind a stand of men's clothes, her white dress holding her softly. She gives every impression of not noticing me but I feel in my heart that she has.

She is fingering the sleeve of an old man's jacket, her hand sliding gently down the tweed as if caressing the lost person inside.

How clean and glossy she looks amongst the racks and shelves of the old and left behind. I gaze again at the ring on her hand. Heavy, dark jewellery and strong perfume; the hallmarks of Elvira. Logical reasons to be drawn to this girl. But perhaps I just need an excuse to look at her.

The woman behind the counter is looking at me curiously. I must act, make a purchase or leave or maybe just ask a question. But what question?

I know her name but I can't bring it to mind.

Then I have that rogue flash of clarity that comes only to the turgidly hungover

'Are you Gabriella?' I enquire loudly

Instantaneously the girl turns around lifting the jacket in front of her and I see her face properly for the first time. There are definite similarities – the direct, amber-coloured eyes, the wide mouth, the delicate bones. Like mother, like daughter.

But she makes no response to my question. Indeed, she appears not to have heard me. She walks towards a mirror and puts on the jacket. The woman behind the counter makes gestures towards me with her mouth and fingers to inform me that the girl doesn't speak. Then she points to her ear and shrugs.

There is nothing for me to do. I smile and nod at the woman and make my way hastily through the door to the bright blue emptiness of summer noon.

I break my vow about not drinking in the day and go to a bar, not one overlooking the harbour, but one up a side street, where the windows are mere slits near the ceiling. If you don't look up it could be night or day. I sip a whisky and think.

Twenty summers ago. I am on an empty train with Elvira. It is raining and we can hardly see the coast as we leave town. She is more drunk than I have ever seen her. More specifically, she is drunk in a manner I have *never* seen her. Not triumphantly 'fuck me now' drunk in a bar as she strokes my cock under the table, not 'fuck you' drunk as she argues with a waiter, revelling in the distaste and embarrassment of onlookers. She is broken drunk and the sight of her chills me to the bone. Not through pity or empathy but through panic. Elvira is the strong one. If she breaks I am nothing.

'Is just the thought,' she slurs, 'Just the thought of never seeing my baby playing on the beach again.' She throws an arm towards the offending unseen shore, bangs her hand on the glass and doesn't feel it.

And I hold her against my chest and hope she doesn't feel me tremble. I think I will have to fuck her, right here in this carriage with the risk of being discovered, to get her to calm down. Fucking usually calms her if she's angry or just too over-excited to sleep after a good night out. For this particular situation then it's the only thing I can think of.

So I try to lie her down on the long seat, tell her it's no good for her just looking out at the rain, that she must still her mind and find peace. I don't actually mean what I'm saying. I just want her to sneer at me, to laugh horribly. I want her to be Elvira. I want my baby back.

'I will never find peace Joe,' she whispers with terrible sincerity. And for all the actress she is I think that this time she is speaking the truth.

I try to kiss her, making comforting hushing sounds, thinking she will hate this and wondering idly if it's a good idea or not.

But she turns her face from my mouth disinterestedly and the tears run down her golden skin. I try to kiss the wetness away and she doesn't notice.

'You will see Gabriella again – of *course* you will.' I try desperately,' But for now it's best she stays with him. You know that – we all agreed. You're *ill*, sweetheart.'

She turns and looks at me as if I'm crazy.

'Ill' she hisses,' I'm not fucking ill, you stupid, *stupid* bastard. I'm ...I'm the thing you can't be as a mother. I'm...'

She thrusts her face so close to mine I can smell the vomit- tainted odour of stale drink.

'...I'm *selfish*!!' she screams, then collapses sobbing on my shoulder.

I put my hand between her legs, pressing softly, once, twice as if she has a wound there and needs to be healed. At first her body is rigid, perversely unyielding, then as the train gathers speed, shaking the tracks harshly and insistently, she looks up at me with eyes full of tragedy. She falls back onto the seat.

'Please,' she whispers.

That's all.

I adjust her skirt, open her blouse, make her legs more comfortable. Through the window the distant lines of the rail bridge cut the smeared sky. The last connection with the coast and our old life. Mist and rain blanket the fields, the river mouth, the white house where her husband lives. Where Gabriella now lives.

Her thighs come up to me reluctantly as if her spirit is fighting me off. She is silent, turning her face from mine but, as usual the wetness between her legs gives her away. I enter her gently, feeling the ghost of her hand on my back, needing it once more, the shadow of her passion. I shiver. I have a sense of foreboding.

Then the train is crossing the old bridge and with its avuncular aid we judder and jerk to desperate, understated orgasm. And she sleeps after that, with her head on my lap. And the erection that comes and goes is not uncertain because of our subdued orgasm, or out of empathy for her grief, but because I too keep seeing a small girl, barefoot in a cotton dress, running along the sand. She is holding my guitar in front of her, almost stumbling with the size of it.

'Careful, Gabriella.' her mother cries.

'I want Uncle Joe to play it for me,' she says

And I remember that when I was a child I thought all my uncles were kind.

I come to with the sound of knocking on my door. I have those merciful 'nothing' seconds where I register physically that I'm in bed and that I have a dull headache, but I can't recall anything else.

'Joe, if you're in there, I'll leave your things outside on the landing.'

I untangle myself from the sheets, pull on my jeans, stumble to the door, now remembering my two hours in an empty bar, then before that – the girl. And so I am anxious

again and need an antidote. And I don't want to drink.

'Linda, hold on. Come and talk to me.'

She is halfway down the sun-dappled hall, her figure neat, purposeful in white trousers and skinny top, her fair hair splashed with the sun. Linda is a woman and a girl. too. She is everyone's family. Sometimes she is too wise, too stable and she gets on my nerves but she's the only friend I have here. I fuck her when I'm down. Sometimes I feel bad afterwards. But she's still a friend and I think she knows that.

She turns and affectedly raises her gold man's watch in front of her. Probably a present from some other grateful bastard. I know she wants me to ask but I really can't think what to say.

'I'll give you half an hour max, Garvie.' she says.

I know she'll stay longer if I ask.

Once inside the room she deposits my washing on the unmade bed and good -humouredly shakes her head at the disarray. She glances towards my crotch. Unconsciously – I think.

'Perchance you have had company.'

She smiles, coming closer to slide a hand down my back. She looks towards the closed door of the shower-room.

I laugh and kiss her forehead.

'Sometimes a man has no choice but to dream.' I tell her.

When I reach for the half empty bottle on the bedside table I hear her sigh. This makes me tense. Just now I don't need her disapproval. I pat the dishevelled sheets and smile into her eyes. When she comes down to me she is soft and resigned.

She smooths the bed herself before she sits down.

'This looks serious, Garvie' she says.

I pour two glasses of whisky. We sit side by side in silence staring into the gloom. The darkness I gaze into is restless, a darkness teased imploringly by the spirit of Elvira. Linda is uneasy too, but I can't do anything about it. All the vague images before my eyes are soured and weighted . A patch of dust there, waiting for the imprint of Elvira's footstep. My jacket here on a chair, perfumed by her fingertips. The air is waiting for the sound of her low voice. Yet Elvira has never been in this room. I have not seen her for half of my lifetime. But always she has been there, waiting for my return.

'I take it you have news of "she who must be obeyed."'

Linda's words come abruptly and my heart thuds. It's as if we both expect Elvira to rush into the room in a brash dress with her mouth heavily painted.

The sad thing is Linda only knows of Elvira through my recall, the finality of my desire. Linda knows that she, herself, is only an antidote, and worse still, that she often isn't enough.

'No... not exactly.'

I take a large gulp of whisky to steady myself.

Then I tell her about seeing Gabriella.

'Could you open the window?' I ask her, halfway through my story.

I am suddenly depressed and afraid of the sunless gloom. I want to see Linda's hair shine bright, her eyes look at me in that knowing way. I also want to her to go to the window so that she won't see me refill my glass.

She stands against the pale rectangle of the sky, a cigarette in hand. She breathes her smoke outwards into the sea-scented air, although she knows I don't mind people smoking in my room. She has something on her mind. A fleeting anxiety comes, annoyance, even. Linda, the eternal figure of good sense, is about to spoil my fun.

But with the blind raised the afternoon sun returns and falls benevolently on my freshly ironed shirts, and despite things I am becoming heartened, less tired. Then Linda turns around but she won't look me in the eye.

'I think I know this girl, Joe,' she says then, starting a fresh cigarette, looking down at her small feet with their painted toe nails. She has painted them the colour of shells. I think of Elvira's dark red nail varnish, her long strong fingernails hard in my back

'I'm sure I've seen her once or twice in the bar.'

She looks at me carefully.

Suddenly there's a purity, a rare magic on my paltry possessions slung about the room. The thought that I might have a chance of seeing Gabriella again.

'I think...' she hesitates then, blows a cloud of smoke in front of her so that I can't see her face, 'I think she's on the game, Joe.'

I get up. Automatically. As if someone has told me to. I walk, a touch unsteadily towards Linda at the window. I look out to the vivid harbour, to the ships lilting contentedly on their anchors. I watch a small craft break away from the rest, go out to sea.

We look out the window, smoking, standing close, our arms touching.

'What makes you think it's her?' I ask eventually.

'Well, the girl I'm thinking of is dark, oriental-looking...'

'Elvira's family were Italian, second generation...'

I say this quickly, with pathetic eagerness, feeling again the caramel skin next to mine, the smell of Elvira, the gripping, the clinging, the pushing away. I feel it all again and I shudder quite obviously, not being able to help it.

Linda clutches my wrist, then relaxes her hold, caressing me gently as if I was a disappointed child. I think how she would have made a good mother.

'Joe, this girl is also deaf and she doesn't speak, as far as I can make out anyway. So...'

'I see.'

I let my cigarette end drop from the window. It drifts forlornly down to the pavement.

Some girls cross the street in short skirts and a lot of make-up for late afternoon. I've been with plenty whores in my time, for Christ's sake. Most of them are nice women, needing the money. Suddenly I feel sickened, annoyed with myself. I take it out on Linda.

'So when did you start encouraging prostitutes in your hallowed establishment. I thought that would be well against your principles.'

She turns from the window and walks towards the bed. I have a moment's panic waiting for her to pick up her bag and go. But

➥

she sits down heavily on the rumpled sheets, stretches her legs in front of her.

'Principles,' she says very quietly, as if to herself.

'I've nothing against... street girls,' she continues in a louder, more considered tone, 'As long as they don't bring trouble.'

She turns to look at me.

'I don't need trouble in my life, Joe.'

Then as if somehow feeling things have gone too far, her tone changes.

'As far as I can see a lot of women sell themselves, anyway. Men too. It's just a question of degree.'

She reaches across to my bedside table, takes a large gulp of my whisky.

I sit close to her, lift her hair, kiss her neck for a while. Too long, perhaps.

'I'm sorry, sweetheart.'

She looks into my eyes, half-searching, half-amused. Then she puts her arms around my neck.

'I don't know, Garvie. I give you a job, even put your washing in with the bar stuff and why?'

I smile at her, shake my head in a mock-woeful way. I begin to get an erection in anticipation.

'You may be past your best but to me you're well worth a shag.' She looks sad for a moment. 'And sometimes I just need a shag.'

She puts her hand on my thigh.

'Fuck me, Joe Garvie.'

mike
Colin Herd

we put masking tape on the floor,
like a tennis court, and played, in our
sweats on the 'lawn' and laughed, you
know: serve, love, deuce, game, set,
then we yawned.

my personal trainer is also my co-
author (in a sense, my muse and
master) his name's mike, and would
you disbelieve me if i said he also trains
gwen stefani? mike you are good, man,
undeniably.

is mike in the room? no, mike's not in
the room. he gives dietary tips too. and
runs a special program designed for
budding brides and grooms in preparation
for their big day. i mention it because
he asked me to.

strictly following
Colin Herd

mike's instructions can be really tough!
but the results speak for themselves, i
guess. a great deal of what he teaches
is really correcting bad habits. my cable
– crossover was completely wrong, barely
beneficial at all to the development of my
chest.
    yesterday, my motivation having dipped,
mike said, think of it as a poem, and knock
out all the unnecessary lines to reveal, eh
(mike is never out of his depth. this hesitation
very rare) the true, sculpted, sexy and muscular
shape of the poem within. he reads the new
yorker every issue. i said: so you think you're
ezra pound now? i'm joining david lloyd.

Three Women Ten Minutes Apart
Graham Fulton

The first,
    halfway up
               an escalator
in the shopping centre,
          with a three foot piece
of toilet roll stuck
    to the sole of her right shoe,
and two little boys
        sniggering behind her back,
and me smiling behind their backs,
with all the people going into
              or coming out
of Marks and Spencer
or Boots the Chemist,
              the second,
       in the Bank of Scotland,
reciting the instruction
WITHDRAW CASH
WITHOUT A RECEIPT
         out loud to herself,
or me standing behind her,
       as if it isn't going to happen
         unless she does,
and the sun shining through
the glass in the door,
            the last,
on the same pavement
        I walk home every day,
    shouting *Why are you*
      fucking running away you pig
to a man 100 metres in front of her,
    or me,
     no-one at all,
  with a little girl in a pink jacket
running behind her
          pushing a buggy,
trying to keep up,
do it right.

How Salt can be a Man
Aiko Harman

She refuses her body, salt.
She wants to remember the sea—
its sharp bite, in every dash
she sacrifices. Every tasteless soup.

At heart, she is a fish woman,
her eyes like bulbs in photos
her cheeks puffed, held breath.
She speaks only of the pure silence
striding lengths underwater
weightless as a shadow,
completely alone.

She wants to mould her body
into a new tool, hone it smooth,
thin as a steel blade,
holding on to nothing,
saltless as a separation
from the sea. Her broken
heart, a conch to crawl in,
now outgrown.

She wants to hear the sea
in her ear like a klaxon, clutch
what she has left behind
in her mouth, a hollow nothing
savour the mute colour
of her own withered tongue
and leave him at last.

The little gothic orangery
Bridget Kursheed

Best work I did there
but I had nothing to do with oranges
the glass panes the cutting of them
and their angles
we had worked on stained glass
and its leading but these
the panes their fine-ness
a meadowsweet head
cut down its shapes
in glass and the curve of it
all to hold oranges
I had nothing to do with oranges

And when we placed the glass there
the rain came in from the hills
we saw its curl
in the glass laid on hessian
in trays from the gardener
he had lent us
before the oranges which might fill them
and then each piece
its position as intricate
as a flowerhead as grass seeds
or crops a harvest of glass
cut and winnowed
with lath and putty
into a shape that caught the hills
each piece of them
their incline and steep upwards
slope in the window's pattern
I could only look out
I had nothing to do with the oranges

Reading the Book
Brian Johnstone

Limp-covered, unprotected, paperbacks
have grown their marks the way a body might respond
to wounds in childhood, accident's distress;

grown them from the chop of steel,
the nicks in blades that sheared them square
to leave raised tracks that curve across the page-ends

like a scar. They bear these too: the indentations
pulsed through covers by some point, that fade out only
as the plot develops, characters begin to grow.

And there the corners start to crease,
each random scalene waiting for a thumb to smooth it out,
to claim the place back from somebody pausing in a past

which left these pits and scores
by accident, from skill a little less than it might be,
or pressing time, preserved here in the strata of a book.

A Sequence of Six Pregnancy Poems
Hazel Frew

Three

There's a word
in the window.

A yes
to attest.

Mallards over
bare-tree bronchi.

In the dark still
near the Kelvin

the two of us
now three.

Minim

We've created this stave
between us
you and I.

And now – you –
the unknown clef
curling on yourself.

A quaver.
Notator in space.

Umbilical.
Attached to me
more than
you'll ever know.

One semibreve
sounding in silence.

A quiet scale
vindicating
our love.

Pang

Leaving my teeth
in cucumber moons

artichokes spreading
like moths

a beetroot
sliced for delectation

sausages dimpling
then splitting

bowls of vanilla
peppered by pods

a sharing of spoons
for two

all of these cravings
driven by you

my burgeoning,
burrowing, baby pang.

Fovea

Linea nigra
an arrow
from plexus
to button.

Pointing
ever dark
gathering.

Tidal sweats
areola
budding nipple.

Your sacred limbs
filamentary in black.

10 Weeks

You're a coil
in a grapefruit

an astronaut
on a skein

size of a strawberry

my little
fruity blessing

defying gravity
treading water

upside down
in your sack

yolk giving way
to placenta

toes taking
shape nicely

ricocheting within.

Pollywog

Pollywog
a tadpole
losing its tail

a sailor
in my ocean

crossing the equator
with eyes wide open

full steam.

Brother Works the Saw

John Douglas Millar

My brother's brow
recedes in salt and pepper
thin

growing wrinkles
spreading spider-like from soft
eyes –

of brown. An arm
of veins, confluence of blood
hand, solid, holds

      A saw that cuts
wood showing
years and weather, where
rain fell and where
              the sun shone

My brother draws the saw
to reveal

In-patient

Extract from novel *Critical Mass*

Kate Tough

I WILL LET these people sit by my bed every afternoon and every evening and I will thank them for coming, when I am able. I am not trying to cause the worry I see when they're leaving but I have no words for them.

I do not want what has happened to have happened. Something has happened. Something happened in my body.

To make a person fear for her own survival; it's cruel. To surgically remove her motherhood-

I do not want what is happening to be happening.

For the duration of my stay I have something that I am doing – I am a patient. My job is to lie in this bed. I do my job well.

Who I would be at home is less clear. And nobody will be there; beside themselves with relief that I am back.

I will have to do things – necessary things – plus other things that I will have to do just to be seen to be doing something.

Doing things makes me tired.

Doing things leads to other things. And things have a habit of changing, just when you'd got very used to them being a certain way.

My heart broke. My body broke.

The bailiffs came for my womb.

What exactly do you people want from me?

I didn't have obsessive compulsive disorder when I came in but I might well have it by the time I leave (an OK trade?). There is precious little to do but notice things and how often they occur:

Times per hour I assess how my wound-site is feeling: about nine.

Times per day I remember to visualise a healthy wound-site: one.

Number of consecutive days with a Tupperware lid of cloud-cover outside: six.

(The sheets, the walls, the sky – all the colour of bone. Am I that colour too? I have no mirror to tell otherwise. Maybe everyone who goes under anaesthetic wakes up in this world of bone, while their previous lives continue somewhere else.)

Minutes per day the nurses listen to a moronic breakfast-radio DJ: one hundered & twenty.

Minutes per day I am now able to breathe behind the radio and tune it out: 120.

Times per day I imagine killing the DJ: none, he's not worth it.

Times per day I imagine being outdoors for hours at a time: one, but it lasts a while.

Times per day I notice that my left foot sits higher under the sheet than my right: about a dozen.

Times per day I speak: zero.

Times per day I make eye contact with the parent who has come to visit: on arrival only.

(I will not cry in a room with a glass half-wall, with a person who has to leave afterward.)

Times per hour I remember what other people have to cope with in life: one, but it lasts a while.

Times per day I imagine a year from now, when things might be very different: zero, initially; now up to two or three.

Times per hour the perma-grin nurse sings out to the woman opposite, 'Feeling OK Hilda?': four.

(I am waiting for Hilda to be discharged or die.)

I make eye-contact with my seven o'clock but it's not my mother, it's Hilary. 'Your mum phoned and asked if I could come. She said she'd been held up at an appointment but, frankly, I think she needed a break.' Hilary handles her coat buttons like they're children who are taking too long over something.

'I have been calling her, you know. She kept saying that you didn't want to see friends yet, but your 'yet' was lasting a long time.' She begins to bend at the knees to sit, but straightens up again.

'I was getting really concerned. Eventually, your mum admitted that you've not actually been speaking – not a word – to anyone. I think she's got me along here to see if a new face can make a difference.' She leaves a gap. I don't fill it.

'They're only keeping you here because you won't talk. You do know that. Of course you know that. You're here because you want to be, Jill Beech. I'm onto you.' Again, a gap from the woman who will never be 'Auntie Hilary' to my kids.

'Just show them you're fine and you'll get home. How can you stand being here?' She has placed her bag on the chair that she stands behind.

'I watered your plants on Tuesday. You have post. You have bills, Jill. They're piling up. If this is what you think you need, fine. But keep it up much longer and they'll turf you out anyway, because they need the bed. You'll end up with a social worker or a mental health visitor or something. Is that what you want?'

I just want to lie here.

'Whatever it is, Jill, we can sort it out. Come *home* and be mute. This is no place to be.' She absently picks up a greetings card from my side-table and places it down again.

'You have us,' she says, re-buttoning the coat she never took off. 'We have a rota drawn up that we're gagging to implement. Leave here, and you will be the extra-curricular project of several people who care about you.' She softens into her first smile. Perhaps I have missed her.

'My freezer is full of soup,' she says, leaving the room with her temporary childlessness. '*And casserole,*' she shouts out, in the corridor... the kadunk-dunk of saloon doors swinging in her wake...

After twenty-eight 'Hildas', while I'm looking out of the window at the Tupperware sky and imagining a year from now, a bouquet is delivered, complete with vase. The card reads:

I forgôt to sit down. You know I hate hospitals. Missing you - a lôt! Don't make me come back there... Hilary x

Half of the lilies are still closed: elongated pods tucked amongst the deep sheen of the leaves. Those flower heads which are open span my hand. The curled-back petals are a bruised blue-pink down their middles. I smell weddings, from the rusty bars of pollen. I lie back and let the flowers happen because a nurse will amputate those sheet-staining stamens as soon as she sees them.

The woman in the next bed woke up after her operation yesterday and was almost immediately transformed into a cyborg of sales. 'You've got your blues, your browns, your pinks... I've only got some of the range here but in this catalogue, see? That entire section. Your corals all the way to your crimsons. Every occasion catered for.'

The cleaner came into our room a few minutes ago with a mop and bucket and hasn't had a chance to start using it yet. She's anxious enough about this situation to interrupt. 'I don't wear make-up that often,' she says, slightly apologetic, 'hardly ever, so it's probably no–'

'Some women – like you, you lucky thing – are gorgeous enough the way God intended. That's why I know you'll be excited by our other products. We're more than just a top-end cosmetics company. In this section,' she says, frantically flicking through the pages, 'here! Here we've got everything you need to enhance and preserve that incredible face of yours *from the inside*. All natural ingredients, nothing nasty. Millions of women like you swear by our Perky Lady drink; you've got your beetroot juice in there, your B vitamins, your calcium, your iron, but it's mild, you won't get that metallic taste–'

A nurse has entered the room and is looking at the cleaner whilst tapping her watch.

'Sorry nursey, my fault,' says the multi-level-marketeer, 'keeping her off her duties. That's a lovely eye-shadow you're wearing, what is that? A smokey-taupe?'

And before you can say bedpan, the nurse is in the chair by the bed getting a make-up demonstration with an enthusiastic, factually-suspect commentary. Twenty minutes later (foundation, eyes, blusher but no lipstick) a more senior nurse type appears and, on hearing her voice, the nurse in the chair leaps up, garnering a lipstick streak down her chin.

'Blame me,' says the pyramid seller, 'but she has such wonderful skin I couldn't resist. Almost as lovely as yours...'

This comment merely elicits a terse eye-roll. As both nurses leave the room, she calls after them, 'Come by again, ladies, at the end of your shift. I'm sure I've a wee something here to add sparkle to a night out.' Then she falls quiet, but not still. She looks about the room appraising its potential. Eventually her gaze lands on me. Somebody must have taken her to the side, though, and explained my 'problem' because she doesn't bother launching into her spiel. She simply reaches over, tosses a catalogue on my bed and says, 'Here, have a read at that luvvie. You can circle the ones you like - not the blushers though, you don't have the cheekbones.'

I almost laugh: there was me worrying whether I'd live or die and it turns out I should have been worrying about my flat cheeks. She probably thinks it would have been kinder if I had died - how could any self-respecting woman carry on with this unremarkable bone structure?

I can't help admiring her spirit. Hospital must be a serious setback to the self-employed. No-one's paying her a salary to lie here.

Looking at her toolbox of tubs and tubes, full of coloured circles and squares, I suddenly realise that all the things a transvestite has to do to transform himself into a 'woman' are no different from the things a woman does, daily, to look like a woman. So who came up with this idea of a woman?

Out of respect for cyborg's need to earn a living, I lift the catalogue and place it on my side-cabinet, to give to my mum, later. She never could resist new slap.

After lunch, somebody sits on the chair beside mine in the day-room. I've never met him before. There is a hospital ID badge clipped to his blazer, so he must work here in some capacity. As a psychologist, it turns out. He tells me that he's heard a bit about my background from the medical staff, but that whatever he and I discuss will remain confidential.

After a bit of eye contact from me, he says, 'I'm not here to make you normal, Jill. You're already normal. Experiencing shock after a cancer operation which removed your fertility - *that is* normal.'

Don't do this.

'I'm here to listen, that's all. No advice if you don't want it. Just a neutral pair of ears. Why don't you try putting it into words? Try telling me how it feels.'

Stop. You're embarrassing yourself.

'I'm not implying I have the answers, far from it. I have personality tics just like everyone else. It's about managing them. Keeping them manageable.'

He obviously hasn't had an intractably silent one for a while. If he had a collar on he'd be unbuttoning it about now.

'I go to the same holiday villa in the Algarve every year – that's how much I hate change. My family thinks it's nuts but they tolerate it. So – there's something about me – why not share something about you? What makes you different?'

My sense of propriety.

'If you feel able to share, I'm here. Or we can set up an appointment. I'd like to hear what's troubling you.'

I'd like it if you skipped back off to Portugal with the two or three, or maybe even four, well-balanced children you doubtless have.

This evening, my seven o'clock is Dad. He walks around my bed to the chair. Instead of sitting on it, he picks it up and brings it round to the other side of the bed. He then sits on it; his back to the internal window. My mother is on the other side of the glass, waiting by the nurses' office (waiting to talk to one of them about me, I presume). No doubt she means well but she's worrying me. Does she think we're at 'decision' time?

'Almost couldn't get parked out there tonight,' he says. Their antics have caught my attention. I maintain eye contact.

'We can't stay too long. We'd like to, obviously, but we can't. Not tonight.' He's smiling, but not explaining himself.

They're moving me somewhere. They've come to say goodbye: break it to me gently before I am carted off. I'm too late. I have fucked it right up. I have to say something.

I inhale the breath I need to speak.

He speaks first. 'We've been wracking our brains. Can't understand why you won't make more... progress. Why doesn't Jilly want to leave there, we keep asking ourselves.'

Mum is still waiting for a nurse to become available.

'We're at a loss. The only thing we could come up with is that maybe you don't want to go back to an empty flat.' He reaches for a bag he must have put down when he came in. The kind someone might take to a gym. Have I driven him to that?

He puts it on his knee. 'Maybe you don't like the idea of being all on your own,' he continues, unzipping the bag and reaching in. 'So... we got you someone to live with.'

Little ears, then eyes, emerge from the bag. He places the unsure bundle on the bed. Very small paws pad clumsily alongside my leg. After some hesitant sniffing, it lifts it head and finds itself looking at me. Its tiny mouth opens in a meow. Sounding more like a baby bird, it does it again. Dad appears to have abandoned it, so it's up to me to reassure the wee thing. I reach for it and it lets me. Holding it to my chest, I say to Dad, 'You're brave, bringing this in here.'

I don't think I've ever seen a smile like that on him. He must love kittens.

'Shift your chair over a bit,' I tell him, 'if the nurse sees this...'

It takes him a few seconds to answer, he's so busy beaming at me. 'Your mum's out there keeping watch. Anyway, I'm seventy. What do I care if I get caught? Well, what do you think of him?'

'He's alright,' I shrug, then smile to show I was teasing.

'Don't you think he looks like Bomber?' he asks. 'Soon as I saw him I knew he was the one for you.'

'How old is he?'

'Eight weeks. Picked him up the other day. We didn't want to move the little man around too much, so we've been staying at yours to settle him in there. Word to the wise, I wouldn't leave it too long. Your mother is getting that look. You know, that look just before she rolls her sleeves up.'

Having lost many treasured childhood possessions to that look, I know if I want to hold on to the objects I've spent the last fifteen years growing quite fond of, I should go home.

'Mum,' I say quietly, into the mouthpiece. She sounds a bit disorientated when she replies. 'Jill? Where are you?'

'In the day-room, on the payphone. I told the night-nurse I was going for a pee.'

'It's nice to hear you. Very, very nice. Have you got your gown on?'

'Yes, don't worry, and the slippers you brought.'

'How are you? Are you OK?'

Squatting on the seat of a large armchair, in the shadows cast by light-pollution, I answer her. 'Mum...'

'Yes, Jill?'

'I never got the chance... I'll never be able to have... any... chil...'

'I know, darling. I know.' She has the grace and courage to talk on, while I cry and cry and

→

cry. 'It makes me sad, too,' she says, 'that you'll never have the joy of your own family. I'd have loved for you to have had a child,' she says. 'It was such a pleasure being a mum to you,' she adds, and many other things just as kind.

Presumably because I have made the decision to take down the bunting on this festival of depression, I wake with a strong yen for flavour. I can't get packed fast enough thinking of the sun-dried tomatoes in oil I will buy on the way home.

In the taxi, it occurs to me that the nurses could have made more of a fuss.

Attendance
Elizabeth Reeder

WHEN YOU DIE she will bury you in some out of the way place and tend to you in the way only the mourning can tend the dead. There will be rosemary and wildflowers and nettles growing there, where you will be buried. Complicated plants. Useful. By useful I mean like the brilliance of light or like sudden, primordial rain.

When you die she will wear a black band around her arm, like a man. She will wear bright dresses when it's hot; a heavy coat when the freeze comes on, but she will wear the black band at all times, so people know.

The band will allow her to tender something unspoken. It will be no big deal when you die. None at all. People die all the time. People who are less loved than you, younger than you, more tragic too. They are also mourned. Her mourning will not be special, and she'll not be made special by it. She will simply be consumed.

In your last days, and after, we will learn that earth has memory of what is given to it. There are places on mountains where people ask to be scattered as ash, and these popular places flourish too green where there should only be rocks and low-growing twisted wood. It's the krummolz zone; thin-aired, weather battered, barely fertile. The generous nitrogen of our bones can be dangerous to that which is used to surviving on so little.

When you are ill she tends to you as only the living can tend the dying. She holds your head as you vomit, sits by the side of your bed in the dark and her weeping takes apart the air of the room and you grow restless, you moan.

You have not been kind but she does not think this, she thinks that soon you will be gone and we, in the midst of illness, are in grief.

I care for you too sometimes, not often, and I move your limbs with neutral sterility and you sleep through my rough handlings. We both know what this is: sometimes absence of love is relief.

The day you die will be no different than any other day. People die all the time. They leave and we all know the shape of this. When someone is gone, but still alive, the loss is the shape of a fist or a fist-shaped bruise. And it's true her lips are dark, like her eyes, and she often holds her hands to her belly, curled over, like she's been punched.

Most of us think of death as absence but it's really about space. Sometimes it's rectangular and three dimensional: rich dirt-black walls which will fit snug to the sides of your box. Sometimes we think of burial as light on waves, the dead scattered into a space which is changed, but only briefly, by their presence. The dead disperse and seem to disappear into the air, into the water, but this is false. You'll be like those plastic bags thrown out to sea. We think they break up, disintegrate into nothing but they simply break down into smaller and smaller plastic molecules, and the organisms they suffocate grow more and more minute.

When you die she will bury you in an out of the way place and even if we witness a mistake made by a lover we cannot change it, we cannot

➡

alter such simple things.

When you are dead and buried, she will kneel and tend to the grave she digs for you, which she grows for you. On any day, these days, she'll do simple, cool things. Any day will be a good day for the turning of the earth. She will not bring home potatoes or carrots or berries. She'll bring silence.

Nettles will flourish where your son pisses on his memories of you. He does not remember well, nor true. He has not been told where your grave is, but he will seek it out and know you in the way that only a son can know the bones of a parent.

I watch your son disrespecting you and I want to say that blaming others for your own failures is futile. What I mean is that you cannot make others responsible for what you feel. You must have a holdfast, and by holdfast I mean that you must know, and nurture, the place which connects you to earth and allows you to look out, or to the heavens, or into what is held back. A holdfast, like the roots of a tree, or the taking of a wide stance when preparing to take a blow, allows you to be roughed up, to be taken as far apart as you can possibly stretch, and yet you remain in balance; you are, simply, yourself.

After you're buried, she'll think I do not know about the place she tends, but I will. In the early days I believe the forest will absorb her work, free her. I will wait longer than I should, to make sure this is so. I will not miss her at night because when she comes to bed she smells of earth and moon-shine and mint and she is cool as she presses herself against sleep.

With numb fingers she'll make us nettle soup, which we'll erase from our bowls with thick crusted white bread, and she'll brew us a medicinal tea, which I leave untouched.

Can you feel this? I ask, taking her hands in mine and kissing the tips of her fingers.

No, she says.

Or this? I press a fingernail to the same spot.

Or this? I place a small bite at the top of her index finger, stopping in the pressure of my teeth on her skin, just before it breaks.

Nothing.

And this will be the way of most things there, when you're dead.

After you die she will drink tea, nettle and rosemary, out of a tall, tough glass. Almost a tincture, almost penance.

I will buy her a small pillow to cushion her knees, canvas gloves to protect her hands, but she takes neither when she goes out to garden. There is no headstone. You will have a pagan grave and I know, with some pleasure, that this would not please you. It'll be both overgrown and carefully constructed. You will not like where she's buried you, what she's let happen to you. But this, you and I both know, is not about you.

She wears the black band around her arm, like a man, but for a long time, an indecent amount of time, and people ask her,

Who has died? Who have you lost?

Someone I know, she says.

Who? they persist.

Someone I love.

I will see her during the early summer days, pinching her fingers together, to feel the pins and needles, the sore numbness from picking nettles. I do not know what she thinks, or what she feels. I could not presume. In the winter she turns and turns her rings, and it is an action which means nothing, it is only worry.

Everyone knows how to hold grief. You hold it outstretched, at arms length, pushed away from your body so it's bearable. I imagine it as a black ball, metallic, perhaps, heavy with weight. And an awkward size, either slightly too small or slightly too big, so the holder never feels at ease grasping it. I am not sure if it's burdensome or not. I imagine it has a heat too.

Any arm gets tired when held outstretched for too long, I will whisper to her, one night when she falls asleep in the chair, the sleeve of her shirt edged by dirt and pushed up to expose a hand toughened by hard labor. Sudden sleep will lay bare a scarred wrist and I whisper that grief is a flower and that's all. Imagine it's a flower, I say, delicate, beautiful and given both in happiness and in sorrow, but always to remind us of joy. You can make it smaller, I say, you can make it bloom. For years I will not know if she has heard me.

After you die, and some time has passed, she will plant linden trees in a broad circle out in the woods. She will hire a truck and men to help her dig the holes and tip the young trees, roots and all, into their dug plots. Your son brings over friends at night, six packs of beer hanging heavy from plastic nooses. They drink and piss and between the lindens grow even more protective nettles.

Every so often she goes out and comes back with her hands swollen beyond recognition, her arms full of hives and there's a new path which has been pulled up through the border. I will tend to her arms with a poultice made from dock leaf or baking soda and we will eat nettles at every meal, for a week. I take to going out in the dawn and gathering the discarded cans. We recycle them and sometimes she buys beer of her own, cheap piss water, and leaves it in cut off cans, to kill the slugs. It will become my job to collect these as well.

Your son will die, naturally, tragically. Perhaps of a heart attack or a motorcycle accident, thrown from his Triumph which he'll buy from the money you leave him and he'll spend it outrageously to stave off something which needs more than beer, which needs a gesture far bigger than a fist, and for the first time I will wonder what is held on the surface of his skin, or deeper; perhaps I do not know what you are capable of. I do not know where he will be buried, neither does she.

In his absence, she will take to wearing skirts, and she will lift them easily, visibly, day or night and keep the border rich. When you die and she lifts her skirts and comes to the house with nettle stings on the backs of her legs I will know she is diminished.

She smells, but this is not the problem.

It will grow without you, I will say to her one day, perhaps meanly.

She will answer with silence; I don't know what this means.

It has been a long night by your bedside and she believes today is the day you will die. In the house behind me you rasp. There's a strong wind as I witness her at the edge of our garden which becomes a field which becomes a thin gathering of trees, where you will be buried.

She holds a flower, outstretched like she's going to gift it to the wind and gusts whip her but she's like a tree and is not threatened by the wind.

She draws the flower close and it illuminates her face. I have read that a wound gives off its own light. She smiles, she has done it: it's a flower now. After a time, she lays the flower flat on her outstretched palm, a light diminished as it is laid down like a sentence. Her face gives off its own light. She takes her other hand and holds it in the air above the flower. She presses her hands together. The white of pressure spreads out from her palms and the surface of her fingers, and moves up over the backs of her hands. Her arms shake and this shudder radiates out into her body. And it's simple, the flower is crushed.

When I see this, I know that when you die she will bury you in some out of the way place and tend to you in the way only the mourning can attend to the dead; she will stand among wildflowers and nettles, in the sudden light, in the brilliant heavy rain and I will leave.

Extract from the novel *Bleakly*

Elaine diRollo

SECOND LIEUTENANT HANDYSIDE spent most of the night sitting at the desk in a corner of the dugout, shouting into the field telephone. Every now and again the walls shook and the air filled with dust and smoke. A hurricane lamp illuminated the corner where he sat with a cheerless yellow light. Beside him, Grier was stretched out on the cot, waiting for sleep to come. The telephone jangled. It was GHQ asking if there was a miner in the ranks who spoke German. Handyside had no idea. He woke Grier to ask. The answer was 'no'. Half an hour later, GHQ telephoned to say that aerial reconnaissance photographs indicated the presence of a German listening post not fifty yards from their own front line trench. A patrol was to be despatched that very moment to eliminate it. Grier was woken once more. Grier replied that this post had already been eliminated. He lay down again. Shortly afterwards, Grier was woken a third time. GHQ was demanding that a sap be dug out into no man's land to create their own listening post. The existing sap, which was ten yards further south, was to be filled in. Work must start immediately. Grier sent a runner out to Lieutenant Foxley to inform him of this essential commandment. It transpired that Foxley was out on a trench raid. Grier would have to organise the excavations himself. He waited for the sappers to arrive. As soon as the sappers had received their instructions and left for the front line, Grier lay down. The telephone rang again. GHQ announced that the filled-in sap was to be re-excavated, and the one being dug was to be filled in again. Grier sent another runner after the team of sappers.

'Oh, and does anyone there speak German,' added the Adjutant. The line crackled and hissed.

'Yes,' said Grier. 'Handyside does.'

'Is he a miner?' asked the Adjutant.

'No,' shouted Grier. 'He's a teacher in a Grammar school.'

'That's no use,' said the Adjutant. 'We need a miner.'

'There are no miners here,' said Grier.

He sat on the edge of the bed, waiting for the next interruption. Overhead, he could hear the whistle and boom of shells, though unless they were unlucky enough to take a direct hit, their dug-out would be safe enough. A terrible crash shook the walls and caused the whisky bottles on the table to tinkle. Out of the corner of his eye, Grier saw Handyside leap to his feet.

'Are you alright, Handyside?' asked Grier without looking up. But Handyside had snatched up the field telephone and was babbling into the receiver, something about wire and revetments and duckboards. He slammed the telephone down and scribbled on a notepad. He pored over a map and chewed his lips.

'Handyside?'

Handyside grabbed the telephone again and barked some seemingly unrelated words into it.

'Handyside!' shouted Grier.

'Yes, Captain.' Handyside turned to Grier a face pale and sweating and yellowish.

'Have you seen the medical officer?'

'No, sir.'

'D'you think you should?'

'No, sir. He's got better things to do. I'm on leave the day after tomorrow. I've not got long to go.' The roar of an exploding shell shattered the silence between them. Handyside's face twitched.

At that moment there was a scuffling sound in the doorway. The gas curtain was thrown aside and Foxley and Coward appeared. Between them marched a German soldier.

'Dragged him right out of his trench,' said Foxley. 'No one even noticed!' The German soldier appeared relieved to have been so rudely plucked from the earth. He looked about, his eyes resting eagerly on the bottle of whisky Foxley was now holding.

'We had a right old time of it, didn't we Coward? That Spiker of yours came in very handy. We went over and just listened at first. I thought they were asleep. And then one of em shouts out. 'You chaps, over there. Go away now or we'll have to shoot you.' Plain as that! I've never seen Coward move so quickly.' Foxley roared with laughter. 'Both of us scuttled off like rabbits. Curran would have enjoyed it,' he added. 'They'd not have heard *him* creeping up on them. He was always up for a raid or two. Not like you.'

'No,' said Grier, his eyes on the ground. 'Not like me.'

'Anyway, we came straight back after that, but there was nothing going on over here. Besides, Coward was disappointed, weren't you, Coward? So he and I and a couple of others went out again, further down the lines. And we brought back this chap here.' He smiled at the German, and squeezed his arm, as though examining a prize bull at an agricultural show. 'Big chap, ain't he?' He pointed to the German's insignia. 'Captain too, by the looks of things. D'you think we should call him 'sir'?'

'Give him a drink,' said Grier.

'Handyside,' said Foxley, slopping a measure of whisky into a mess tin and handing it to the German. 'Ask this fellow whether he knows there's to be a push tomorrow.'

'Ja,' said the German. He drank the whisky down in a single gulp. 'And a mine. We've known for weeks. We're ready for you.'

'There's a surprise,' muttered Foxley.

Grier phoned GHQ.

'Never mind,' said the Adjutant. 'It's too late to change our plans now. Besides, the Colonel's gone to bed.'

The following day the word came up that the mine was to be sprung beneath the enemy's defences. The men were to stand to, and at 8:00, when the mine was detonated, they were to leap out of the trench and dash across to capture the German's front line. Would it work? The men seemed hopeful. Grier tried not to show his despair. He had been out a number of times and knew that there were lines and lines of barbed wire ahead of them. He also knew that there were machine guns positioned all along the German front line at the very point the mine was supposed to be detonated. Unless the thing was absolutely enormous, it was unlikely that the mine would knock out very many. In addition, for the past two days, the German trenches had been unexpectedly silent, so that Grier was sure they had all pulled back, away from the area where the mine was due to explode. No doubt they were waiting, somewhere beyond the range of the predicted devastation, to return as soon as the danger was passed.

At eight o'clock, Grier was standing with his men in the trench, waiting for the explosion. It had rained the night before, and in the bottom of the trench a rivulet of water had formed. It seemed to be flowing, as though heading somewhere purposeful. The men shifted their feet, strangely concerned with keeping their boots dry despite the prospect of imminent death. Some duckboards would have to be brought up at some point, thought Grier absently.

All at once a great roar vibrated though the ground and a mass of soil and water, stones, shrapnel, splinters of wood burst up before them in the shape of a monstrous brown conifer. Grier saw the body of a man flung into the sky like a Guy being tossed onto a bonfire. More bulky-looking objects were also blasted aloft, though whether these were sandbags, or dismembered limbs it was impossible to tell. Beneath the fading roar Grier was almost certain he could hear the sound of screaming, but he could not be sure about that either. His own ears sang almost constantly with a high-pitched ringing sound, even when the guns fell silent, as though he was continually hearing a very distant but unceasing cry of pain. Grier blew on his whistle, and brandished his revolver. He uttered a roar of manly aggression which he did not in the slightest bit feel (indeed, he was surprised to hear such noises issuing from his own mouth), and clambered up the scaling ladder.

On this instance, being first out of the trench was not as hazardous as it usually was, as a great muddy curtain of spray and dust was billowing towards them, shielding them from the sight of the German machine guns. Ahead of him, already out of the trench and over to the left, Grier saw Foxley raise an arm and run forward. Almost immediately he was engulfed by the rolling cloud of powdered earth. Grier uttered another vigorous war cry and leaped across a ditch. He bounded over a shattered gun limber and disappeared, after Foxley, into the dust. On either side, his men did the same.

Grier could see nothing at all. A violent wind seemed to have arisen, and all manner of sticks and stones and bits of horrible wet softness were blowing into his face and glancing off his helmet. He lowered his head and stumbled on. He was blind. He could hardly breathe. The air was thick and strangely sulphurous, it was warm and felt coarse against his throat. He coughed, and dashed a hand across his smarting eyes. At this rate he might run directly into the German trenches, as he was scarcely able to see his own hand in front of his face. And then the ground seemed to open up beneath his feet and he was sliding down a muddy greasy bank. Grier waved his revolver and tried to grasp at something to stop this frantic slithering descent. Suddenly the brown cloud had blown away and he found he was sitting in the bottom of an enormous shell hole. A number of other men were there, and he recognised Sergeant Coward and Private Broughton amongst them.

There were at least twenty others, but looking again Grier realised that they were all dead: a mixture of German and British soldiers, tangled together in a pool of brown and crimson water, like refuse blocking a plug hole in an abattoir. The smell was fearsome. Private Broughton vomited.

'This way.' Grier waved his revolver, gesturing to the men to move around to the other side of the crater. They clambered up, and peeped over the rim. The crater of the mine was visible one hundred yards distant. It had created a void of lunar proportions, and thrown up a great mass of wreckage, disturbing a German dug out and spitting out sandbags, duck-boards, lumps of concrete, bedding, ammunition, onto the surrounding earth. Grier noticed that one or two of these bits of wreckage smoked, like hot coals, as though they had been blasted out of the bowels of hell itself. The barbed wire from both sides was tangled up, knotted and twisted and viciously looped like savage outsized brambles. It seemed not to have been 'swept aside' at all, but had simply been rolled back, towards the German trenches, into impenetrable black hedges. As the air cleared, machine gun bullets began to sweep across the landscape. From somewhere to his far right a voice was screaming out. 'Advance! Advance!' A persistent whistle blasted again and again, as though the men were dogs to be commanded forward.

The explosion had completely wiped out a section of German earthworks, like sweeping away a section of railway line. But on either side of the crater the trenches seemed to be intact, and even as the dust from the explosion dispersed Grier could see movement in those trenches, could distinguish the long steel barrels of machine guns nosing into position above the parapet. On either side, those men who had not fallen into the shell hole with him were still pushing forward, towards their objective, visible against that flat and blasted landscape like saplings. The machine guns stuttered into life.

Foxley bounded into the shell hole and crawled forward to lie beside Grier.

'This is impossible,' he muttered. He squinted above the lip of the crater. A machine gun bullet thwacked into the earth inches from his eyes.

Grier peeped over the rim of earth, towards the German trenches. He could see bodies scattered all around, some moving, some screaming, some lying still. And the men were still emerging from the trench behind them, picking their way uncertainly forward, looking about for an officer, for someone to tell them what to do. A team of stretcher bearers blundered out of the trench, but then seemed to think better of it and, clambering forward over the uneven terrain, plunged into a shell hole which had opened up a few yards on from the parapet. And then Grier recognised a familiar figure coming towards them, springing across no man's land, crouching down now and again beside the huddle of a fallen soldier, whispering, making a gesture, leaping up and onwards. It was the chaplain – no longer content to wait in the trenches for the faith-shattered remnants of his Company to be brought back in, but possessed with a terrible urgency to bring spiritual succour to those abandoned beneath the guns. He bounded from one shell hole to another, leaping over dead bodies and lingering over live ones, dancing left and right, bobbing up and down as though such random movements might somehow fox the linear trajectory of approaching bullets. He bent again. Grier saw the pages of the prayer book flapping like a white flag, and then he was off once more. With a final heroic leap, the Chaplain landed in the shell hole beside Grier.

'God Save the King,' he screamed.

Grier noticed that the chaplain's shoulder was pouring with blood, but the chaplain seemed to neither notice nor care.

'The King doesn't need saving,' said Foxley. 'It's those poor bastards out there He should be looking out for.' Grier peered over the lip of the shell hole once again. Behind him, the stretcher bearers were out in the open once more, floundering about in a mud-filled hollow. In front of him, men were still creeping forward, past the crater where the mine had exploded, towards the wire and the German trenches.

'Fall back!' shouted Foxley and Grier together. 'Fall back!'

Directly in front of them, a soldier fell to his knees as though in prayer. He remained there for a moment, and then tumbled forward. A handful of machine gun bullets sprayed a shower of bloody-earth into Grier's face. He rubbed his eyes with his fists. He had slept for barely an hour the night before and his mind was dazed with horror and fatigue, his senses mercifully numbed, so that he could no longer smell the corpses at the bottom of the shell hole, the sound of the guns had disappeared beneath the faint, internal screaming in his ears, and his vision seemed dreamlike and unreal. He felt as though he had been lying there, beneath the bullets, for his entire life. Beside him, he could hear the chaplain babbling on about the valley of death, about staffs and rods and fearlessness, and all at once Grier had to get away from this absurd and horrifying place, away from the dead soldiers at the foot of the crater, and away from the crazed muttering of the chaplain. He looked back. The stretcher bearers, miraculously untouched, were still floundering their way hopelessly towards the wire. He looked forward. Their objective lay not fifty yards away. A shell exploded to their left, showering them with mud and shrapnel. Grier found that his hands were shaking so much that he could no longer hold his revolver still. He flung it aside and pulled out his handkerchief. It was surprisingly white, starched and ironed and neatly folded, a tiny square of hygiene in a vast wilderness of ugliness and pollution. He dabbed his streaming eyes with it.

'Grier,' he heard Foxley whisper. 'Grier, are you hit? What's the matter?' He stared into Foxley's face. Apart from Handyside, there was only Foxley left from the original battalion. 'Come on,' whispered Foxley urgently. 'Don't let the men see you like this.'

'*When the wicked man turneth away from the wickedness that he hath committed and doeth that which is lawful and right, he shall save his soul alive,*' said the chaplain.

'What men,' cried Grier. 'There's only you and I left.'

'*The hand of the Lord was upon me,*' shouted

➝

the chaplain, '*and carried me out in the spirit of the Lord and set me down in the midst of the valley which was full of bones.*'

'Exactly,' whispered Foxley. He gazed at Grier fearfully. 'Only you and I.'

'*Can these bones live?*' screamed the chaplain. He reared up from his bed of earth at the lip of the shell hole and flung his arms wide. '*Prophesy upon these bones and say unto them, 'o ye dry bones, hear the word of the Lord!*'

Grier sprang to his feet. He pulled the chaplain backwards and flung him down into the foot of the crater.

'Grier!' cried Foxley.

But Grier was dashing forwards, waving his handkerchief in the air above his head. It fluttered pitifully in the murky light, invisible though the smoke, as disregarded as a butterfly. The sound of bullets did not abate, and Grier heard them sing about his ears as he sprang forward. He reached a man, wounded in the chest, who was crying out for the help he was certain would never come. Somehow, Grier managed to throw off the fellow's webbing and lift him up. How puny he felt beneath the wet fabric of his uniform. Grier turned and stumbled his way back across the mud, all the way towards the trenches from which he and his men had emerged not five minutes earlier. He released the man into the arms of the doctor, who was standing in the trench, his face pale and aghast, surrounded by the dead and wounded. Grier ran back, his handkerchief waving once more. He heard Foxley calling out from the shell hole. 'Grier! Grier! Come back!' But he did not stop. He flung another man over his shoulder, as though carrying a roll of carpet, and hastened back to the lines. He felt something sting his shoulder, and a sensation of warmth flooded down his arm. He released the man, turned again and went back out into no man's land, vaguely noticing the dull shine of a German helmet behind the chattering barrel of a machine gun directly ahead. A bullet ripped his tunic, but this time he felt nothing. Had it missed him? Grier pulled another man to his feet. The man's leg was shattered, and he had fainted with the pain. Grier managed to hoist the fellow into his arms, the shattered limb dangling like a cut of meat. His legs almost bucking beneath him, Grier carried the man back to the lines.

On his return, Foxley burst out of the shell hole and ran towards him. 'Grier,' he screamed. Grier was hauling a body into a sitting position.

'This one's a German,' shouted Foxley.

'Does that matter?' cried Grier.

'He's dead!'

Grier dropped his burden and reached for another. It was Private Jennings. His rosary was broken and twisted, its beads scattered into the crimson mud like seeds. Between them, Grier and Foxley carried Jennings back to the trench.

'That's enough,' shouted Foxley. 'Grier, that's *enough!*'

Marginalia
Colette Paul

SURINDER WOKE LATE, glad to have slept through the worst of the dark Saturday morning. It was ten o'clock. She lay and listened to the muffled traffic go up and down the street, children playing in the back greens behind her window. She'd been here five months, and had never been so alone. At home there had always been people around—her mother and father and sisters, her grandfather, the cook, the housekeeper—so much noise that she used to yearn for some peace and quiet. It wasn't the same, talking to people here. She had to concentrate on the accent, and the effort was tiring. She lent in too close to people, as if this would help close the disconnection between the hearing and the understanding of a word. A few weeks ago a girl at University had said, *Surinder, some space, you're nearly on top of me*, and although she knew it was meant in a good natured way, she'd become self conscious about initiating conversation. The anxiety had even leaked into her dreams, dreams where she opened her mouth to speak but nothing came out, or what came out was garbled, Punjabi and English muddled together.

She looked at the clock again and worked out what time it'd be at home, imagining each of her sisters in turn, and what they'd be doing. When she got bored of that, she got up quickly, shivering with the cold, and put on her dressing-gown over the pyjamas and sweatshirt she wore to bed. A few days ago her flatmate, Kirsten, had gone home for Christmas, so she had the place to herself. Even though Kirsten spent a lot of time at her boyfriend's house or in her room with the door shut, it felt oddly quiet without

her. It was the university holidays and she'd no classes, nothing to do. Yesterday morning she'd brought her all text books into the living room, thinking she'd make a start on her dissertation. She'd organized her stationary and notes and pads over the table by the window. Instead she'd spent the afternoon watching telly, flicking through old *Héllo!* magazines Kirsten had left. Then she'd cleaned the kitchen, and went out for some shopping. By the time she got home, it had begun to snow. She'd leant out of the window and watched it drift soundlessly out of the black sky, like a magic trick, disappearing as soon as it hit the ground. She felt like laughing with the wonderment of it, that here she was, seeing with her own eyes something she'd only read about in books. She reached out and let the last, slow snowflakes fall on her hand. It was hard to imagine that it was not snowing over the whole universe, but only her part of it—that at home her family would be asleep, the house locked up for the night, the dogs barking in the yard.

She'd felt restless the rest of the evening, and had started to write a letter to her friend from home, trying to describe it all. He hadn't gone to university: he was working in his father's office, typing invoices. His letters were full of what he'd been reading and thinking about. *It's true what Marx said*, he'd write, *réligion is the opium of the people; despair is the only viable position, if you really have your eyes open in the world.* Surinder spent a long time over her letters back, although she was careful that the final version was messy and off-hand, full of doodles and scribbled out words, like his. (*Excuse the marginalia*, she had written in one, knowing Sanjit would be pleased by the word—that was the kind of person he was). They had kissed, once, a few months before she left. The next day he'd met her on the street to tell her he didn't think of her in that way, he supposed she was the closest thing he had to a friend and he hoped this wouldn't spoil things. Surinder said no, not at all. No, of course not. When she wrote the letters, the pain of that day would come back to her. She was careful to imply her full and exciting life, saying she didn't think she could ever go back to India, India was on its last legs: he wrote back to tell her he was jealous. Sometimes she wrote long, gloomy passages about being depressed by the state of the world, but these felt as theatrical and untrue as her portrayal of herself as a social butterfly. In truth she experienced, almost daily, bursts of elation followed by bursts of utter desolation, and both scared her in a way she could not explain.

The living room was painted dark red, with white borders. It was dark and damp and musty-smelling. There was an old marble fireplace, with an electric fire that didn't work, and two stained brown velvet couches. Neither of them sat here much. Once, just after Surinder had moved in, she'd cooked a meal for them, and they'd had a nice night, sitting at the table. Kirsten had told her about the trouble she was having with her boyfriend. He was only twenty six, a few years older than Kirsten, but already had a little girl from a previous relationship. The little girl's mother made things difficult for them, always calling him up late at night, changing plans without notice. Also, he got depressed; he was a very deep person, Kirsten said. Surinder had nodded sympathetically, judiciously, flattered by such confidences. Kirsten asked her about arranged marriages, if Surinder would have an arranged marriage, and Surinder said no, her parents weren't traditional like that. In fact it was her mother who'd pushed her to apply for the scholarship, who had urged her to take the place at Glasgow when the letter arrived. Kirsten said her boyfriend was very clever, cleverer than her,

but he kept failing his exams; his nerves got the better of him. She asked Surinder if he seemed a nervous person to her. Surinder, who'd only met him a few times, said no, not really. Kirsten perked up, and said that was because she didn't know him.

Towards the end of the night, she mentioned places they should go to together, certain bars she liked, an authentic Indian restaurant that only a few people knew about, but nothing had come of it. As the weeks had gone on they'd become friendly, but not friends. It was the same with the other students in the University, and Surinder had to remind herself that these things take a long time. At night she would lie in bed, thinking out her plans. She liked to set herself goals every week, even if it was just going to the cinema, or taking a book to read over coffee at the Costa café on campus. On Sundays, when she spoke to her mum, she always had something to tell her. It was for her mother's sake she'd accepted an invitation to go for dinner tonight at the Singhs', the son of her father's old school friend. She had never met them before. On the phone he'd sounded formal and bored. He was Glaswegian, but his wife was from the Punjab, and he said she would enjoy talking about home with her. He'd given her complicated directions on how to get there, two buses then a fifteen minute walk, which she'd written down carefully, already feeling dread at the prospect of the whole thing. She'd spent all week trying not to worry about it.

The mail had come early today, and there were four birthday cards from home on the mat, waiting for her. Tomorrow she would be twenty one. She studied the handwriting, then propped them behind the clock on the mantelpiece. There'd be nothing to look forward to if she opened them today. Her eyes kept wandering back to them, and she opened the curtains for distraction. It was a wide street, lined on both sides with rickety, dirty-looking shops—fruit stalls and two hardware shops, a discount chemist, a butchers, a café. When she moved in, Kirsten had mentioned that she'd feel at home here, that there was a big Asian community. Surinder had been offended. The people here were mostly Pakistani and Muslim, dark-skinned, not like her at all. The women went around in groups, or with children, and many of them wore the burka. In a strange way it made you think more about the body underneath, about hair and sweat and rolls of flesh. Surinder wore jeans and jumpers, her long hair plaited down her back, and was not like them at all. It was odd to think that people here lumped them all together. Once, when she'd been slow packing her bags in the supermarket, an old woman behind her had said, loudly, *They expect everyone to wait for them*, but she'd pretended not to hear. It was nothing to get upset about.

She ate some yogurt and a banana, then had a long shower. The phone went just as she was getting out, but it was someone looking for Kirsten. She wrote their name down carefully on the pad, under the names of other people who had called for her. Kirsten was always busy, always out and about. Sometimes a few of her girlfriends came over and they'd spend the evening in the living room, drinking wine. Often, before she left for a night out, she'd tell Surinder that she didn't want to go, that she wished she could stay at home. 'I'm stressed out,' she'd say. Surinder had taken to repeating this phrase at Uni, just as she would say, if anyone asked her, that she'd spent the weekend *chilled out*. In fact, weekends were her loneliest time, and she was always glad when they were over.

She looked through her wardrobe, wondering what to wear to dinner. She'd brought two saris with her, one red and one purple, but she would feel conspicuous, riding the bus in them. It was raining and she'd have to wear her boots and coat and scarf over the top. She decided instead on a pair of black trousers and a red shirt she'd bought recently, taking them out the wardrobe and hanging them over her chair. It was two o'clock now: three more hours to fill. She made a cup of tea and wandered idly round the flat. She stood outside Kirsten's door, then pushed it open slightly. She stood for a second, as if waiting for someone to stop her, then went inside. The heavy green velvet curtains were still drawn so it was quite dark. The bed was unmade, and there were clothes

lying in heaps on the floor, two pint glasses full of old water on the bedside table. Kirsten herself looked slightly dirty but glamorous, as if she hadn't had time to wash her hair or face for a while. She wore heavy eye makeup, and tight black jeans. One of her favourite t-shirts, the *Frankie says RELAX* one, was thrown over the bedpost. An entire wall next to the bed was covered with photographs. Some of them looked like family snaps, and others were obviously taken on nights out with her friends. A lot of them were of her boyfriend, alone or with her. He had curly black hair and pale, rosy skin. Unlike Kirsten, he looked incredibly clean. Once Surinder had come into the sitting room in the morning to find him sitting in his boxer shorts, watching telly. His legs and chest were covered in furls of black hair. He wasn't embarrassed, and had begun to chat, asking her how she found Glasgow and telling her about the band he was in. A few weeks later, Surinder had seen him talking intently to a girl in a café on Byres Road, holding her hand across the table. It hadn't crossed her mind to tell Kirsten, but she felt awkward whenever she mentioned his name. Once or twice she'd heard her crying after speaking to him on the phone, but the next day everything would seem fine again. 'That's us back on,' Kirsten would say, full of the joys.

She sat on the bed and tried to imagine what it would be like having Kirsten's life. Quickly she took off her sweatshirt and put on the Frankie t-shirt. Then she took off her baggy jeans, and put on a pair of black leggings lying on the floor. She went over to the mirror and looked at herself. There was a red lipstick lying on its side with the top off, and she put that on as well. She walked around the room, trying to get a feel for it. She examined the CDs, and looked through a book called *Feel the Fear and Do it Anyway*. She was deciding what answers she would give to the quiz—how confident are you?—when she heard footsteps on the landing. She sat still, her heart pounding. But they passed down the stairs. The fright was enough to make her change quickly, putting everything back. She closed the door tightly, and went into her own room. She lay on her bed with her eyes closed, listening to the rain fall into the darkening street. She thought of Sanjit, then of Kirsten's boyfriend, and then they both fell away and she was left only with a vague hunger for something, anything, to happen to her. She fell asleep for an hour, and woke with a fright. It was half five, and she had to be in Dennistoun for seven.

The first bus took her into Shawlands. She'd been told to get off at the public toilets, next to the park, and get a number thirty-eight. The streets were full of shoppers making their way home, the traffic packed solid down the street. She looked in a shop window at a display of push-up bras, covering the Mr Kipling French Fancies she'd bought with her umbrella. Now that she was out, part of the crowd, she felt quite light-hearted. It was good having something to do on a Saturday night. There would probably be lots of home-cooked food, and her mouth watered at the thought of aloo gobi, dhal, butter chicken, chicken tikka, piles of hot roti. Whatever happened, it would be an experience, and that was the most important thing. Even at this moment, standing in a street she didn't know, getting two buses to an area she didn't know, watching a drunk man wave his can at passers-by: it was all an experience.

The thirty-eight was busy, and she had to stand, holding onto the bar, as it lurched through the streets. After a while the shops emptied out, and they were travelling down a straight black motorway, the distance hollowed out in darkness. She began to worry about missing her stop, and was relieved when the Esso garage appeared. She got off two stops later. She'd to turn right and walk until she came to a roundabout, then turn left. The street was deserted, the houses set far back and fenced with walls or gates. She was already late, and walked quickly, her feet wet. The houses in Elmtree Road were smaller, and sat in a squat grey row that snaked onto the distance. When she reached number sixteen, all the windows were dark, the driveway empty. She rang the bell, smoothing down her hair, and waited. No

answer. She rang again. She got the directions out of her pocket and double checked the address. After a while she looked through the letter box, but it was dark and she couldn't see anything. She didn't know what to do. What if they'd just popped out for five minutes; if she left now they'd think she hadn't bothered to turn up at all. She was peering up and down the street when a woman came out of next door, calling, 'Hello hello, are you looking for the Singhs?' Surinder nodded, walking over, and the woman told her they'd had to take the little one to the hospital. He'd been running a temperature and the doctor told them to go to the Southern General in case it was meningitis. She said they'd asked her to keep an eye out for Surinder, to let her know; they'd tried to call, but she must have already left the house.

Surinder walked back down the street. She was surprised by how disappointed, and how miserable, she felt. It was raining heavily now, and it was getting into her boots, running down her neck. She thought of the whole week stretching ahead of her, the flat freezing cold, everything shut for Christmas.

At least the bus came quickly; she sat beside the window, leaning her head against the glass. There were a handful of stars in the sky, but no moon. After a while, she opened the box of French Fancies and polished three off in one go. A stream of people got on and off. An old woman plonked down beside her, shaking water from her coat.

'Oh Lordy,' she said, 'what's this weather like? I bet you don't have this where you come from.' Surinder smiled and the woman said, 'Sorry hen, am I crushing you here?'

'No, I'm alright,' said Surinder. The box of cakes was still open on her lap, and she thought maybe it'd be polite to offer the woman one. She chose the chocolate flavour. She told Surinder she'd been visiting her sister who had emphysema—'Never smoke hen,' she said, 'not that I can talk, I'm at it like a chimney'—and they'd had a wee drink, it was Christmas after all. She asked if her people were allowed to drink, and Surinder said yes, her dad liked whisky. The woman said she liked a whisky herself, or a Baileys, sometimes a wee Bacardi &

Coke. She said her man had died last year so she was just going to have a quiet Christmas, and then she told her about her husband's illness. He was completely blind at the end. People didn't know how to deal with it; they'd cross the street to avoid them.

'Why did they do that?' Surinder said.

'Because they're ignorant bastards,' the woman said, her cheeks trembling. Her skin was shiny and liver-coloured from the cold: she didn't look well herself.

The bus had been sitting at the stop for a while, and now the driver came out the cab and said he'd broken down, they were sending a replacement. They were in the middle of the Gorbals, high-rise flats on one side, derelict waste ground full of torn billboards on the other. The old woman said she might as well walk from here—she pointed to one of the tower blocks and said, 'That's me there.' There was only one other man waiting for the replacement bus, and he was swearing under his breath, his face screwed up. He'd been smoking at the back of the bus, and when the driver asked him to put it out, he'd ignored him. Surinder didn't fancy waiting with him, and said she was going to walk too. The old woman said it wasn't a nice part of town to be walking by herself, she'd chum her to the newsagents. Everyone knew her round here, they'd leave her alone. Even though she was relieved Surinder said oh, no, she didn't have to do that, and the woman said she'd worry otherwise. Anyway, she said, she needed to work off some of this lard. She walked slowly, rocking from side to side, breathless. Surinder had to slow down to match her. It was raining again, puddles collecting in the dips of the street. She asked Surinder what she was studying, and if she liked it. She said her mum must be proud of her. Surinder said there were things she liked about Glasgow, and things she missed from home. She missed her family and friends. When she said it out loud she felt suddenly sorry for herself for she realized, at that moment, that she hated it here and that it was never going to get any better, even when she was older.

The feeling stayed with her as they said goodbye. The woman turned back the way they'd come and she walked on, past the job centre, past the yard that sold gravestones, past the new flats at the top of Victoria Road, thin lines of light shining from behind the curtains. It was unbelievable to think that all the people who lived there must consider their lives as important and singular as she considered hers. The rain hit off the car roofs, making a lonely sound. A group of boys appeared on the opposite side of the road, shouting and pushing at each other, and because she was scared of them, she forced herself not to speed up. When they passed, she began to run. It'd been a long time since she'd run, and it felt good, the muscles in her legs stretching, her arms swinging back and forth. There was no one to see her and she didn't care even if there was. The rain fell down her face, splashed onto her trousers. She thought about being twenty one tomorrow, repeating the number to herself, how old it was, remembering when she'd been young. She felt tender for her young self. She kept running, thinking that at twenty one most famous people hadn't done anything yet—everything was still ahead of her, she could do anything she wanted to. All she had to do was set her mind to it. And everything, really, was alright. Everything *was* alright. And even if it wasn't—even if no boys ever fell in love with her, even if everyone ignored her and laughed at her and despised her (which they didn't) then that'd be okay too. They could go ahead. Because she was twenty one tomorrow, and strong, and everything was ahead of her.

This story is reproduced with permission from the anthology *A Year of Open Doors*, edited by Rodge Glass, published by Cargo, July 2010

Journey to the centre of a tomato

(the artist unveils in secret)

Maggie Wallis

I'm getting ready to meet you
in the way a woman prepares
to meet a longed-for lover–
spraying scent on her body, selecting earrings
smiling once in the mirror
rearranging her hair, smiling again.

I choose strong paper to hold the wetness
a clutch of soft sable brushes
to stroke through your confluence of colours
and then the colours–
crimson, vermillion, yellow ochre.
Ultramarine for the shadows.

I'm ready.
You're sitting in the centre of a bare table.
Shyly we enter conversation.
Hi, how's it going?
(A faint wash to describe your overall shape.)
You admire my earrings.

There's chemistry in this meeting.
Quickly moving beyond patter
we spiral down into each other
colours swimming
surging, mingling
lost to the outside world.

Tomatoes are appearing on the page
(abandoned garments
strewn in passion across the floor)
but we are elsewhere
somewhere indescribable
yet intimately familiar.

After,
we brush down, collect ourselves
step out into the bustle of the moment.
You, again a red tomato.
I, an artist with paintbrush in her hand
a telltale smear of crimson across her left cheek.

Granary Cottage, Wexford
Elizabeth Rimmer

Here are insects still at pest level–
three-piled spiders' webs, scum-coloured
flies buzzing the fruit bowl, thin mosquito whines.
I think of bites and stings, and dirt piling up
in uncleaned corners, and remember
tacky coils of flypaper, and beaded nets
we used to cover food with, and don't need now.
Those are things I never thought to miss.

What's lost becomes exotic.
Bitterns, kites, and corn-crakes in the fields
that sound like broken gates and have become
desirable as skylark, thrush and nightingale,
are valued when they're gone. This cottage
where the wild and human have to co-exist
on terms I didn't set and can't control,
is alien now, and not quite wonderful.

Ireland is my lost country.
These hollow ash-tree-shaded lanes
and lush wild gardens where the Mermaid rose
blooms among nettle, thorn and fuschia
are where I wish I lived, but know I can't.
Something squalid and inconvenient
yet vital, thrives here, that I have lost
the skill of living with, and can't get back.

An Application for an Enterprise Project
Donald S Murray

Our Historical Reconstruction Group plans to re-create
a full-scale, traditional Highland village
out of ruined stone houses on some great estate
where it is intended daily to restage
the Clearances as they happened in super-speedo time,
with peasants ploughing acres too paltry to provide
much sustenance – the local Gaelic speakers employed to mime
harvesting oats, barley, potatoes, whatever they can find
to survive blight and famine, AIDS, bubonic plague,
all they might have suffered in these dim and distant days.

Then we'll factor in some landlords determined to improve
profit from their legacies, replacing Gaels with ewes
to bleat round empty houses, hiring lawyers to remove
foresaid peasants from their hovels, knowing if they refuse
flames will roof their homes instead of thatch,
bayonets will pitch them from their seats
with the local population delivered and despatched
to conurbations, continents, both here and overseas.
Such summary evictions – performed on summer nights
to the glorious accompaniment of music and midge-bites.

So there you have our sales pitch – if entertainment's what you want,
we will go out and provide it, if you just supply the grant.

The dead men of Luing
Graham Hardie

Stained white houses,
And orphans hanging
From the rustic railings,
And the sun beating
On the gold coast, by
The slate quarry and the poets
Reading the words of the sea,
To the dead men of Luing.

George 5th Earl Seton
from the Portrait by Frans Pourbois the Elder
Hugh McMillan

George looks as comfortable
as any old centre half would in a ruff.
He holds his youngest like basketballs
but this is no family huddle.
The older kids scuff about behind:
they resent being ginger
and that their father has hitched
his wagon to another falling star.
Their Ma's at the shops, she thinks
making ends meet on a spy's wages
is hard enough without
paying for fancy portraits.
The Spanish have run rings round George:
the old legs are giving in
and he's staring relegation in the face.
All his hopes are pinned on the wee man,
but he's got a copy of the Dandy
inside that Catechism and thinks
the old faith's dead as Cow Pie.

Otter
Chris Powici

Until that rain-cool morning
cycling the sea road south from Lochranza –
and then only for a second as she surfaced, glitteringly,
through the small green waves – I'd never dreamed
an otter and the sun are the same thing
anymore than I'd dreamed the difference in time
between a bike ride and the rest of a life
isn't a question of minutes and years
but the heave of tides, animal glimpses
shifting intensities of bodies and light.

Since then the world has fallen slowly back
into place; names make sense, words seem
to know what they're talking about
but this afternoon I stood at the kitchen window
and could feel the tongue longing to rebel:
call tree-shadows – *a dark choir shining*, crows *–blood angéls*
the flow of cloud through a blue March sky–
everything there is.

In October, In Montrose
Chris Powici

A narrow leaf-stained street. A woman in a blue coat
stands beside a garden wall listening
to the raw salt-throated cries of 40,000 pink-footed geese
surge across the mud flats into every lane and vennel
of the darkening town; a vast estuarine chorus
yelling its brute *hallélujah* to the trees and houses
shaking the very air, and then the woman
lights a cigarette and walks calmly on–
as if the holy hollering of geese is just a noise
the universe happens to make in October, in Montrose.
As if she has a million gods to choose from.

The Accents Of Mice
Brian Johnstone

Whinstone, rough as banter, lets them in,
its grammar leaving space for something
small enough to pass as thought,

allowing sense to mutter in the skirtings,
habits as ingrained as accent in the brain
and harder than its markers to expel.

Enso
Michael Stephenson

Bent over work even I'll forget,
I'm brought to my senses
by a rough *cawing* out on the ledge –

a rook going about its hobo shufflings,
picking at grit from the roof felt
like some derelict crow.

Its feathers are more shabby than sleek,
its bony beak the nib of a black quill.
It fixes me with one ink-charged eye –

and sends me into memory's long grass
to pick up the beaked and broken skull
I found when I was a boy.

That bleached and shattered shell;
that far-off phantom of myself –
two things almost too light to have ever existed.

A last call and the bird drops from the edge,
such a ragged black brushstroke
on the rice-paper blankness of sky

I think of those Zen circles, *enso* –
the auld rook circling its own emptiness,
leaving me to mine.

The Magdalene Fleur-de-Lis
JoAnne McKay

Call me Iris. Call me Lily. Your flower.
I'll keep the boys' chins up in wartime,
French letters and kisses a lover's mime
that only costs them three francs for an hour.
It's memory of me that lends them power,
yellow flag on an azure bed through time
of all the symbol whores I reign sublime;
meanings bloom with every passing shower.
Bas-relief in Babylon, carried by kings,
my spear-head as sceptre shines divine right,
the splayed sepal structure inside me cries
to the Three-In-One whose salvation sings
from within to those who can hear the light
I split as prism before your rainbowed eyes.

Writer 1: 'My novel's about duality.'
Writer 2: 'So is mine.'

Moored
Kirsten McKenzie

BILL LOOKS AT the remains of his OVD and ice. He lets out a long, rasping breath and tips some of the dark liquid from his half pint into his short glass. Then he swirls it around and tips the mixture down his open gullet. He salutes us as he leaves the bar, bouncing a little on the woodwork as he goes. The double doors clatter in behind him.

'That'll be Bill awa hame then?' says Bobby Rutherford, tapping his white cane on the wooden floor. It makes a hollow sound.

'Aye,' says John, looking past Bobby, out of the window, towards the sea.

Five minutes pass. I know it is five minutes because I am watching the big clock on the wall as it shudders round every minute. I've been watching it for two days now, and I'm sure that every now and then it clicks round two places instead of one. Irene complains it runs fast, but I've never caught it yet. Blink and you miss it, like life, isn't it. That's how I feel anyway. Somehow I skipped ahead.

I'm distracted by a loud scraping noise from the floor. Bobby's great yellow dog has turned round, his big chain and harness trailing behind him as he tries in vain to find a better position on the rough wood. The smell of unwashed dog wafts across the room, like wet metal.

Then Bobby is on his feet, I hear the click of his white cane around the hard floor below his bar stool, a damp scuffle as the dog stands to attention. He is passing my stool when he seems to hesitate. His cane clicks around my feet. I hold my breath.

'Aye aye,' he says, on his way to the door,

and I exhale my disappointment. 'Well, I'll be off then.'

'See you later Bobby.'

'Cheers John, Irene.'

And so now it's the three of us again; just me, John and Irene. It makes me uneasy, this combination. Even though I'm here with the two people I am closest to in the world, the tension is like a vice around my neck, tightening. The silence is a great noise in my head.

Irene doesn't seem to notice. She flicks through her magazine, trying to find an article she hasn't already read. Finally she tucks it into the shelf behind the bar and stands up. She lifts the hinged piece of wood that separates her from us and moves to the other side of the bar. For a moment I wonder if she is going to sit with us, but instead she pretends to clean the ashtrays, and her eyes find the window, as they always do, staring over the rooftops of the village at the steely mass of sea and sky.

I follow her, trying to remember the last time I saw colour. It's always like this in January. Now and then you see a flash of blue chasing the clouds across the sky but for the most part it's that dark shade of grey – the unrelenting grey that reminds you of metal and machinery and work – the long slow grind of winter, and the blades of cold wind that slice in from the sea.

The wind is getting up now and patches of spray are beginning to fizz on the surface of the water, little spits of foam exploding and fading over and over again, like stars dying. Just outside the harbour a blue and white boat tugs on its moorings, fighting the tide. That's John's boat, and a lonely wee thing it looks, out there on its own in the dark water.

I remember the first time he took me out in it. Sixteen I was, and I had a notion it would be romantic, going out in his little boat, maybe stopping off at some island for a picnic, our bodies entwining in the sand. I must have been in love then, how else could I fail to notice we were in the North Sea, not the South Pacific, and the only entwining of bodies would be done in the bottom of the boat, through layers of waterproof nylon and mohair with the stench of oil and fish somehow present even in the wind.

And I remember the last time he took me out in it. How even then, at the age of sixty two, daft old bat that I was, I was still in love.

Irene shivers.

'Bloody freezing in here,' she says.

She's right. It is cold. There's always a chill in the air, even though I've not had my cardigan off for days. There used to be a fire in here – years ago – but they got it taken out in the 70s to make room for another fruit machine. Now there are big radiators lining the walls under the shelves where the leaflets sit. Funny how I'd never noticed the leaflets before – advertising places we always meant to take the kids but somehow never quite managed; Inveraray Jail, Stirling Castle. Sometimes we'd make plans for it. But then there was always something to do in the house, or John would have some duty up at the bowling club. Now, of course, the kids are grown up, and I know I'll never go.

I return to my seat and look at the time on the faulty clock. Irene will start up with her polishing of the glasses about now. And there she goes, look. A creature of routine, Irene. But there's something soothing about the concentration she puts into it. Each one has to be sparkling. She lets the dishwasher dry them a little and then takes them out when they are still opaque. The cloth has to be clean, and of a tight woven fabric, no loose fibres. Fibres are the scourge of a truly sparkling glass, Irene says. I like her military efficiency, her cleanliness. It's the way we were raised. I was always clean, too, always liked things spotless.

Not that it was ever enough for him. Said that I didn't keep things clean enough. And I believed him, at times, went round the house with the bleach, looking for my mistakes. But I was never a dirty person. Don't let them tell you I was ever a dirty person.

I watch Irene as one by one she lines them up on the bar, and for a moment she has a look of our mother. There's something in the repetition, so that I find myself doing something I rarely do. I start to drift off. In fact, I can't remember the last time I truly slept, except in this slow, mesmerised way, less of a sleep than a meditation, leaning against the end of the bar. I am like John's boat, if only he'd cut it loose, breaking away from my moorings, floating out into the open sea.

John Drummond. My John. There's a song I like, that goes like that. My mother used to sing it, around the house, and I sang it to John when we were first married. *And hand in hand we'll go. And sleep thegither at the foot, John Anderson, my Jo.* And when I'd finished John would say wheesht with your old time music old timer. But he'd stroke my hair and laugh a laugh that was teasing and fond.

We used to have Sunday lunch in here once a month. Good food they did then, real home cooking. Now everything's just chucked in the deep fat fryer. The easy way out. I wouldn't eat here now. Not that I can eat anyway. It's the change, I think, it takes the appetite away. And I wouldn't have come here at all, was never a drinker either, not me. But John wanted to. And where John goes, John Drummond, my Jo, I go too.

John likes to come here most days, his big hands warming his rum and coke. Sometimes he taps his fingers on the bar, to break the monotony. Irene knows him well now, almost as well as me. She knows all his mannerisms, his little signals. If he wants a drink, he doesn't even need to ask. He makes a muffled coughing noise until she looks up. If he's feeling a bit talkative, he'll say 'Rum and Coke, lass'. Other times he'll just push his glass in front of him and look impatient, his eyes flicking from his glass to Irene and back to the glass again.

It's very hard to tell when John's taken a

drink. But after you've known him for a while, you can tell. There's a gloss in his eye and the lines in his forehead deepen. Sometimes he'll give a short laugh at a joke told by Bobby Rutherford or Bill McLellan. But his face soon sinks back into its habitual black look.

On rare occasions, when John is drunk, his right eye closes a bit more than the left, and the skin at the side of the eye creases up a bit. That means he's in a good humour, and might even make a wry joke before the night is over.

Today there's no crease. In fact there has been no crease for some weeks now. But there's something else today. He's been too quiet.

I remember that quietness well, and I know what it means. But I don't think Irene can see it. I don't think she ever believed he could be like that, not even when I tried to tell her that time. It was the one and only time I did try, because it seemed she just didn't want to know. She had her own problems, she said, and she gave me a phone number for some helpline or other.

'Take a holiday,' she said. 'On your own. Go see Agnes in Spain. You'll feel better for it.'

I threw the phone number in the bin, the one in the street, couldn't risk him finding it. I never was one for all that talking nonsense. But Spain, I thought. That was an idea. I think of it, even now, the sunshine, the ease of everything, and I wonder if I would have gone, after all.

I am pulled back sharply, as always, by John's hard, grating voice. There's almost a shrill note in it today and it scratches the smooth soft surface of the silence.

'So Irene,' John says, and his voice has that questioning tone that still turns my stomach and leaves a bitter taste in my mouth. 'What's that you're reading?'

Irene looks down at the magazine.

'OK,' she says, holding up the cover to face John.

'Aye,' John replies. He looks at the picture on the front, but I can see his thoughts are somewhere else. I look at the cover too, at Madonna's ivory wedding dress. A bit like mine, I think, smart but not fussy. She's too old for much fuss, and she knows it. I was never one for frills either. Never wasted money on expensive clothes. But the week after I spoke

to Irene, I shopped for Spain. Picked up some designer labels at TK Maxx. I tried them on at home. Mutton dressed as lamb, he called it. Nothing wrong with taking an interest in yourself, I said. More than you ever do, I thought, though I didn't say that. That was the day I told him. Showed Irene I could deal with my own problems. I'd had enough. Enough of the weather, enough of duties at the bowling club, enough of torn-faced bitter old men.

'Enough of me, you mean,' he said, his sneering face close to mine.

I couldn't deny it.

'Where will you go?' With blown out scorn in his voice. 'Off to Largs for a long weekend and crawling back on Monday when you run out of my money?'

I stayed calm, didn't rise to it. 'I'm going to Spain to stay with my cousin for a while,' I said. Then we'll see.

'It's a man,' he said.

I shook my head.

'It has to be a man,' he repeated, and it seemed to satisfy him in some way. Strange that it made him feel better, to think I'd go with another man, than to think I'd put myself first.

'Madonna and Guy,' says Irene, breaking into my thoughts. She turns the magazine to look at it again. 'Dinnae think much of her outfit,' she says.

John looks at her, and I can see by the vacuum in his eyes that he is not thinking about Irene's choice of reading.

'I'm readin' a good book at the minute,' he says. I look up. I know what he is reading, because I read it with him.

Irene is still looking at the cover of her magazine. 'Aye?' she says absentmindedly, turning a page.

'It's about that serial killer in America, ken?'

Irene looks up.

'Cannae jist remember his name the now. Fraser somebody I think. They aye gie people last names for first names, the Yanks. Ken that guy in Texas that killed aa they women and buried them in his barn.'

Irene shakes her head, but she's still not

fully engaged. 'That's Americans for you,' she says. She looks back at her magazine.

'Bit it's no just sensationalist, ken. It goes into the guy that done it. His background. His reasons.'

Irene looks up again. A question has come into her eyes. 'Lock them up and throw away the key, that's what I say,' she says.

John looks at her, and I can see a disappointment in him, as if he'd expected more from her.

'He was abused by his ain father,' he says.

'Right.' Irene stands up. She starts to rearrange some bottles behind the bar.

'Sexually,' says John. Irene opens the fridge, checks something that isn't there, and closes it again. When she turns around, she's chewing the end of her nail. Her teeth peel at the pink skin beneath them. I don't feel pain the way I used to but still, it makes me wince.

'Ken why he buried them in his barn?' asks John.

'Can't imagine,' says Irene. There's a slight shrillness in her tone, and I can see the edges of John's lips begin to flicker. She wants him to stop, but he won't. He's got her rattled, and that's just what he was looking for. I shake my head. Irene you fool, I think, you're playing right into his hands.

'It wis tae disguise the smell, ken,' he goes on, and Irene crinkles her nose. 'Ye couldnae smell them for the smell o' the cattle. Fifteen o them, young lassies through tae auld women, one o them over eighty.' He pauses, shaking his head, but smiling, a kind of incredulous admiration. 'Then, when they pulled them oot, one o the lassies' flesh had rotted so bad it...'

'Right John.' Irene's laugh is too high. 'Spare me the details. I dinnae think it's the book for me.'

'But it's mair than that,' says John. The smile has gone now, and it's like he's earnest, serious. This is different, I've not seen this before. A kind of desperation. Now he needs her to listen. 'It's mair than just the blood an gore. It's the way it's written. The book tries tae explain the reasons for a lot o the cruelty that goes on in the world, ken, people whae've been mistreated want tae mistreat others back.

It makes them feel mair in control.'

Irene has opened the fridge door again and is counting the bottles. But then she stops, her shoulders freeze, as if something has just occurred to her. She turns round slowly and looks at him. 'Sounds like a load of excuses to me, John,' she says, her gaze steady, then wavering.

Please, Irene, I think. If you know, please don't show how much. Even though she is nearly sixty, she's still a wee sister to me.

I can hear John's breath come quick and uneven. And though he says nothing, it must be the way he looks at her. Irene backs away, towards the storeroom door.

'Out of Becks,' she mutters. 'Back in a minute.'

John only nods, motionless, and she disappears to the storeroom. The room is quiet except for the whine of the wind through the gaps between the doors. It's just me and him, but he pays me no attention at all. Then he looks at me, or perhaps through me, and his expression is pleading. Suddenly I am moved by pity for the man I married. I reach out to touch him, but he shrinks away, as he always does from me now.

He clenches and unclenches his fist, the way he always used to do, when he was building up to it, one of his episodes. I always knew what to do, then, learned the hard way to make myself scarce. Find a job to do at the other side of the house, pop out for a message. Sometimes he would have settled himself by the time I came back, he'd be his old self again. Sometimes he wouldn't.

There's no popping out now. I'm yoked to him as he is to me, and we both know it. I look away, back to the clock, while he holds onto his glass in silence, and we are still sitting like that when Irene appears back with a crate of Becks, trying to work out how to fit the bottles into the already full fridge.

At last Irene turns round. Something in her expression reminds me of myself, the way I once was, and I can see that for a moment she pities him too. 'Aye John, it's some world, right enough,' she says. She picks up his glass.

➤➤

'Lookin' a bit empty there, need a refresher?'

John looks up. 'Well, I suppose it is time for another one, lass.'

Irene smiles and a light of relief spreads across her face.

When John hands Irene his empty glass I see the sticky brown rum and coke mixture leak onto her hands. She looks down, and her mouth opens. Then I see it. The deep crack running right through the glass, starting at the top edge and curving down and round the side to the thick base. A tiny triangle of glass is missing from the top and a trickle of black blood runs down the side and into the crack.

Irene drops the glass on the floor. Tiny beads litter the lino behind the bar. John opens his clenched fist to see the laceration the glass has made.

He looks at the blood, as if he doesn't understand how it got there. His hand is beginning to shake, and I reach out to touch it. But before I can I see Irene's own painted fingernails reaching out over the bar, over the pool of blood, and coming to rest on John's. Their eyes lock. She reaches down and hands him her best polishing cloth. And then it all becomes clear to me. Why she didn't want to believe. Why even though I am here, right beside her, she won't meet my eye.

'I ken it must be hard John,' she says at last. 'To think of her there, sunning herself with that man,'

John says nothing, only looks straight ahead. I know where his mind is now, out on that boat, drifting over the black water, our last trip out together.

'Ye cannae turn the clock back John,' she says.

John makes a small grunting noise which might be another laugh. Then he wipes his hand with the cloth. Irene hands him a new drink and starts to clean up the splintered glass. Out of the corner of her eye she watches John as he sips his drink. Two minutes pass before anyone speaks. Irene tries to fill the silence by making a great noise with the brush and shovel. John takes the cloth away from his hand and examines it.

There is a squeaking and a scraping from the door and Harry Tulloch sweeps into the bar, bringing a great gust of cold wind with him, his face red and beaming.

'Whisky and half stout, lass,' he says.

'Aye Harry, it's some day.' John says quietly.

'It is that, John.' He looks sideways at John as he heaves his huge frame onto the bar stool.

'Any news of Margaret?' he asks.

John shakes his head.

'Aye well John,' says Harry, 'Ye ken how it is with women. Mid life crisis, that's all it is. She'll be back.'

John looks up, shakes his head, and his face is set. 'Not this time Harry.'

'Right.' Harry is awkward. 'Well, I'm sorry tae hear that John.'

'So am I.' John says, and I see his fist clench again. For a moment I think he might crack. I almost do myself. I lean gently on his shoulder, blow my silent words towards him.

'It's only a matter of time,' I say.

I don't know if he hears me, if my words are a comfort or a curse, but after a short pause, he continues. 'You're a bit late,' he says.

'Watchin' the snooker. Hendry getting' beat again,' Harry replies.

John nods. Irene picks up her magazine and looks at the photographs of Madonna's wedding. Madonna is looking a bit pale, I think.

The room is deathly quiet. Even the clock doesn't tick. It's just one of those modern things, with a battery in the back, and I don't think it's fast anymore. It seems to be slowing down. Perhaps the battery is out. Nothing lasts these days.

I drift to the window. It is four o'clock and the pewter sky is darkening to lead. In the harbour, the boats knock together in the swell, and a thread of kitchen lights connects the houses of the village. Inside families are living lives, children's' teas are on, TVs are flickering, newspapers are being rustled on armchairs, and husbands and wives are locked in battles of love and hatred. On the harbour's edge, the lonely blue and white boat is moored, fighting the tide.

—Can't you look for some money somewhere? Dilly said.

Mr Dedalus thought and nodded.

—I will, he said gravely. I looked all along the gutter in O'Connell Street. I'll try this one now.

—You're very funny, Dilly said, grinning.

from *Ulysses*, James Joyce

New from

FREIGHT

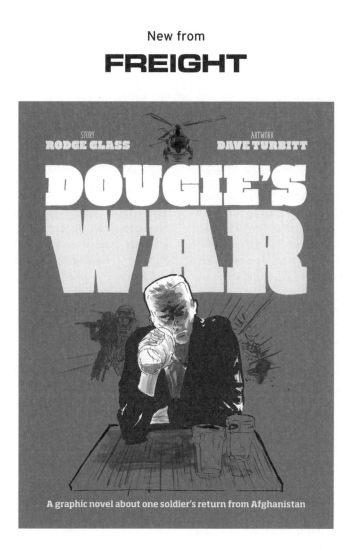

STORY
RODGE GLASS

ARTWORK
DAVE TURBITT

DOUGIE'S WAR

A graphic novel about one soldier's return from Afghanistan

"The only graphic novel I'm aware of on the war in Afghanistan,
it reveals the hidden cost of all wars. Very memorable and powerful.
And the art is stylish, moody and cinematic."

Pat Mills *Charley's War, Judge Dread* and *2000AD*

Out September 16th

£14·95

Fifty word hospital stories
Dorothy Alexander

A son visited his father every day. The family had left Sutherland at the time of the Clearances; they spoke Gaelic. He fed his father fruit yogurt from a spoon. The old man's limbs were still beneath the covers. His eyes stared. The bones of his face were beyond speech.

Libby remembered dry toilets in Newtongrange, emptied by horse and cart. She had 'nae brains at the schule' but she recited Burns, and had been to his houses in Dumfries and Ayr, and to his mausoleum. She liked the statue of him at the top of the street in Dumfries.

The woman in the pink dressing gown was going home tomorrow. She lived with her brother; he did the cooking. Her nieces would get everything ready. She had had a miscarriage and a baby who died but what could you do? In those days you just got on with it.

I shouted the contents of Liberton Church newsletter to a woman of ninety two who was very deaf. My loud voice telling of the Minister's recent holiday and the success of the drop-in cafe made it hard for the woman opposite to speak to her husband. She lost her temper.

Dod maintained underground conveyor belts at Burghlee then Bilston Glen. One Monday he didn't go in; him and his pal Jimmy Moffat had spent Sunday in the club drinking. Jimmy was killed that morning when the roof fell in. Dod never went back. He took a job with his brother.

I asked if she would like a visitor. No, she had visitors yesterday. She was having more tomorrow and wanted time to write a note because there were things she needed. She hoped to be going home soon but she wasn't desperate. I asked some questions. She answered. Time passed.

Her voice was one used to being in authority. She was waiting for a care package to be put together. She knew she needed looked after now. I asked where she lived. Merchiston she said. But no, that was her memory doing its thing. She had lived there with mama.

The man with the oxygen mask had fallen and made a right mess of his face. He'd need a buzzer at home now. He lived on his own since his wife died. When he came in they'd put him in a ward full of women but that was too upsetting.

When mama died she and a friend bought a bungalow at Cramond but she hadn't been there for years... months. She seemed flustered. Her expression implied disgust: hurt, fragile disappointment. She was tall and straight with short hair that stuck out a bit. She was sitting on a thin cotton blanket.

She loved spending the whole day at the National Gallery. She would have lunch and if the weather was nice and the gardens were lovely... She used to take her car; it was just a small car and she could park nearby but the tramworks had put paid to that.

The woman in the pink dressing gown was going home tomorrow. She had been six weeks in the Western General before coming here. She was looking forward to seeing her garden and her friends. One of them had been in the room two doors up but she had died yesterday.

John the physio had been to talk to the woman next to Libby about shoes. Libby sank back into her pillow and pushed her hands through her hair. He's a nice lad – he takes me oot. She was laughing. I tell the nurses I've been to the woods wi John!

'My name is Mrs Edwards.' Her voice was small. She was all in black, her clothes streaked with dried food. 'You've got a lovely view of the sky,' I said. 'That's all,' she replied offering her hand. 'My name is Joan Edwards. This is a terrible situation to be in.'

I put blackcurrant juice from a small carton into a beaker. She drank a big mouthful and nodded her approval. 'Sweet – beautiful juice.' She had big, bewildered eyes that searched out mine. 'This is a terrible situation.' I poured some more juice as she spoke. 'My name is Joan Edwards.'

Libby's neighbour asked for her shoes. Libby said the smell of them keeps me awake at night. Her neighbour kidded on that she was affronted and they both laughed. I pushed a zimmer within easy reach. They're our motors said Libby – hers is a Ferrari and mine's a Ford Escort.

Thawing
Ewan Gault

THE MOON'S FACE pressed snub-nosed against the night, watching him familiarly. Stitch walked by an abandoned car sunk deep in snow. Its passengers, unfashionable lamp shades and old pillows squeezed tight against the windows, trying to glimpse the glittering glow. Another fall and they would be buried with the stubbly rice fields that rot and grow. He watched his shadow shimmer and slink before him. 'Looking at the same moon briefly.' That was what she had written. He wondered if it was possible. Not now when it was lunchtime in Scotland, but later, when he woke. If she looked then it would be the same moon, surely.

He rubbed his numb cheeks, thick-gloved fingers feeling foreign on his face. A sharp gust of embarrassment caught him as he remembered the night class. Practising introductions, he'd brought in his curiosities: stamps, coins, photos of friends, a Tourist Information guide to Scotland written in Japanese. Pages marked so that they fell open at relevant pictures; 'This is Glasgow, where I used to live.' An evening skyline shot from the south bank of the river. He worked out where his old flat was. The magazine was at least a year old. He wondered if he had been somewhere amongst the tenements made unfamiliar in silhouette.

He concentrated on the grind of snow under his boots. In the middle of the last field before town a farmer had left a slaughter of rotten tomatoes, a gaping wound in the white. Animal prints could be seen weaving this way and that. Some were obviously bird tracks but others, rabbits or deer he guessed. He wasn't sure what wild things lived out here.

Stitch felt glad there was no one about, that he didn't need to smile so hard. Going through his pack of photos practising the words for mother, father, sister, friend, he'd forgotten that she'd still be there. A soft, pale, slim, slip of a thing, he'd said and she had given a much-photographed smile and revealed her perfect sharp teeth. She didn't look so soft as he opened his mouth, unsure what he could call her.

As he passed the sports hall next to his house a sheet of snow slipped down the roof and slumped with a dead thud to the ground. Once inside he wrenched off his boots and tip toed across the tatami matting. The darkness crowded with the crackle and spit of melting ice, the ticking of his kerosene heater warming itself. In bed fully clothed he remembered her attic flat; kicking off blankets heavy and stuffy as hospital beds, tangled legs, the cool of sheets, the smooth of thighs.

Stitch squeezed his mouth, eyes, ears shut, wanting to sink into sumptuous silence but the slow clicks of the heater's fan and the drip of melting ice wouldn't let him.

Later, somewhere among the ruins of a dream, the sharp noise of something solid would come to him. It is a sound that wanders about in his head that he will struggle to recognise. Then it will click. The measured steps of a girl practicing dancing in high heels on the wooden boards in his kitchen. He should be curious but the sound reminds him of a sentence repeated on a typewriter. He thinks the girl may have slept near him as he wrote on this typewriter.

It seems a good memory.

At 6am a muzak version of Edelweiss blared out of the tannoy speakers followed by static and the staccato of Japanese instructing the populace to do their morning calisthenics. Stitch was meant to be working in the Board of Education's office today. Working wasn't really the word. He knew it'd be another dull day loitering with Internet.

Down the hill and over the bridge the ducks bobbed up and down the edges of the river, water in the middle too fast. He felt he could watch them paddling ferociously up the same stretch again and again. An old man rattled by on an oversized bike, wobbling in surprise at the sight of him. At home someone would have said something like, 'you're not going to jump' and he would have said, 'Nah it's not high enough.' He leant over the side, the water stormy with clouds of thawing snow. If he was a duck he'd just let himself go.

He slumped in front of a laptop and checked his inbox. Three messages but nothing from her. She would be in bed now or out in a club or a pub. Just the thought of that used to sting him with jealousy. He would look at Scottish newspapers on the Internet, to find out the weather in Glasgow. Mild with showers, cold but clear, he would stare at the symbols wondering which was best.

'Good morning, Mista Lichard,' Iwasaki San smiled.

'Ohayo Gozaimasu,' he dutifully replied.

She offered him the sweet tin, his fingers trying to negotiate the minefield of Japanese delicacies as he muttered 'Arigato.'

That evening he went to an Onsen with a friend. They lounged in the hot outdoor pool, smelling the sulphur and watching the tangle of lights in the town. After a while the pool made his skin prickle and he climbed out into the snowy night. It seemed a great thing to be naked on the frozen hill. He wanted to feel the flakes land on his skin, before they melted. Nobody had touched him in months. When he turned round Yuski was looking at him in a strange way.

The drive home was a short one. He tried to fall asleep before the heat of the pool left his body but heard a patter of tiny rodent feet running in the space above his ceiling. He tried to ignore it. His room was secure, it couldn't crawl its low black belly over his bed. But a clatter of bottles in his kitchen sent him charging furious, throwing open sliding doors to see a fat retreating rat, clambering round his sink. He stood in the dark with a wooden kendo sword and heard the beast, gnawing. That was what it was doing now. Chewing and clawing at the wooden panels, trying to find a new way in. He balanced on his bed and pressed his cheek to the ceiling listening to the creature's urgent noises. In the kitchen he made himself a cup of tea. It was freezing and he wrapped a scarf around his head. He swilled the last of the tea through clenched teeth, went to the toilet and heard the rat's pitter patter feet following him. He returned to bed, closing all the sliding doors and listening to his own breathing in the night.

She comes to him again through dreams that feel like memories and memories that feel like dreams. He can't remember her opening the door. (The door is locked.) It sounds as if she struts the length of his kitchen trying to find a way in. She stamps her feet. She would look imperious, wretched. The clicks of her heels follow a pattern. She is dancing in the dark. A heavy body of snow slumps from the gymnasium roof. It sets a dog barking. He sits upright in bed and feels that he was near something beautiful.

In the morning Stitch eyes his bag of bread suspiciously. He sits looking at lumps of snow, amazed that they could have come off his boots and still not melted. He feels that he should shiver but he no longer really notices the cold.

He is in a Shognakko today teaching eight year-olds. He arrives at the Cocho Sensei's office and is plied with dark chocolates and heart attack coffee. A monster's head, with bells on the mane and a body of pale blue material is presented. For the first lesson he is to slowly

➤→

dance his way into class (making sure the bells ring) whilst the pupils throw beans at him and shout, 'Devil in, devil out.' He presumes this is a ceremony to usher in the spring, to drive away evil spirits.

For the rest of the lesson he holds up pieces of plastic fruit, the children repeating their names after him. There is a moment of panic when he forgets what a peach is. He pretends to take a bite. 'What is this?' he asks, revising a phrase the students learnt the week before.

'Peach,' they roar as one.

During break he escapes the stuffy staff-room and goes out with the kids. They don't seem to realize he is a Gaijin, and even if he is he can still play. The younger ones speak to him, their faces serious but patient. They will understand him better than anyone. Today they take him by the hand to build Yukki monsters. In the middle of a snowed over baseball field is their work in progress, a huge head similar to the mask he wore in class. They quickly finish sculpting the horns, shaving off the sprinkle of night snow. The Cocho Sensei appears with spray cans and everyone begins colouring the face. It delights him, this spraying paint on snow, watching the shades fade and glow. They work until the bell, all the crazy colour combinations that children can come up with. When he leaves he looks over from his car. The bright reds have faded to a faint blush, the burning eyes only a suggestion of yellow and green.

That night the rat follows Stitch, scuttling above his ceiling, faithful, familiar. He plays some radio J-pop but even this doesn't drive it away. When he holds his breath it stops, when he walks its pink feet follow, when he dreams it claws at the wooden boards between them. Before he leaves he opens a packet of rat poison. The box has an anime picture of a light grey rat, goofy and bucktoothed waving a white handkerchief in surrender. Stitch pours two sachets onto a saucer. He leaves this invitingly near the corner where the creature last got in. The pink pellets remind him of the sugary sweets children offer him at school that fizz in your mouth.

Out on the road the footing is treacherous, half melted slush, tire-crushed, refrozen. He passes a buzzing vending machine, all the multinational drinks of the world, plus green tea and little medical looking bottles that have something to do with erections. Japan has more vending machines than any country in the world, providing refreshment without the need for human interaction. Every year a surprising number of people are killed when a machine topples on top of them. Statistically speaking vending machines are more dangerous than sharks.

Stitch enters a bar called Shiro. There, kneeling around a low table are the people he works with, their faces made soft by Sake and the end of a long day. He smiles at them but his cheeks are a little numb.

Once everyone arrives the Head of the Board of Education gets shakily to his feet and embarks on a speech. Stitch watches the listeners as they stare demurely at the floor and feels like a child with eyes wide open during prayer. He notices himself smiling at a joke he doesn't understand but is more comfortable doing this than sitting in silence as those around him laugh. A rousing frothy 'Kampai,' the clink of drinks, then everyone begins to eat.

It is not long before the drunken party reach for karaoke books. It is a good moment. Stitch has secretly been learning a traditional Japanese song that he performs to everyone's amusement. Sugnawara Sensei, for whom not knowing the words or tune to a song has never been a problem, struggles to his feet shouting 'You Keith Lichards, I be Mick Jagga.'

The rest of the evening is spent supporting others' stumbling English until the chorus, which will hopefully contain as many LaLas, or NaNas as possible. He feels more useful than he has all week. On the way home Sugnawara Sensei is full of praise, 'Lichard San, gentleman, greatest man, stay here, three years, five years, forever.' He hears the river rushing by in the dark and hopes that the ducks have a place to go. He is not sure he can imagine it.

In the flat he notices the rat poison is gone. He peers behind the oven half expecting to see the stricken beast foaming at the mouth. There is nothing. In some ways he would have liked a body.

He lays his futon on the tatami matting and turns on the telly. The news is showing a night time fire fight in Afghanistan, the same brief shaky footage on a loop. The power-cut buildings captured on a night vision camera, glow, unreal, emerald green. Stitch turns the volume down low, the dull explosions and crackle of machine guns lulling him to sleep.

Sometime during dawn he hears a rustling from the kitchen. There is something in there snuffling and his heart goes with a panic. Stitch reaches for the wooden kendo sword. He creeps, sneaks, but whatever has been making the noise is silent now, listening. He slides the door open.

There on a seat sits a girl. There are snowflakes in her long black hair that are slowly melting. She wears a red polka dot flamenco dancer's dress. 'You've travelled a long way,' he says. She picks at holes in her laddered tights. He notices her dress is wet, that it wraps and wrinkles tight to her skin. She slips her foot from a shoe with a broken heel, lets it fall to the floor. There are droplets hanging like dull jewels from the curls of her long black hair. She stands up, seems to lean her face towards him for an age. She doesn't smile, doesn't frown but kisses the side of his neck, barely a kiss at all. He feels the warmth of her slow breath and the cold damp tip of her nose.

She has been coming here for weeks, dancing in his shivery kitchen while he huddles under a blanket watching Japanese game shows, trying to stay warm. All this time and she has never come to his bedroom, with the quilts and duvets and the temperamental heater. He ushers her in, hands her a tracksuit. He tries to occupy himself with igniting the heater but finds his head turning to see her struggling to find the leg of the trousers. When she has these on she faces him, all skinny ribs, nipples pink and pointy. He passes her a T-shirt and baggy woolly jumper. The fan on the heater has started but the igniter clicks away with no sign of lighting. He presses the red button and watches anxiously a faint quivering flame begin to grow.

In bed he wants to trace the shell of her ear with the back of his finger. Foundation and smudged mascara have gathered far from the sweep of her eyelashes. His alarm goes off and he kills it with a bang. She murmurs, snuggles softly.

'Is the room too warm?' Stitch asks. She moves further under the covers in response. He gets ready for work. He would like to stay but has things to do. It is for the best that she gets some sleep. Then they can talk, he is sure she understands. She looks at him blankly and he is in truth a little frightened.

He drives to school sending up great waves of brown slush. Classes are accompanied by huge lumps of half melted snow slipping off the rooftops and falling to the earth. The students cannot be stopped running to the windows to see if they have landed on anybody. There is a feeling of chaos, of something coming undone.

As soon as Stitch gets home he knows the dancing girl has gone. There is no sign of her though the pillow seems a little wet. He thinks he can smell a faint hint of perfume but he has been chasing smells up dead ends for weeks now. An urgent sounding announcement trips over itself from the tannoy speakers. It could be anything from the timetable for this weekend's Taiko competition to a warning that North Korea has let off its nuclear arsenal.

He tries to sleep and must succeed in dozing off as the nine o'clock sound of Moon River playing over the Tannoy nudges him awake. He gets to his feet and goes to the door, looks out at a night sparkling with frosty stars. There is a plane flying into the distance, its frozen slipstream caught in the moonlight like a stitch in the sky. It is flying due west. He knows this direction well for it is where he sends his thoughts. It reminds him of the dancing girl. He rubs the starlight out of his eyes and returns to the shivery air of his flat.

Once inside he tries to put on the kerosene heater but the ignition ticks away without catching. He fiddles with the dials to the side of the heater, ignores the incomprehensible instruction manual bound in dust and goes to bed.

➻

Sometime before Edelweiss chimes across town and the dogs start barking a sharp tapping noise can be heard. His eyes fling off their covers. The girl is back. He rushes to the kitchen leaving a trail of blankets, hats and scarves. But the noise is coming from outside the front door. It doesn't seem like dancing, sounds more urgent than that. He opens the door, the sound stops and he has no idea what was causing it. Then it starts and he sees himself looking at the bright red head of a woodpecker, its folded black and white wings. There on the frozen trunk of a long dead tree it is battering its beak. The sun is almost up. It is the start of spring. The bird is making itself a home.

Shady Chills and Hot Throngs

Naming the Bones
Louise Welsh
Canongate, RRP £12·99, 400pp

Welsh's fourth book is as much a mystery/crime novel as a wink and nudge to the particular 'academic life', where sexual partners are passed around more readily than the latest tome on literary theory, colleagues can be found propping up the bars around campus and office desks are more likely to contain fast-emptying bottles of whisky than student essays.

Dr Murray Watson is a member of the English Literature Department at Glasgow University, which solid stone buildings contradict the instability demonstrated in nearly every arena of his life. The first half of the novel shows us Murray's descent into a general shambles: the topic he spends his sabbatical researching (a biography of Archie Lunan, a poet who had published one collection before his early, unsolved death) is influenced more by personal obsession than an existing body of work; his girlfriend, unfortunately already married to his boss, leaves him under particularly unhappy circumstances; and his family life undergoes changes seemingly designed to emphasise his loneliness.

His ties to the university weaken as his passion for Lunan inflames, and Murray spends more and more time chasing scant leads about Lunan's short, turbulent life. Midway through the book, another setback launches Murray towards the Isle of Lismore, his attempt at a personal escape disguised as a research trip.

There are enough twists to save the book from predictability, but never is there the sense that things will remain unresolved for long. Each time it appears Murray has reached an obstacle, something clears the way, and even when Murray reaches the point of giving up his research, the reader is confident that he's merely saving his energy for the climax and conclusion. The novel is thoroughly paced and planned with fluid and measured writing that demonstrates Welsh's dexterity, while not always being conducive to a nail-biting, edge-of-your-seat pageturner.

As always, Welsh excels at sensual description of misfortune and discomfort. Awkward or embarrassing encounters, the burn of whisky sucked straight from the bottle, rain down the back of a collar – the language comes alive in these moments and leaves us grimacing along with (or at) the characters. At reading the climax of the novel, readers would be forgiven for thinking that Lismore is made of nothing but mud, wind and rain – we almost feel the gales and the cold stickiness palpable to the reader as Murray himself.

Likewise, the parts of the book set in Glasgow and Edinburgh crystallise effortlessly for anyone who has been to those cities – and simply burst into colour for those who haven't. Stepping from the shady chill of a bridge into the hot throng of Edinburgh during the Festival, an early-morning view over Kelvingrove Park, the cawing of drunk youth outside The Viper Club: in these moments the book rings true and we have no trouble envisioning Murray; and indeed are walking right beside him.

Beneath the layer of who's-fucking-who and whirlwind of pubs and grizzled men, this is a novel concerned with how to access the truth held by others, how to even recognize it, or know how to look for it. "Authenticity... was it authentic?" muses one of Murray's old professors. "It existed, I held it in my hands and it impressed me. I think it had something better than authenticity. It had integrity, and that's all the truth we can ever hope for."
Cheshire Cat

Alice in Gumshoe-land

The Existential Detective
Alice Thompson
Two Ravens Press, RRP £9·99, 168pp

Any book with existential in the title either takes itself terribly seriously or not at all. This, together with Alice Thompson's reputation as an 'intellectual' writer, meant I approached her fifth novel with caution.

Unlike many of her contemporaries, Thompson isn't in thrall to realism. *Justine*, her debut, was a lyrical mirage reclaiming female sexuality from the male gaze. Other novels feature fragmented journeys across sci-fi America, amnesiac women shipwrecked on remote islands and tales of beasts roaming Scottish estates. Anti-realism continues here in a noir Portobello populated with Russian hoodlums, high class bordellos and cocktail chanteuses, more akin to Ellroy's L.A. As with her Wonderland namesake, keeping company with this Alice demands stepping through the looking-glass.

The detective of the title is William Blake – not the 18th century Romantic but a Camus-style *étranger* – haunted by the unsolved abduction of his daughter. A shambling gumshoe, Blake is employed by enigmatic scientist Adam Verver to find his amnesiac wife (a recurring Thompson leitmotif).

What follows is a detective story refracted through David Lynch's lens. As Blake tries to piece together the fragments he gleans, he loses his own grip on reality, becoming prone to ambiguous, incapacitating visions. A fortune-telling machine dispenses cryptic advice pertinent to the case and Blake becomes infatuated with a barroom singer who might be the missing woman or his daughter, or both.

Thompson loves symbolism even more than Puvis de Chavannes and has been quoted as admiring writers like Golding. However, while the Nobel winner mainly employed a single over-arching symbol, here they come thick and fast; we're bombarded with unsolvable jigsaws, items in red (hair, dresses, mirrors), irises, blind men who see, cameras like eyes... The effect is disorienting, certainly Thompson's intention.

The Existential Detective has its weaknesses. Third person narration slips into pedestrian passages of didactic prose. One example, a description of Will's penchant for prostitutes would be more effective as a scene with an actual prostitute and some dialogue. And the whole novel is from Will's point-of-view apart from two short sections at the end. Having spent the entire book in Will's company, this feels like cheating.

There's a subplot about computer games which suggests Thompson is a fuddy-duddy. She's partial to a cliché (men nursing drinks, moths towards a flame) and still hides clumsy adverbs in her text. Finally, although perhaps intentional (I deduce from Will's ex standing 'like a Byzantine artwork, two-dimensional...'), some of Thompson's minor characters are so lightly drawn as to be devoid of substance.

However, she is capable of passages of great beauty. The skin of young prostitutes reminds Will of onions made from sheets of tabloids. She is also an erotic writer of great skill, building the sexual tension then presenting scenes of ambiguity. As with *Justine*, she likes the duality of female sexuality in moments of simultaneous power and submission.

Ironically, for a writer revelling in dream-like playfulness, the most successful passages are focused on Will's experience losing a child. Reminiscent of Ian McEwan's gut-wrenching first chapter in *A Child in Time*, these feel born out of experience; that is the novelist as mother.

While it is tempting to judge Thompson on what she is not, she is to be commended for what she is – highly original. Readers should not expect a conventional detective story but prepare to be drawn into an unsettling netherworld of charm and lunacy, both serious and anarchic, much like Lewis Carroll's 150 year old tale, just with more sex.
Behemoth

No mean PC

Shadowplay
Karen Campbell
Hodder & Stoughton, RRP £18·99, 467pp

Karen Campbell is emerging as one of the most promising writers of the so-called tartan noir variety, in the company of commercial powerhouses like Denise Mina, Val McDermid and Alex Gray.

Her third novel featuring policewoman Anna Campbell, *Shadowplay* gives equal weight to the pressures, challenges and occasional pleasures of holding down a job where expectations are high. Juggling family responsibilities, living alone and one's own ambition can be onerous. Anna has a humanity whereby she is in turns fierce, determined and overwhelmed. Linda La Plante's DCI Jane Tennyson is an obvious comparison but Anna Crawford is very much Campbell's own unique creation.

Shadowplay weaves together three main storylines – the stabbing of an Asian teenager, an elderly woman missing from a care home and a police officer who is being stalked by a gang of neds he has antagonised. In the process of investigating each of these cases it is clear that police enquiries are less about leaps of faith and more about hard graft, due process, and keeping on the right side of colleagues and communities where councillors and local hacks are to be treated with respect and caution in equal measure.

We can be sure that Campbell knows what she's talking about; she was a serving policewoman in Strathclyde for seven years. Her knowledge and experience of procedure, routine and the banter between officers rings true. A special mention here for Anna's boss, 'JC' Hamilton, the Sue Sylvester of Giffnock police station, whose put-downs and political manoeuvrings demonstrate that women in authority can be just as competitive, abrasive and focused on their own career as any bloke. A scene where JC gets her shoes cleaned is very funny, demonstrating even tin-pot tyrants feel compelled to exercise their power.

The crimes that Anna investigates are those you would expect to find in any metropolitan city and the way in which they are handled by the author is equally matter-of-fact. The disappearance of the 88 year-old from the home where staff struggle to provide care without the use of drugs, though a genuine mystery, is not played out with high drama. But the real gems are the set-pieces where Anna comes into conflict with colleagues and crims, trying to separate the good guys from the bad and sometimes mistaking one for the other.

Glasgow is described with real panache. Those sections of *Shadowplay* where Anna observes the changing features of the town hints at the range of Campbell's talent: for example, 'Queen's Drive was a dark dead-end, fringed along one side by the fat gnarled oaks of Queen's Park itself. This should have lent the street an open perspective of rolling hills and rural ripeness, even on the dankest days. It did not. It was as if the park itself was bursting out, too full of oily green to be sustained.'

Anna's own inner dialogue maintains the pace as she bounces between job, relationships and family. Her own state of mind is a place where her personal dilemmas, prejudices and petty thoughts are exposed, warts and all, and become motivations to which she occasionally falls victim. Her fraught relationship with her mother, who becomes seriously ill, also creates opportunities for the reader to gain insight into Anna's insecurities.

Recent press hints that Campbell is on the verge of TV success. A fourth novel is already in the can. A graduate of Glasgow University's creative writing factory, it looks likely that Karen Campbell's place amongst its illustrious alumni, who include Anne Donovan, Louise Welsh, Zoë Strachan and Rachel Seiffert, is assured.
Sharik

At the Crossroads

Between the Sheets
Lesley McDowell
Overlook Press, RRP £16·99, 365pp

Relationships are strange. Sometimes inexplicable even to those intimately involved, how much harder then, for the outsider to reach a truthful understanding, with only letters, diaries, memoirs, and fictionalised accounts to go by.

In *Between The Sheets*, Lesley McDowell attempts to do just that by considering the 'literary liaisons' of nine women writers including Simone DeBeauvoir, Martha Gellhorn and Jean Rhys. Defying prejudice and re-examining their lives, McDowell argues that none of these women were the victims they have been portrayed as; rather, they knew exactly what they were doing, they *chose* their relationships, and their writing benefited.

This is not an easy case to make. We hear how Hemingway raged at Gellhorn, "throwing things at her, shooting bullets through windows" and, in his 'better' moods, opened the door with "his drawers down, ready for sexual play." We read of Rebecca West's humiliation at being "shut up" in the country by H. G. Wells, a subservient mistress and unwilling mother. Nevertheless, McDowell argues that there were benefits for all these women: their male literary partners helped them develop as writers, edited their work, and opened doors into a literary world; the women went on to write works directly about or heavily influenced by their relationships.

But, as McDowell herself points out, all the women already had ambitions, in some cases established careers, before they met their literary partners. They *were* writers; they did not need a lover to tell them so. After all, just because a woman's writing has been influenced by a relationship, is it fair to assume that she wouldn't have written about something else, had the relationship not taken place? We cannot know if never-produced work would have been worse, or better, than the writing that was published. But the men, it is argued, helped to *get* them published.

That is the truth and the tragedy. These women simply did not have the support that male writers had. We hear how George Barker, for example, was aided by John Middleton Murry, his work passed up the ranks of (male) editors to be lauded by T. S. Eliot. At the same time, Elizabeth Smart – before meeting Barker and completing the seminal *By Grand Central Station I Sat Down and Wept* – was being told that women shouldn't write for a living, and her poems "should be written and then destroyed." These women needed a literary partner because they wanted collaboration, discussion, debate, and, unlike the men, they were unable to find it elsewhere. So were they using their men? Was it a professional strategy? McDowell is not here to judge. She presents the many personal and professional contradictions and concludes, "What they gained far outweighed what they lost."

The gain referred to is literary immortality, and it makes me slightly uneasy. 'Writing' is placed up on a pedestal – where writers are always a little too inclined to put it – and I'm not convinced it justifies the mistreatment these women endured. Nevertheless, interesting, intelligent, flawed women do tend to be attracted to interesting, intelligent, flawed men.

Given how different the nine women were, it's unsurprising that McDowell's argument holds up better for some than others. Did all these women's relationships really benefit their writing? I'm not so sure. But I am sure that they had reasons for making the choices they made. I do not see any victims here. McDowell's writing is as intelligent as it is engaging and whatever the conclusions, this thought-provoking book is not to be missed by anyone who's been through one of those interesting, inspiring, fatally flawed relationships.
Golden Monkey

The Unsettled Will of the People

And the Land Lay Still
James Robertson
Hamish Hamilton, RRP £18·99, 670pp

Many is the reader whose heart is unlikely to skip a beat at the prospect of 670 pages devoted to the development of Scottish nationalism since the Second World War, but James Robertson, who has made the murkier byways of Scottish history his speciality, clearly believes that this is a subject of hectic passion. Ultimately, *And the Land Lay Still* does make a persuasive case that the nationalist story is a convulsive one, a subject leavened by hope and compromised by deceit.

Grand themes demand a grand scale; the cast of characters here is necessarily vast, and Mike Pendreich acts as the point of contact between them. A photographer like his more celebrated father Angus, Mike is organising a posthumous exhibition of Angus's work. Struggling to find a narrative thread to his father's portraits and snapshots, he recalls his own formative years amongst Edinburgh's bohemian demi-monde. We then swap perspectives to follow others tangentially connected to Mike. Most interesting by far is Peter Bond, a former intelligence officer wrecked by alcoholism who was involved in the semi-official operation to discredit nationalist movements in the 1970s. There's also Don Lennie, a war veteran and socialist, unable to forget the disappearance of his friend Jack Gordon, even as his own family life falls apart. Tortured by the Japanese during the war, Jack had survived the prison camp by conjuring up an idealised vision of his homeland, and Robertson seems to suggest here that nationalist passions can incarcerate as much as they can set free.

There's an initial impression of much sprawl and indiscipline, but the book is skilfully constructed, and there's nothing to fault in its architecture. Mike ends up being little more than a cipher though, and it couldn't have taken a great stretch of the imagination to bestow a foot-fetish on the otherwise sympathetically portrayed Conservative MP, David Eddelstane. Many of the minor characters seem to lurk around the narrative for no other reason than to bulk it up.

Such voluminous ambition tends to be awarded the benefit of the doubt, but where the novel collapses is in the sentence-by-sentence quality of its prose. Rather than allow historical events to form the warp and weft of his characters' daily lives, Robertson rarely misses a chance to lay down a shameless page-and-a-half info-dump of undigested exposition. Confused about the development of the Poll Tax? Don't be: 'The poll tax – or community charge, as it was officially known – was born of the Scottish rates revaluation of the early 1980s.' We are helpfully reminded that the National Gallery of Photography is 'located in the former High School on Calton Hill, a building that in the 1970s was earmarked as the future home of the Scottish assembly; then, when that came to nothing, it was mothballed during the eighteen years of Conservative government.'

Sometimes Robertson hits the right note; when the shattered spook Peter Bond drunkenly hallucinates his former handler. Elsewhere it's like reading an over-cautious politics essay, where the author labours his point. No one can hold an opinion without declaiming it unconvincingly, and step by haggard step we're led through clunking interior monologues as each character puzzles out his position on the Three Day Week, say, or the Korean War ("North Korean Communists were rampaging through South Korea and it looked like they'd have the whole country wrapped up before the clocks went back. Certainly before the newly established United Nations could agree how to respond.") The more vibrant stories are squashed under this leaden weight, and this frustrating didacticism undermines what should be an interesting book.
Montmorency

Nature Remains

The Ice and Other Stories
Kenneth Steven
Argyll Publishing, RRP £7·99, 192pp

Kenneth Steven is known as a children's writer, so it is no surprise that most protagonists in this interesting if ultimately underwhelming collection of stories are children. Whether adolescents on the verge of maturity or young children waking up to a sensual appreciation of the world, they occupy a privileged position, connecting with and experiencing a primeval nature – often in extreme states of ice, howling wind or storms – from which adults are excluded.

Here, human life is contingent whithin the larger contexts of nature and weather. In the title story, Lewis, dependent upon the depth of ice on a lake to get to an island in its middle, realises how igloo-like is the hut in which he spends Christmas, while in *Lemon Ice Cream*, a young immigrant to New York from Sicily, realises that 'the snow and the light are bigger... than all of us together.' In *The Gift*, a family realise 'everything [becomes] drenched and frozen in the end' when their child dies of pneumonia.

Because children are more at the mercy of seemingly unknowable – yet human – powers in the form of adults and rules, they are presented as being able to communicate with specifically non-human nature in a way that the adults cannot. *Conquering* establishes a theme that is repeated in later stories. When the protagonist, Michael, sneaks out of bed to get conkers from a tree, child and weather become entwined in a higher sense of being: 'I galloped with the wind; I felt I was part of the wind myself.'

In *Teddy Fry*, adolescent Danny is mesmerised by an entry in an elderly man's diary of his youth, "golden bell of light". Danny impulsively runs to the scene of the light, where he finds a plaque commemorating the man's dead friend, showing an inscription "of two boys leaping, throwing a ball between them." Danny feels "that the ball [is] the sun." It is a quietly effective story, showing Steven's talent for subtlety and illusiveness.

When human relationships are broken or stripped away, what remains for Steven is nature. In *Billy*, when the title character dies, the teenage protagonist cannot sleep, and lies awake listening to "the wind [that] came in big gusts and was loud in the trees; it banged over the dustbin and sent it rolling up and down the path. A branch tapped in Morse code against the window, and I understood every message it sent." When humans are unable to communicate, nature remains, and does their job for them.

Read as variations on themes of youth and nature, these stories work well as companion pieces. Although a little uneven – *The Ice* seems more fleshed out than *A Christmas Child*, for instance – and with an occasional clumsy ending or heavy metaphor that upsets the balance of the writing, Steven manages to create vivid and atmospheric images of childhood anguish and anxiety.
Mr Mistoffelees

A Feast on Hunger

Sushirexia
Edited by
Gordon Jenkins and Robert Smith
Freight, RRP £9·95, 240pp

Sushirexia is a collection of stories showcasing the work of students from Glasgow University's Creative Writing MLitt course. In their lively Preface the editors Gordon Jenkins and Robert Smith, both graduates of the course, tell us of the blind distribution and scoring system they adopted in the selection of these 32 short stories. Reflecting the different levels of development in the writers, each story, is woven with a strong sense of place.

Published by Freight in a handy, portable, the anthology's theme of 'Hunger' encouraged a wide variety of stories from the selected authors. While some are perhaps more reflective of food than of hunger, there is an astonishing array of subject matter here. No story is predictable in terms of theme or exposition.

Though all have merits worthy of mention, there are some, at least for this reviewer, that stand out. *Thwarted Little Redskins* by Martin Shannan, who previously published *The Tin Man* under the 11/9 imprint questions the success of therapy as cure through the eyes of persistent blusher and sceptic Rory, whose hypnotherapist tries to convince his patient that their blushing is caused by a hunger for self-worth. The hunger for a job in *An Act of Desperation* by Arthur Ker sees the protagonist resort to extremes in the hope of academic promotion, provoking both empathy and dismay. Duncan Muir's sinister *The Crabman and the Fishwife*, with its hints of cannibalism, contains a wonderful passage where the fishwife, Irene, cooks and eats lobster for the first time, inducing revulsion and appetite in equal measure.

The anthology takes its title from Jackie Copleton's story, in which we find the character Hazel struggling with obesity. The narrative is strong on observation, and on society's obsession with weight. The subject matter may be serious, but Copleton creates humour through double-lensed observation: Hazel, observer and observed, offers a bland commentary on the mixture of responses she receives; her GP's concerns about her 'behaviour' regarding food, insults from a junkie in the street and a wilful lack of engagement from a skinny woman in the Sushi bar.

Some stories explore dialogue and voice through intimate snapshots of life. *Lily* by Vicki Husband, is a touching story of human connections and frailty where Lily remains one of the few tenants in a city high rise. Fiona Ashley's *Whit Div Ye Want Me To Say?* has a strong narrative voice which sustains its register very well. Without heavy-handedness or contrivance the narrator speaks in honest, direct language on her realisation that she is unable to conform to society's expectations, unearthing her hunger for a woman and the judgement she receives from her mother as a consequence.

John Jennet, 2010 winner of Glasgow University's Sceptre Prize for new writing, succeeds in evoking the isolation and beauty of Scottish island life in *Won with the Egg, Lost with the Shell*. Deftly weaving the mythical with the everyday, life in nature and actions against nature, the gentle tone belies the harsh consequences for a stealer of birds' eggs.

Sushirexia reflects the diversity and the quality of Glasgow's creative writing graduates and it is to be expected that these authors will, in the future continue to contribute to the health of Scottish literature's bounteous feast.
Jabberwock

Come Join Us

Chosen
Lesley Glaister
Tindal Street Press, RRP £9·99, 368 pp

Lesley Glaister's new novel gives us two tales in one. The first begins in suburban Sheffield with the unusual family of Dodie, her depressed, estranged mother Stella, her teenage brother Seth, and her strained relationship with Rod, the father of her young son Jake. After the horrifying suicide of her mother, Dodie learns that Seth has travelled to New York State to join a religious organisation called Soul Life. When Dodie visits the religious cult's complex, she is both blocked from access to Seth at every turn and coerced into joining their life herself.

With many questions raised this part of the narrative pauses, and we move to the self-recounted tale of Melanie, Stella's sister. Abandoned as teenage girls in mid-70s Sheffield, by the emigration of their father and death of their mother, their ramshackle existence is disrupted by the shiftless but charismatic hippie Bogart. He begins sleeping with Melanie and the three eccentrics form an uneasy but stable relationship, soon challenged by Bogart's drug-induced religious visions – visions that eventually lead him to form the group that will become Soul Life. After many twists and turns, we return to Dodie and her attempt to escape the cult

The novel's strength lies in the depiction of the cult's steady, rapid, chillingly plausible brainwashing process. Soul Life allows Glaister to play with some of our basic fears – confinement, loss of control, loss of will, disruption of our sense of time. But the book also illustrates the disturbing way in which these restrictions become things that subconsciously we wish for, even find comforting.

Glaister expertly builds up a picture of a complex, interrelated network of family members, friends and rivals. Characters and events echo, mirror and contrast with each other, often in ways that the reader only gradually becomes aware of. Although Bogart's religious teachings are satisfyingly debunked, there are other uncanny, potentially supernatural elements hovering around the edges of the story. These function all the better for never being fully explained to us, adding to the somewhat unsettling tone. Dodie herself, around whom most of the action revolves, never quite seems fully fleshed-out, but again this is a shrewd move, as it allows the reader to become a proxy, immersed in the present tense of the story.

The book is not without its shortcomings. When it comes to Melanie's narrative, there are perhaps too many potentially pivotal moments in the plot, meaning that over time they lose their impact, especially as the character's behaviour becomes less plausible towards the end of her story. Melanie's section of the novel is also longer than Dodie's, leaving the overall novel somewhat unbalanced. Nevertheless, as a convincing portrayal of a fascinating phenomenon, *Chosen* works admirably well.
Hound of the Baskervilles

Scotland: Now or Then

The Year of Open Doors
Edited by Rodge Glass
Cargo Publishing, RRP £13·99, 220 pp

To be truly successful, any short story anthology must present itself to the world with a degree of self-confidence bordering on arrogance. For the annual New Writing Scotland anthology, the conviction of being an unrivaled barometer is in part founded on the publication's long history and its place in the country's literary establishment.

For other publications, though, especially those put out independently – often on a wish and a prayer for the art, rather than the money (or even academic kudos) – the belief has to come primarily from those involved.

On some occasions, of course, the 'arrogance' of such anthologies is certainly justified, given not just the talents involved but also their legacies. The literary shadow of 1985's *Lean Tales* (Cape), which brought together Alasdair Gray, James Kelman and Agnes Owens, is significant. A mere 12 years later, the Kevin Williamson-edited *Children of Albion Rovers* helped validate the new *Rebél Inc* generation of Scottish authors that included Irvine Welsh, Alan Warner and Gordon Legge.

Now, 13 years after that successful volume, award-winning author Rodge Glass and independent publisher Mark Buckland have taken it upon themselves to produce a new collection to follow in those illustrious footsteps, gathering together specially commissioned or previously unpublished work by a new generation of writers born and/or resident in Scotland. Their brief for the anthology was, it would seem, deliberately non-restrictive – 'Scotland: Now'. At least on the surface, the result is an anthology celebrating the diversity of an early 21st century Scotland that is defined by the people living here, rather than just lines on a map.

Of course, between 1997 and 2010, there have been other notable Scottish fiction anthologies, including the Neil Williamson/ Andrew J Wilson-edited *Nova Scotia* (Crescent Books, 2005) which successfully mapped out a different picture of modern Scotland through its now often overlooked tradition of the fantastique.

So, what does *The Year of Open Doors* bring to the party? On the surface at least, it too gathers writers from across Scotland. The writers in turn bring a variety of literary techniques – from Sophie Cooke's playful transcript of one side of a secretive conversation, to Aidan Moffat's terribly polite 'confession' from a senior citizen in West Kilbride – and tackle everything from a drugged-up club night on the Clyde to a genuinely touching island tale of making gates out of the flotsam from the sea. All to the good.

These are stories about 'Scots' of all ages and creeds, from the lonely Indian girl trying to get through Christmas to the cultural misunderstandings that can flare up between young children. Some, it has to be said, are more genuinely lyrical than others – the work of Alan Bissett and Kirstin Innes, for example, clearly benefit from their experience in spoken word performance.

Yet, while *The Year of Open Doors* presents a snapshot of an intrinsically diverse, modern day Scotland, its focus on 'Scotland: Now' translates into a collection of tales about people who all too often look to the past, fear the future or try to lose themselves in the present. And giving the prominent final slot in the anthology to Kevin MacNeil's tale — in which a lone Scot distastefully gains some personal redemption from a failed romance in his attempt to save a young girl from the 2004 Asian Tsunami – hardly signifies the unselfish, outward looking nation that Scotland supposedly wants to be.

There's a lot of good writing here, and this is an anthology that doubtless has the arrogance to strut its stuff but it is sadly less than the sum of its parts.
Yeti

New Views: recent collections from Bloodaxe Books and Red Squirrel Press

Scottish poetry dares to make a statement. A selection of books from poetry powerhouses Bloodaxe Books and Red Squirrel Press illustrates that some Scottish poets find inspiration in historical events, taboo topics and exotic places. Though these poets stick to composing in tried-and-true forms, they take risks in their content, characters and choice of narrative.

Kona MacPhee's *Perfect Blue* (Bloodaxe, £7·95) contains the most succinct sequence within the selection. 'A Book of Diseases' describes illnesses that were once difficult to cure. Clinical fact and sensitive perceptions are expertly intertwined. In 'Leprosy', MacPhee describes the skin's diminishing sense. Each stanza begins with a statement about touch: 'yet sense can lie... and sense can be deceived...and sense can even die.' In 'Scarlet Fever', the sufferer falls ill on the commute home. In the middle of the night, he realises the severity of his illness. Bewildered, he stares at the red lights of his alarm clock that 'might be a guiding beacon or a warning / it all depends on whether you know how lost you are.' Set in World War Two, 'Gonorrhoea' describes how soldiers' were warned against venereal disease. Bromide tea was doled out to stifle their libidos. MacPhee closes the poem with this cheeky couplet: 'and Private Fenton claps his hands around / the shrapnel-wound that used to be his balls.' Yet the highlight is 'Typhoid'. From 1902 to as late as 1997, female asymptomatic carriers were detained for life in the Long Grove mental asylum, Surrey. The women's longing for their previous existences overpowered their daily life. MacPhee choice of fragmented language feels appropriate: 'here she is that one / open face no-mask one / white clothes always a smile.' Overall, this sequence reads like a suite of music. The tone and form of each poem adapts with the content, allowing each poem to lead on naturally to the next.

While MacPhee describes frailty with subtle imagery, Cheryl Follon writes about human weakness with colourful phrases and glittering symbols. Her collection *Dirty Looks* (Bloodaxe, £7·95) is a brazen set of poems about how sexual desire is both debilitating and liberating. These poems are unashamed to employ blatant sexual references and scenarios. 'Auntie's Snaps' describes photos of male genitals. Similes include 'a car's oil-dipper' and 'soft as a lady's ballroom slipper.' Like the 'Little Britain' gag of which this poem is reminiscent, the result is a tongue-in-cheek commentary about sexual standards. Similarly, Follon uses irony in her poems of animals. A devious wolf uses cheesy lines to coax a bird to the ground: 'How about I pick you a posy? / Women like that sort of thing.' The blatant symbolism of this poem is matched with a poem about a rooster – also known as a cock – that struts around town in new clothes. The townspeople encourage him to take off his clothes: 'Let the blood flow! I'll hold your coat.' Furthermore, the carnival ambience of the collection is reflected in the many poems about the Old South. The sultry powers of 'Lady Voodoo' is likened to that of a spider 'with a sack of silky eggs inside her.' The collection's bizarre characters, jazzy rhythms and unrelenting sexual imagery are meant to destabilise the reader's notion of gender.

On the other hand, Stuart Conn plants his poems firmly in a domestic setting in *The Breakfast Room* (Bloodaxe, £8.95). His sequence 'The Loving Cup' explores the minutiae of a steady marriage. Though at times squirmingly sentimental, the poems imbue a sense of reassuring wisdom and contain delightful images. Conn begins with a description of the loving cup itself, a double handled mug with the initials of a couple intertwined. This cup is, as Conn states, 'brimful of memories that can never spill.' Continuing with the intertwined imagery is 'Early Morning', which describes the coupling of pigeons; birds that mate for life. Though their cooing disrupts the narrator's morning routines, he eventually lets them be: 'Worse things / to have outside your window than so decorous a love-in.' The poet looks back in 'The Life Ahead', where the memories of a life together blend in with each other. Ordinary events such as holidays in Provence, walking across bridges, walking home from concerts, and visits from family and friends can be expressed in the mantra 'I love you'. The scent of vanilla is the motif of one of closing poems, whereby the scent of perfume reminds the narrator of stealing biscuits in his childhood. This feeling of being submerged in the poet's memory never dissipates.

A similar focus on reminiscence is alive in Eleanor Livingstone's *Even the Sea* (Red Squirrel Press, £6·99). This debut collection from the poetry director of StAnza has the air of a photo album containing modern Scottish images. This motif is introduced in the opening poem, 'Shorehead lost and found'. Livingstone writes: 'signs declare – Leven bay / Fish Bar and Restaurant / Real Spice, Currys, Pizzas.' These observations lead to the poem's clincher: 'Mac Tours – real Scots / showing you the real Scotland.'

This 'real Scotland', according to Livingstone, who lives in Fife, also contains seasides, dogs and flowers. The poems' slow pace and similar arrangement on the page allows them to blend into each other. Both 'Dysert at dusk and One more River' describe the day's close, with 'nets gathering in / the echoes of the day' and 'when the low sun / walks on water.' In 'Bluebells', the narrator recalls blushing in front of an admirer while clutching bluebells; thirty years later the bluebells are a symbol of unity between them. The strength of Livingstone's work comes from these small but significant realisations.

Whereas Livingstone's work seems to float along, Andy Jackson pins his to the page with full stops. The poems in *The Assassination Museum* (Red Squirrel Press, £6·99) contain very forthright phrases.

Surfacing illustrates his brisk style:
> His rent is due. He works tonight.
> The empty quarter calls. He leaps
> from running boards, his eyes alight
> and whistles while the city sleeps.

It is interesting to note that though Jackson employs a formal structure of measured accents and rhymes, he merges these poems with artworks. Supplementing this poem is a photo of a man on a bench. The street ahead of him holds passing cars and trucks, and his head is turned to the right. It's an ordinary scene, but functions as an additional visual for Jackson's poetry, which focuses more on capturing the narrator's voice rather than tracking images.

Much like Jackson, Kevin Cadwallander also employs traditional forms. Most phrases in *Sagrada Familia* (Red Squirrel Press, £6·99) are capitalised, resulting in emphasis placed on each line's first word. This causes Cadwallender's poetry to sound heavy; however, the weighty tone matches the content. Love poems such as 'Rewiring Houdini Revisited' benefit from a deep tenor: 'You wrap your arms and legs / Around me, skin-chains, soft links / The kind that take a lifetime to break.' The serious, and sometimes ironic, tone also suits the sequence entitled 'Casey Diem poems', which was co-written with Deborah Murray. Cadwallander waxes lyrically about the love life of bees: 'Glued to you by song / By words sticky and strong / By wax and waning moon.' Cadwallander's traditional poetry has the touch of W. S. Graham, and he pays tributes to friends and influences Adrian Mitchell, Tom Raworth and Pablo Neruda by writing poems for/after them. The hefty collection – almost a hundred poems – illustrates a sensitive ear and a lyrical turn of phrase.

These collections reveal the wealth of topics that currently inspire Scottish poets. From incurable illnesses to the couplings of bees, it's clear that poets are finding their art in all kinds of sources.

Puss In Boots

Scottish Friction

Dreams and Other Nightmares
New and Uncollected Poems 1954–2009
Edwin Morgan
Mariscat Press £9·99

Edwin Morgan's new book ranges across decades' worth of thoughts and dreams from Scotland's postmodernist conscience. No swansong is evident here, and new readers would be forgiven for thinking it the work of a younger mind than the nonagenarian grand makar himself. In part this is because the collection covers a staggering fifty-five years, but later poems show his imagination still cradles its starry sparkle.

As those familiar to Morgan's work will expect, the essence of these poems is a seriously playful exploration of the nature of existence, space and time – via dreams, fantasies, nightmares and remembered liaisons.

Morgan is not blind to circumstance, his poems of senescence are particularly affecting. In 'Four A.M.' the narrator wakes 'as if to a warning'. Nothing seems amiss, but mortal night fear teases him: 'So was there some black power / Pawing the window glass, / A Grendel from the morass / Come to claim me at last?' Such isolation is offset by the focus, concentration (material and spiritual), and philosophical optimism of restricted existence in 'From a Nursing Home'. Here, grim reality '–Now that you are down to one room, / ... / Have you started thinking about it? / ... / First and last things. Don't say you've forgotten.' contrasts with optimism brought by the intense proximity of treasured objects: 'Careful, careless, carefree – we are alive / With whatever equanimity we can muster / As time bites and burns along our veins.'

Previously unpublished poetry from 'Pieces of Me', takes a picaresque, instamatic journey from childhood 'Glasgow', via first death 'North Berwick', lost love 'Rutherglen', war 'Sidon', and sexual pleasure 'Amsterdam'. The repression ('Arran'), blackmail, and sometimes-violent milieu of 1960s/1970s gay Scotland is graphically present in 'Glasgow' and 'Happiness', while 'Glasgow Gay and Lesbian Centre' is a hopeful celebration of acceptance.

As always, Morgan's love poetry crosses arbitrary definitions of sexuality, as in 'The Quarrel', 'Amsterdam Revisited', the exquisite simplicity of 'Morvern', and delicate understatement of 'Skins' where: 'Naked now, we have no salutation. / The bodies we don't know / don't know each other or themselves. / We introduce the stranger to the stranger.'

No Morgan miscellany should want for some concrete. In this regard 'Zoo' and particularly 'Rainbow', don't disappoint. Riffing on the old mnemonic 'Richard of York gave battle in vain', it contains the marvellous sequence 'ram oafish yesman grasp belt invoke vanboy'. Other familiar Morgan tropes are also present, from aliens, 'Encounter'; to wordplay, 'Norwegian' and 'A Pleasant Flyting'; mysterious visitations, 'Resistance'; and humanity's insignificance in the cosmos, 'Beginnings' and 'Geode'.

For different reasons, three poems stand out. The first 'Scottish Fiction', a collaboration for Idlewild's 2001 album *The Remote Part*, is Morgan at his most makarish, most socially engaged: 'It isn't in the mirror/ It isn't on the page / ... / It's asylum seekers engulfed by a grudge / ... / Do you think your security / Can keep you in purity / ... / Scottish friction / Scottish fiction'. Buried on page 23, 'Heaven' is a weary meditation on what might await us all: 'We have seen too many films / to be bowled over by many mansions' and resignedly 'We tiptoe up the stair / to the last room / with the last key / and get it to growl / round in its hole'. This collection is a worthy primer on Morgan's epic poetic mission across space-time. Appropriately, it ends with a 'Riddle': 'I outstrip the moon in brightness, / I outrun midsummer suns. / ... / I claim this honour, I claim its worth. / I am what I claim. So, what is my name?' The answer, fittingly, is Creation.
Moby-Dick

Incidents in the Mall
Ewan Morrison

#15. The Price of Life, according to Pope Jim

If your car was refused exit at the barrier of the multi-storey car park of Scotland's largest mall then, you would have to push a button and speak to the parking attendant. As you did so, a queue of frustrated drivers would inevitably start to form behind you. The voice over the intercom may then announce that it will open the barrier to let you out, or it may ask you to come to the payment booth to resolve the issue. As the cars behind rev their engines and faces swear at you through windscreens you must then find and follow the signs to the payment booth and fight your way through the fume clogged air. You might become incensed that some little man can humiliate you in this way, implying as he has, that you are a liar, a thief or an imbecile. By the time you finally locate the tiny booth, you are ready to scream at this idiot sitting behind his protective, probably bullet-proof, glass, who has not even turned to greet you; who seems, in fact, to be joking with some colleague beyond your line of vision.

Look, you shout. This is a bloody outrage!

Now Sir, he says slowly with a thick Southern Irish drawl, what seems to be the problem?

His smile is disarming, but you don't want to be disarmed. There are now twelve cars parked behind yours and honking has started.

Look, you shout. I need to speak to your superior!

He pauses for a second and smiles, Well,

apart from God almighty, I'm the one next in charge down here, he says.

A minute later, after he has taken the ticket from you, smoothed out the crease that was causing the scanner to fail to read it, you find yourself apologising to the lovely man for the inconvenience you have caused him by your own stupidity.

This man is Jim. He is forty-nine years old, the father of three sons and a daughter who he proudly boasts is the first in the family to ever make it to university. His nickname is Pope Jim, or just Pape, but he has never declared any faith. The name was bequeathed to him by Rena, one of the cleaners in the mall car park. She is a sectarian, a true blue royalist, a racist, and despises almost everybody. Hearing Jim's accent she must have assumed he was a catholic, and since his ticket box looks a bit like the confessional booth the joke stuck. Every time Jim has tried to speak to Rena she has vented a deluge of obscenities, even on work related subjects, like the time he said: Excuse me Rena could move your trolley, you're causing a traffic jam, she'd shouted back. My arse, ya fuckin Papist paedo! Rena the cleena, he calls her in his sing-song voice. She'd be great at the old ethnic cleansing, jokes Jim.

If you have time to spend with him, Jim will be grateful for the company; he'll even invite you into his booth for a cup of tea and to hear his stories. He tells one about a guy who tried to kill himself on the top floor, but he usually leaves that one till last, while he lures you in with cheerier tales.

➥

On a sunny Sunday in June, two elderly ladies in a red Fiat Panda were stuck at the barrier after having neglected to insert their card in the scanning machine. A large queue formed behind them as they at first tried to reverse then to do a U turn. They had failed to notice the 'attendant help-button' or, it seemed, any of the other cars that were having to reverse to avoid impact with them. The old ladies however, managed to hit four vehicles and so set people panicking. Jim ran towards them and was nearly knocked to the ground when they accelerated for the barrier, then crashed through, snapping it in half, before spearing their car on the concrete security bollards. The back wheels of the car were stuck a foot in the air and still the old dears kept revving the engine, smoke coughing out of the exhaust. When Jim knocked on their window they smiled and neither apologised nor showed any distress – Don't worry about us officer, one of them said, We're just on our way. Thelma and Louise, Jim calls them. Thelma and Louise.

The old people. Jim feels sorry for them. They used to have a town centre and market stalls, he says, now they come here, wander about by themselves, like wee lost kids; they spend the whole day, buying endless cups of tea, reading their newspapers in the toilets. It's not right. There was that ancient old skinny bloke he came across, up on the fourth floor, standing there in his socks, no sign of his shoes anywhere around, the old fella didn't even have a shopping bag. Standing there by the down-ramp – not even on the pedestrian-safe walkway – a dangerous spot on a blind turn where the cars head down from the top level. Jim had gone up, asked if he was all right.

Mind yer own bloody business, the old man yelled, I'm waiting for ma bus.

Waiting for my bus, Jim repeats, that's a good one. You have to laugh eh, or you'd weep. The fourth floor, eh? Waiting for ma bus, waiting for ma bus.

Jim repeats himself a lot, which is understandable, given the nature of his job. Sometimes, he laughs so much it seems like he's crying. People often ask him –Why the hell do you do this job? And for so long? He's

been here since the mall opened, twelve years before, people in his kind of post usually stick it a year. Why?

Well, I used to be a prison officer ...and before that I was an undertaker. He grins. I don't know, I suppose I'm a people person.

You might laugh and sense that he is trying to keep you longer in his booth, stringing out time till the suicide story, the promise of which is what's keeping you here. Sensing that you might be about to leave, he finally begins.

This guy has come to his window, this would be a year back; the guy is respectable looking, mid thirties, bald headed, smart dressed.

Now, Sir, Jim says. He always says Sir, or madam, very polite – What seems to be the problem? – The choice of the word 'seems' is crucial, it defuses blame on both sides, and it is always 'the problem', not 'your problem' - Jim explains this and tells you he has done three different anger-management and conflict-management courses; and as for the Irish accent, yes, he came from the south originally but he finds that people are less aggressive to him when he hams it up. There are reasons for this that he'd rather not go into, which are reminiscent of tactics that African-American slaves have historically used to outwit their masters. The customer's always right, eh?

The bald guy is brandishing his parking ticket and explaining that the barrier wouldn't open for him and the screen said Ticket Not Valid. He's shouting that his ticket is bloody well valid cos he only paid for it five minutes ago.

Jim checks the time and the ticket – and the guy paid for it twenty minutes back. Jim waits for a gap in the rant and points this out.

You saying I'm lying, the man is shouting, you saying I'm a fucking...

Jim quietly shows him the printed time on the ticket – paid: 11.04. And while the guy interrupts and yells over and over No, no you, you listen to me, Jim explains that car parking is by the hour, so if you park from ten till eleven, that's one pound twenty and if for two hours – then two pounds forty. But the guy is yelling, you fucking people, this is a dictatorship, you miserable little fucks, drag us all down to your fucking level. And Jim, has to use all his reserves of patience and training to explain that since the man had taken so long to find his car, twenty minutes in fact, he had entered the new hour and so a further payment of one pounds twenty pence would be all that was required to clear the outstanding balance.

Money, more fuckin...! So if I stand here another hour, two hours even, taking this shit, I'm gonna have to pay you for the fuckin privilege, right? Are you fuckin kiddin? Are you listening to me? You're not listening to me. Fuckin listen to me, man!! They always scream Listen to me, Jim says, even if you're not saying a thing. You can't even say, I'm not saying a thing, cos they scream, you're not listening to me. Round and round the roundabout Jim says, round the roundabout.

So, to end it, Jim says the only thing he can say. The truth of the situation. People don't like the truth, it makes them angrier, but what else can you do?

 I'm sorry sir, but those are the rules, Jim says. One pound twenty. I don't make the rules, I don't like this any more than you do.

No, course not, ya fuckin moron, you're fuckin dead already! All you bastards! Dead!!!

The man punches the wall beside Jim's window and runs off.

This was nothing new for Jim. Every day, there are about twenty people yelling No-one said I couldn't pay at the barrier. There are those that tear up their tickets, only to have to come back five minutes later to apologise and beg to be released. There have been people stuck in queues, screaming, I've got my pregnant sister here. Let us out - she's going into labour!, and a stroll to the car reveals that there is no pregnancy, not even a sister. There are those who have lost their tickets and when they are informed that they must then pay for a whole day's parking, which comes to twenty-four pounds, even though they've only been there for half an hour, they throw their keys away in disgust. There are those who can't find their car and insist it has been moved without their permission. There are those who enter and seeing the car park is full, try to reverse down the one-way entry route into oncoming traffic.

Jim has been spat at, punched and had a wide variety of objects thrown at his reinforced glass window, including cans of Irn-bru, cell phones, pre-packed sandwiches and on one occasion a soiled disposable nappy. His day is, in fact, little more than the long hours of waiting for precisely such incidents to occur.

So Jim thought nothing of it, until he sat himself back down and looked out and was surprised to see that the man's car, a vw Passat, was still parked to the side and the man curiously absent. He gazed down at his monitor and at his tea, which was now cold, and before he could reheat it in his microwave, he got a call on his walkie-talkie from Security.

Charlie Papa (which means Car Park) – we have a Delta fifteen – area five.

A Delta fifteen was a jumper, and area Five was the top floor. Jim scanned his monitor and found the image among the fifteen views of the car park. The guy was standing on a tiny ledge, (intended, it must have been, purely for ornamentation), his arms behind himself, gripping the concrete.

Jim skipped the stairs and the lift and ran up the down-ramps, dodging the traffic. Cars honked around him and he went over on his ankle. He staggered up the last bit and broke onto the top floor.

The jumper was still there, but there was someone beside him, not security, or the police, but Rena the cleana.

On ye fuckin go ya baw heid! She was shouting at the poor guy, Wan less of you cunts an we'll all be happier. It was clear to Jim that Rena had never done any courses in conflict management.

The guy was trembling, looking down at the fall. Jim made it to his side, but could not get a word in.

No, you an all, what is this? Attack o the fuckin papes – you an all then cunt face, oer the edge ye go, the both o ye.

The bald headed man seemed confused, as Rena was ignoring him, pointing her mop handle at Jim.

But dinna fuckin come crawlin tae me tae clean up yer fuckin brains! Rena then turned and walked away, trailing her trolley.

Sorry about that, Jim said to the man on the edge. She's got a hell of a mouth on her.

The bald man seemed suddenly embarrassed. He reached out and climbed back up over.

The police and ambulance took some time to arrive and Jim couldn't leave the guy there standing shivering, so he led him to his booth and made him a cup of tea. Once the guy had calmed down and Jim had showed him the spot on the CCTV cameras where he'd been standing, the guy broke down and started to tell the story of his life. Jim never repeats the personal details to anyone when he recounts the tale. All he says is there was a moment there, when he said to the guy, One pound twenty, eh? If I'd known you were going to do that, I'd have let you off with it, hell, I'd have paid it myself.

One pound twenty, eh! The guy repeated and then started laughing. The price of a life, eh?

Would you have done the same if it was twenty pence? Cos ten years back that was the price.

Of life? The guy asked.

No, of the car park, said Jim.

When the police arrived they found the two men roaring with laughter.

One pound twenty, they both said over and over. One pound twenty.

This is the story, the way Jim tells it. He has many others of things he has seen in mall car parks, as he has worked in several others before. Things you wouldn't believe, he says. Things you wouldn't believe.

#8. The Burger King

Every day, a man comes to the mall and takes the escalators to the fourth floor food court at six p.m. exactly. He is thirty-six years old and has never before enjoyed either shopping malls or fast food. He orders his meal from Burger King because they have a new Healthier Options menu. He comes to the mall because he cannot eat unless he is surrounded by people. He fears returning to his empty flat and cooking a meal

for one. He finds the silence overpowering. He gets panic attacks, dizziness, nausea. Before he started eating in Burger King, over six months he had lost two stone in weight.

The reason for this is that he was once married, with three children, and he was the family chef. His Bolognese sauce was famous at dinner parties. He cooked an impressive roast sea bass with green salsa; he followed recipes from the River Café Cookbook and entertained many guests and their children.

He now sees his children once a week and the place in which his now ex-wife hands them over is the mall, because it is a neutral space, without prior emotional associations. It is not her place or his, it is somewhere in the middle.

His National Health Service psychiatrist was concerned by his weight loss and said he would starve to death unless he got over his fear of eating alone. It was suggested that he should try to eat in public places; cafes, railways stations, even the canteen in the local hospital. The mall was not on the list, but he found that, in the half hour before seeing the children, before hand-over time, surrounded by the noise and bustle of people, he could eat without stress or fear or vomiting.

Since eating in the mall he started to regain his strength. He would love to share what he eats with his children. The only problem is their mother has them on a strict health food diet and she looks down on many of his choices of living. As a result, his daily Burger King meals are a secret he has not told anybody. Before meeting his children he scrubs his hands and mouth in the toilets and eats mints or antacids, to hide the smell of the fast food, as once before he had done with cigarettes, with alcohol.

In the mall he has noticed that there are other regulars in the food court. They are not there to shop, only to eat. They are old men. They never learned how to cook, perhaps, and have now lost their wives, to cancer, to old age, to things unspeakable. They sometimes exchange smiles and nods of the head with him as they eat, as if they know.

He looks forward to the day when he can eat like a normal person, alone in his own home. In the meantime, his favourites meals are: the BK veggie burger and the Flame Grilled Chicken Salad, which includes crispy lettuce, red ripe tomatoes, crunchy carrot, cabbage and sweetcorn, wearing the latest designer dressing.

Sometimes there are women, young women, and he thinks them too beautiful to be eating alone. But then he thinks, going up and chatting to strange women was what led to all this in the first place.

And he's come to look at his former self and to think: My God, what a snob I must have been. Look at me, licking the mayonnaise and ketchup from my face, with that bloated happy feeling. I'm no different from anyone. Look at me, the king of burgers. The burger king.

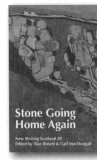

'If I had listened to the critics
I'd have died drunk in the gutter'

Anton Chekhov

Whit a Man Wants
Stephen Nelson

When ah sit doon
tae meditate in the mornin,
it becomes clear tae me
that ma inner man is,
in fact, an inner wuman.
Noo don't get me wrang–
there's nuthin sexual,
trans-sexual or even trans–
genderific aboot aw this. Naw.
It's simply that ah feel
inside me a beautiful
feminine thing I can relate
tae wi a certain degree ae affection,
offerin masel lovingly, yes,
and that ah have, indeed,
a most delicate lady forming,
as it were, somewhere
between ma heart
and ma abdomen, with whom
I share tender moments of
the most exquisite
gentleness.

They tell me it's
the beginnings
ae tantra or some mad
Jungian thing, an esoteric
roadmap to ecstasy that
the high beings ae heaven
shared wae mankind
some 40,000 years ago
or thereabouts.
So be it!
Ah jist hope ah don't
hiv tae gie up coffee
or red meat or anythin
like that.
Ah mean ah'm aw fur
tantric bliss n everythin,
but a man's gote his limits
efter aw. Fair's fair.

East Chevington Opencast
Richie McCaffery

Me and Tommy were drunk, playing rogue golf on site
when the plane came down. We didn't see the bang
or the blistering fuselage fall apart like a meteor.
But we saw its frosted tracks, etched in the sky,
that was Pan Am 103 – 'Clipper Maid of the Seas'.

When we got back to the office, orders came through –
'collect any debris' from that wilderness
of spent farm soil, threshed for coal, the Opencast.

We got in the Defender and started the search.
Somewhere in the ponds of tadpoles and murdered dogs,
in the reeds and spotted orchids we'd find lost luggage.

Tommy was dying of lung cancer, he tried to hide it
but his breathing was like a tyre pump in custard
as he defiantly sucked on his Dunhills.

Each time the blasters blow open a new seam,
I think of star-crossed lives, the omens of comets,
and Tommy, lying snugly in his pine overcoat.
The tremors break at my desk and my pen jerks
like a polygraph.

Emigration
Mark Ryan Smith

Scotland,
folded like a paper cone,
funnelled its folk to this place.
Glasgow became the hinge;
on either side lives swung.
The gangway lay waiting
to lift feet from native land;
arms, like the last strands of root
at hairst, held to those left wondering
if they had been right not to go.
Letters would come,
with words moving east, to home,
and west, to hope.
America:
can you ever box the compass?
can you ever make the broken parts whole?

The Captayannis
Marion McCready

The Firth has birthed a sugar ship.
Cormorants as black as the Furies
have commandeered her starboard.

A part of me crept inside her
while she slept in my womb,
smaller than a plum.
I imagined I could keep her buried
like a treasure. But even the Captayannis
could not keep her cargo.

Beached on sand banks, she has leaked
Caribbean cane for thirty years.
She has turned the river to syrup.

I've been awake for days,
the window translates morning
into my room. Clouds glide like continents
above the yacht-mottled Clyde.
I daydream of cormorants
and crystalline, plums with appleseed hearts.

The Greenock girls in their silver heels
do not see the sugar ship.
She has been there all their lives.

Subconscious Relationship to Success
EP Teagarden

When you stop on the bridge
to watch the water
is it flowing towards you
or away?

Book Launch
Eveline Pye

Part of me is in this book, my blood is splattered
on his porous pages. He asked me. *Do you want to
be my inspiration?* I told him no. Did he not hear me?
For all the good it did. See the books stacked up and
nothing to protect me from the mental equivalent
of date rape. Was it my own fault? After all, I talked,
I did, and he listened, and it soothed me back then
to have someone really listen but it was never worth
this. I've been a fool but, well, I've endured worse.
Wait for the applause, stand up, smooth your skirt
as though creases count. Smile, stroll to the exit
and remember, you are a nonentity, a nothing.
No one is looking at you.
                    No one knows *she* is you.

The Art and Craft of Fiction
Kevin Williamson

The business of money, to the writer
is like catching bubbles, to a child.

The publishers formed a guard of honour
at the bar, for the malcontent.
Guinness and wine. Good cop, bad cop.

'We've received a letter, a *legal* letter,
from lawyers representing a powerful
and influential client. An unhappy woman.'

The author gripped his glass of Guinness
with both hands. 'Aw, aye?'

'Their client states that you've insulted her,
libelled her, accused her of filth and depravity,
not even bothered to change names or details.
They're going to sue us for every penny they can.'

The writer picked up the letter,
scrutinised it, passed it back to the publishers,
drew deep from the well.

'Why didn't you tell us it was about your ex-wife?'
'We didn't even know you had an ex-wife.'
'It was supposed to be fiction, for fucksake.'
'There's rules about what you can and can't do.'

There was a silence that spoke in many tongues.
Some serious, some not.
'You must have something to say about it?'

And he did. Just the one word. 'Bullseye.'
And that was that. Ripples on the pond.

The Art of Discretion
Andrew Elliott

I know it reflects very poorly upon me
but much as I admire almost all of her poems
what I really want to know are the things she got up to
when the mist like the minds of however many people
get around to reading this poem of mine, pressed
up the hill – not put off by rocks, abundant
vegetation, the steepness of the climb, the moon's
insoluble shadows – to press against the glass
like all those eyes, against this page, circling slowly
round each other, spawning from the mist they're made of,
so many brief, competing visions that they overlap
and slide away into each other and make it all so hard
to know what were the things that she got up to –
in the middle of the night and here, in this of all places –
safe inside the house of Lota de Macedo Soares.

Believe
Adam Hofbauer

FEEDBACK FROM THE microphone in the Houston Hilton, an audio spike in Conference Room A. The projector clicks on and the audience shifts. I clear my throat.

I look you in the eye and I speak with certainty.

'It is my belief that the most significant developments in our history have not only already occurred, but have been obscured from us, intentionally, and under the funding of our own tax dollars.'

Click the laptop and begin. The NASA logo glows behind my shoulder.

Folding aluminum chairs lined up in rows in hotel conference rooms. The Blue Room. The Chester A. Arthur Ball Room. Vast, angular spaces, never with a single window. Tables with arrangements of coffee makers, cups, sugars, red plastic stirring straws, bagels, plastic knives. At night, the sound of vacuums being pushed down long stretches of carpet. The sandal claps of family feet on their way from the pool back to their room.

'There is a great Truth out there. It's the most important Truth that has ever been, and there are elites, groups of men with too much power, who think that it is in our best interests not to know about it.'

Click the laptop and go on. The Masonic flag flicks into view.

Beneath the fixtures and the fluorescents of the Orlando Hyatt's main dining room, the crowd lets out a knowing murmur.

Life in projectors. Life in programs. Life in the 3:00 slot. Dinners beneath the glow of Waffle House signs, signs the color of bees, at watch above highway exit ramps. Denny's soaks everything together in syrup, into a single wad of glucose. Catch dinner in a time crunch, eating one handed on the highway from out of your lap, pollution-pink hot dogs still dripping with stale convenience store water. Mustard out of packets and soda out of Styrofoam. I gain five pounds a month, fifteen in a summer. If I did this all year I'd weigh three hundred pounds.

Stay fit. Pushups on the hotel room floor between the bed and the wall. Crunches in the bathroom before your conference slot. Stay clean shaven, collected, with tie knotted and slacks pressed, shoes matching my belt. Careful to avoid the ear marks of the images that instantly scream out that a crackpot is in the room.

Come well rested, no bags under the eyes; under the influence of no pain killers, no uppers, no downers; no alcohol before dark, some caffeine but just enough, clear head; fact, no opinions. Show no signs of being unhinged. Keep criminal record clear. Make no unnecessary associations. Sign up for a limited number of e-mail lists. Political affiliation: independent. Make a point to be just visible enough, just enough on grid.

A voice spikes in my ear, I hear my name from far down the hallway of the Knoxville Holiday Inn. 'Don? Hey Don.'

A man rides long spidery legs towards me. 'It's Randy,' he says. 'Randy Sullivan from Springfield Tech.'

I try to place the glasses, the face, the white

collared shirt, the widening paunch. All these guys start to look the same. He chuckles, 'It's the bald spot isn't it? It's bigger than it was then. But you look great. How have you been? I haven't seen you since Tulsa.'

His face pops into my memory. 'Randy,' I say, shaking his hand again, this time as an old friend. 'Of course, I'm sorry. Yeah, I guess it has been since oh-seven.'

'I figured someone like you would be around more often,' he says. 'I've seen your name on programs here and there, but only in the summer.'

'I teach high school science most of the year,' I admit.

'Oh, Don,' Randy says. 'You've got to get on this year round.'

All around are handfuls of men in out-of-style glasses, neck beards, unstoppable guts. They drag wives, they drag infant sons, mini vans, all these heavy lives. They drag it all with them all year round.

'Gotta pay the bills,' I say. 'Can't do it all on book sales.'

'Bills?' Randy scoffs. 'After all the cover ups your tax dollars pay for and you're going to stand there and tell me about bills? We're a family Don. We take care of each other when the times get bad.'

During the school year, stick to their curriculum. The school wants it straight, biology, astronomy, geology. Give the people what they want. Commit a million little truth suicides. Bite your tongue. Smile and nod. Tell them Mars has always been a planet. Swallow the evidence that it was once a moon. Swallow the evidence of long ago exploded planet V. Long for the off season. Long for the real year. The lunar year and the real lesson plan.

'Stick to the book,' Principal King told me the day I was hired. 'We hired you for your astronomy background. None of that moon stuff.'

Hands raise in the back of the room. 'Mr. Marsh,' asks a girl in dark make up, too much make up, big wide child eyes, 'What do you do during the summer?'

'Yeah,' comes another voice, a boy, peach fuzzed, skinny-armed, 'I heard you drive all over the place and give talks to people.'

'Well,' I say. 'I used to be a consultant for NASA. During the moon years.'

Another hand, another face, a boy asks, 'I heard we never actually went to the moon.'

'Oh,' I say. 'We went there. We went there all right.'

Spring break comes and I'm all motor. Six dates and six hotels in a week. I'll be bleary eyed and coffee raddled by morning. Bring on the road again and remember.

Click the laptop. Images of the pyramids of Giza.

Memorize, the longitudes, latitudes: 33 degrees, Masonic obsession with; 19.5 degrees, Egyptian connotations and links to extra-dimensional physics. The dates April 20th, 1972. June 20, 1969. Cydonia. Nansen. The lander, the lander. Armstrong, Aldrin, Crowley, Hitler. These are the fish in my head.

Speak slowly. All words chosen carefully.

'In 1953, the Brookings report indicated the strong possibility that contact with an extra-terrestrial civilization would lead to massive civil unrest.'

Let the words on the slide speak for themselves: '*If super intelligence is discovered, the [social] results would become quite unpredictable... of all groups, scientists and engineers might be the most devastated by the discovery of relatively superior creatures.*'

'The riots that resulted from the 1938 broadcast of *War of the Worlds* gives us a good example of this.'

Somewhere in Alabama, hands raise in the Dixie Ballroom. A man in coke bottle glasses, a liver spot on his cheek, a wad of Redman in his lip, he asks, 'But isn't there evidence to suggest that this broadcast was a test? Put together on purpose to see how we would react?'

Give the canned response without a pause to think. 'Of course. And it seems that we failed that test. The actions of NASA have been based on a belief that exposure to other civilizations could have disastrous effects on our own. But there are other reasons why the Truth has been kept from us.'

There are only so many questions one can ask of the truth before it starts to shine through.

A plane comes in above The Baltimore Regency, these hotels always by the airports. The Dwight D. Eisenhower conference center is stocked with plastic looking muffins, red eyed pastries, strawberries on black plastic plates. But all that matters is the coffee.

Click the laptop and continue. Frame LO-III-84M. The Shard. Frame RM-IIX-19R. The Castle. The Temple. The Face. The Sphinx.

Speak very carefully at this point.

'As we can see, this slide clearly indicates a shadow from this non-natural and clearly artificial structure, a shadow that is against the natural grain of the image. Based on the height of observance, this object is roughly one mile high.'

Click the laptop, continue. The Tower. The Dome. The City. The Pyramid.

'It is unclear how old these lunar ruins actually are. At the very least, it has been many thousands of years since their desertion.'

I will be the one to hold nothing back.

Still in Baltimore, feedback jumps from the microphone.

There is always feedback from the microphone. No one knows how to run an audio system anymore.

Outside, in the Regency reception area, men stand in huddles of two and three, checking their programs. A line of tables covers the long wall of the room. Larry Gibbs is here, selling his new book claiming to have unearthed photographs of a tunnel system in the ice of the northern Martian poles. He's not drawing many visitors at the moment, so he's leaned over to the booth next to his, and is talking to Bob and Jean Tripplehorn, who operate the Lunar Mission web site. They're just here to pass out business cards. At the center, drawing the biggest crowd, is a table marked, 'Truth Teller Party'. Under this, in smaller letters, the words, 'Gabe Davidson for regional representative.'

The humidity hits in Georgia. The air sits still in the Lincoln Room of the Savannah Regency. Hands raise. The crowd is skeptical and you know you're losing them.

I'm cornered by a woman when she finds out what I do in the off season.

'We have to get this into the textbooks,' she says.

'I agree.'

'This is the truth. This is what could change the world. What could save the world.'

'Yes. You're right.'

'I think that you could be our messenger here. You could start in your classroom. Move out into the rest of the school. The district. Just teach it. It's the truth.'

'Oh, sure. I've got an astronomy lesson coming up after the break. It kills me to teach it every year the way they want me to.'

'So don't. Teach it your way. Teach the truth.'

There's the real crime. You could be put in jail for doing this. Come to every hotel in the country and speak the truth and no one looks up. But the minute you insert the truth into the education, you become a target. You cross that line they've drawn, that they don't want to see dissent on the other side of. We all know the story of Galileo.

'We're ahead of history, aren't we?' I say to her.

School starts in a week. I look around. I see the same faces everywhere. The same aging geologists. The same old married couples, self publishing their books. They need me.

Drive homeward, plans in head stacking and unstacking. Hit home with belly fire, purpose in mind. Scrap the old ways and head to Kinkos. For the first time in years, I smile about the thought of going into school.

Students stare slack-eyed and miserable. Back in class and not expecting a thing. Sometimes the best audience is a captive one. Lay out the black folders on their desks, one by one. I ignore the looks they give and make small talk.

'I hope everyone had a good spring break. Did anyone do anything interesting.'

One by one they answer. I'm stalling

and it's killing me. Their stories about family vacations, about sitting around doing nothing, about picking up a few more hours at their jobs. It's not that I haven't missed them, it's not that I don't want to hear what they did all week. But there's something I want to get to.

'There's been a little change in the lesson plan,' I announce finally. I turn towards the overhead projector.

The students start poking through them before I've even said what they are. They pull out the printed copies I've made for them, the black and white Xeroxes of the Face, the Tower, the Castle, the Sphinx.

'What's this Mr. Marsh?' asks one of the front row, straight-A honor roll girls.

I smile, big, too big, 'I told you at the beginning of the year that we'd be spending a lot of time on astronomy. Now, that's still true, but you aren't going to be needing your textbooks on this one.'

'What's Cydonia?' asks one of the back row hooligans, his hair spiked, his lip pierced.

Someone in the back chuckles as he points to one of the pictures and says, 'It looks like a face.'

I clear my throat. I've already placed the first slide on the overhead projector. 'Patrick,' I say, 'Cut the lights.'

The projector switches on. The crystal towers of the moon come into view behind me.

'That textbook of yours is pretty in-depth,' I say. 'But there are a few gaps. What do you all think this is?'

By the time the bell rings, I'm breathless. It took a while for what I was doing to really hit them. Some of them were sure it was a joke until pretty near the end. But I made certain no one left without knowing just how serious I was.

For homework I gave them the telephone number to NASA's service hotline, and passed out a script for them to follow when they called.

I stand in the hallway, watching them go. The rest of the classrooms empty, and soon the hall is choked with kids. My next class starts

to filter in. I've got a set of black folders for them too. If all goes well, by the end of the day NASA will have received almost one hundred and fifty calls.

In fact, they're already on their phones. One of them hides half-inside her locker. Normally I'd tell her to put the phone away, but given what I know she's doing, I let it pass. The caller glances at me. She nods and points.

I watch them as they show the folders to their friends, pulling out the images I've given them. I watch the Truth spread. They shoot me glances, nervous, avoiding eye contact. I don't blame them for not knowing what to think yet. But by the end of the month, their little heads will be so full of revelation, they won't know what to do.

One of them shows the folder to a teacher across the hall. Mrs. Henderson, the geology teacher. She looks at me. Now she's staring. More than a few people are. I duck back into my room, ready for my next class. And as I pass out the black folders to thirty more kids, I think back to the words the principal spoke to me the day I was hired.

'I'm serious, Mr. Marsh,' he said. 'Stick to the textbook. Just the facts.'

But that's the thing about facts when it comes to science, isn't it. They just keep on changing.

More than anything, I want them to know. I want them to realize we aren't an accident. We aren't alone. Great minds have come before. They watched us in our infancy. They brought us pyramids. And one day they fell. But we can learn from their mistakes. Some would hope to obscure the truth. But I reject the idea that we would collapse under this knowledge. I think it would set us free. To return to the stars from which we were formed.

Take my hand, for I am reaching out to you. We have been living in a box. I offer you the box cutter. I offer you a world inside the sun.

Hands raise outside of Washington D.C. The crowds will soon be growing. I can feel it.

'We can see clearly that this image has been

➤

doctored. And yet there is still no denying the artificiality of the structures.'

Hands raise in my second period astronomy class.

'Mr. Marsh,' says one girl. 'I heard in the hall that you're going to tell us about aliens.'

Ignore the nay sayers.

Touch the overhead projector and continue. The Lunar Surface glows red behind my back.

'Could someone get the lights?'

Feedback from the loudspeaker. 'Mr. Marsh,' comes the voice of the secretary. 'Principal King would like a moment with you in his office after your class, if you don't mind.'

I can feel it. Today is the day they start to change their minds.

'Of course,' I say. For some reason, the kids giggle. A note passes in the back.

'Can you feel that?' I ask the class, my hand trembling. 'Something good is happening.'

Special Terms

A Carnbeg Story

Ronald Frame

FORTY-ODD YEARS AGO, in the late 1950s, Kevin's parents kept a small hotel, in a good road at the back of Carnbeg. The McIvors called their guests, the majority of them, 'discerning', which meant genteel types, nicely spoken but either close with their money or not flush with it, who appreciated crisply laundered linen and silver service, and who didn't mind the fair step it was from the shopping streets if that allowed them to be thrifty with accommodation.

Some others did slip through the net, commercial travellers and doubtful foreigners, even actors at the theatre. But that only happened when Mrs McIvor wasn't on phone duty to judge from their accents before accepting a booking; both her husband and the girl Noreen, her stand-ins, lacked that sixth sense for who would fit in and who wouldn't. Even on high-days and holidays, when Carnbeg filled up, Kay McIvor had her standards, and the hotel rooms were occupied then as ever by Abercrombie House's usual sort, men in tweeds and cavalry twills and ladies who walked out in sensible shoes and were unfailingly hatted.

The Nivens came every September, after the Carnbeg Festival, when the arty brigade had gone from the town.

They were in their early fifties, twin brother and sister, both unmarried. Tall, fine-featured, with long-fingered hands. (Kevin's mother had taught him to notice guests' hands, from the moment they were first drawn from gloves: you are born with the mark of grace upon you, new money will never buy you those slim tapering appendages.)

Mr Niven was a lawyer in a small market town up north; Miss Niven lived alone in the old family home down near Duns. He was clean-shaven, well-scrubbed, balding; she wore her greying hair in a French roll, favoured pearls (two strings) to flatter her clear complexion, didn't like to be seen reading with her half-moon glasses. His two three-piece suits, one flannel and one tweed, carried a faint odour of mothballs; she smelt of talcum powder, the heathery fragrance which Scotswomen prefer to English country gardens.

They came to Carnbeg to visit an aged uncle in an eventide home; to call in on a lady living out Loch Bragar way, who was a friend of both from long ago; to do some shopping; and just to savour the town's fresh air delights, as they did annually for these six days.

The particular year Kevin would remember best of all the years they put up at Abercrombie House was the last one, when the Nivens were out of their usual routine.

The standing reservation had had to be cancelled, and they didn't make their respective journeys until the third week in October, arriving on a Tuesday, which involved them in staying on until a Sunday. Mrs McIvor wasn't able to offer them their customary single rooms, the best ones at the front on the first floor, with the high ceilings and connecting door between which gave an illusion of greater space.

Mr Niven elected to take the remaining single, decently sized but on the landing between the first and second floors, while his

➥

sister had a small double on the second. At their special terms, of course. In those days before phones in bedrooms, at least there was only a half-flight of stairs between the rooms if either should have pressing need of the other.

The Nivens were very typical Abercrombie House specimens. They read *The Scotsman* for news about their own country and about England and the world beyond. They preferred the simplest choices from the menu: Scotch broth, baked sole or cold silverside or tongue salad, a helping of steamed syrup pudding. They tapped the barometer on the wall in the hall, to check weather pressure. They had Cash's name tapes sewn into their outerwear.

At the same time they weren't quite typical. It registered with Kevin that unlike the others they didn't pay court to Miss Campbell-Gunn, who had a way of winkling out of fellow-guests all, or almost all, about themselves. They also steered a wide path round the Reverend Gilfillan, who entertained colleagues in the ministry at his table in the middle of the dining-room; from fifty yards both brother and sister could spot a dog-collar approaching along our Clune Road and make off in the opposite direction. Miss Niven read historical novels: not Georgette Heyer or Jean Plaidy, however, but Mary Renault, who wrote about the inverted morality of the Ancient Greeks. Her brother supplemented his *Scotsman* with a copy of the distinctly liberal *Manchester Guardian*. It was Miss Niven who wore the signet ring with their father's initials engraved on it, and Mr Niven who used their mother's coral and silver filigree cigarette case.

They both of them were, and were not, what they seemed to be.

That was also the year of the trollop.

Kevin heard some of the guests tut-tutting about the young woman with frizzy red hair who now regularly paraded the pavements, before they became unkempt grass verges, on the Carnmor road on the edge of town.

The Learmonths, who had taken ten years to adjust to the McIvors running a hotel after initially protesting to the Council, were back in a complaining frame of mind.

Kay McIvor's reaction, expressed when she thought she was alone with her husband and could let her accent slip, was a curious one to Kevin.

'Well, the lassie's got to make a living. Just like the rest of us.'

Jack McIvor told his wife she'd better not let anyone hear her say *that*, and she asked him, well, didn't he agree, but he only grinned, then threw back his head and laughed.

Kevin became especially aware now that the Nivens were keeping him in their sights.

They seemed to detect that he was a more observant boy than many of thirteen years old. Or maybe the presence of a youngster among the predominantly middle-aged and elderly clientele discomposed them.

Mr Niven was armed as usual with a smile, non-committal and professional, but a smile nonetheless; while his sister, who probably had to make do for most of the time with her own company at home in Duns, found it more difficult to unbend enough to humour the owners' son.

Even when they were sitting in the lounge reading the newspaper or a library book, Kevin would catch a furtive sideways glance of the man's eyes or his sister's moving off him, and found it unsettling.

That was the same year when, in the springtime, Jack McIvor had taken Kevin aside, in an embarrassed way he must have meant to be Significant, to advise his son that, well, to be frank, but not to alarm him, it's just that he thought, a little word of warning, about... well... that Kevin shouldn't let himself get too close to any of the guests. You know? He should keep a civil tongue in his head and, preferably, a smile on his face. But he should keep himself to himself. And if he ever suspected that anyone – in particular, any of the chaps – was trying to be friendlier than Kevin in thought he should be, then Kevin must tell his father. Promise, Kevin? Yes? That's all right then, end of conversation, they wouldn't say any more about it, they'd just presume it never came to that—

Kevin made his escape. He pushed through the baize-lined door marked 'Private' on the other side, into the wee corridor that connected to the hall of the hotel, very glad to get away from the awkwardness of the subject. His mother was sitting behind the reception desk, clearly biding her time. She smiled up at him as he blundered past.

So many smiles in this place, it occurred to him. The smiling house, even when the smiles were in a language he only at best half-understood.

Why did Kevin's mind switch to film star David Niven whenever he saw Mr Reginald Niven?

Yes, their guest was six foot or so, lean, with old-fashioned manners. But he didn't have a moustache (clipped or otherwise). Also he was a decade or so older than the actor, or looked as if he was. Why did Kevin make any association between a bachelor Morayshire lawyer on reduced tariff and the wealthy star of those mild Hollywood sex-comedies he saw the posters for outside cinemas?

Who was *their* Mr Niven's equivalent of Mitzi Gaynor, Anne Vernon, Ava Gardner?

She was called Senga, the girl on the Carnmor road: that silly modern Scots name which is 'Agnes' reversed. One of Kevin's schoolfriends had discovered that her rates started at two pounds seven and sixpence. It seemed a very precise sum, in return for they didn't know what. Another boy at school said Perth used to be Senga's beat, she would be standing about near St John's at the time of the Kirk Commissioners' own assembly in August, when the city was host to hundreds of Church of Scotland elders. 'I expect *they* get special rates!'

First impressions might have persuaded you this neighbourhood was too quiet, and unsuitable therefore. But on second thoughts, there was always traffic circulating round the town; they lived in the age of the car, and it was straightforward enough to make a quick exit from Carnbeg to the country back roads, or even – once it got dark – to conveniently vacated family homes.

Mr Farquarson from No 27 across the road spoke to Mrs McIvor one day in passing.

Kevin listened to how his mother responded. Her reply surprised him. She told the man, oh *that* business, yes, she'd heard; something should be done about such behaviour, disgraceful really, she'd be getting these parts a bad name, the hussy.

The words came out with perfect-sounding sincerity.

Kevin's mother had been pretending to Mr Farquarson she'd needed to have her memory jogged about the girl. But Kevin had seen her, not once but several times, looking from the car as they drove along the Carnmor road; she had slowed as they came nearer, so that the object of her scrutiny – the said 'disgraceful' Senga – was obliged to go stepping off into a side-road, to get away from them. As they picked up speed again, his mother would adjust the driving mirror, keeping an eye open for the girl, and then later reserving her attention for herself.

Smiles. And eyes, always watching.

In the hotel Kevin would catch the Nivens exchanging glances as their fellow guests' conversation swilled round them.

The talk was entirely predictable. Moral prejudices abounded, the social status-quo was upheld, the intellectual life was disparaged by their preferring to talk of dogs, horses, gardens, golf, curling.

The Nivens would swoop, silently, on some remark. They would seem to be secreting it, storing it away, for discussion later between themselves.

A comment about the lower orders, about some Unionist junket, about Women's Guild politics or kirk session shenanigans. Only the subject of sex, treated always under the guise of another matter – a husband's workaholism or business trips away, a wife's indifference, what gets shown in cinemas these days, the cut of the new fashions, the current mania for showers in people's bathrooms – kept their eyes downturned, as if *that* was the final taboo to them both.

↦

But as the *Guardian* was shaken out and the bookmark removed from the latest Mary Renault, Kevin thought it must be a bluff, because the Nivens surely followed different mental tracks from the other Abercrombie House regulars.

Clune Road householders were becoming indignant about 'that slut' who was lowering the tone of the locale. Mr Learmonth's brother was an advocate, and was looking into the matter to 'see what redress we might have'.

The Learmonths were what Kevin thought of as their poshest neighbours. They hadn't had much to do with the McIvors in the past, being ringleaders of the faction which had originally objected to their opening a hotel. Kevin's mother was intrigued by their 'connections', the ones she read about in the social pages of magazines, which must have been why she succumbed so easily when Mrs Learmonth stopped her in the street one day and courteously asked her for support.

'Oh *certainly*, Mrs Learmonth.' Kevin's mother was using her best front-of-house delivery, vowels stretched and exaggerated. 'You can count on me. If there's anything I can do, anything at all ...'

But by now Kevin's father was taking the girl's side. 'The underdog', he called her in the privacy of their own quarters. Kevin's mother retorted, with starch in her voice, that 'dog' wasn't really the appropriate gender, was it? That evening Kevin heard them having words. His mother went to bed early, always a bad sign.

It was Kay McIvor's habit to try to find out from the guests some details about themselves, the more concrete the better. She wasn't as adept as Miss Campbell-Gunn at the task. Sometimes – for instance, with the Nivens – it was a case of guesswork, surmising from a scatter of clues.

She had answered the phone to their Loch Bragar friend. A bright-sounding lady's voice, she reported to her husband, lively-ish. And Mr Niven, when he came on the line, had called her 'Kitty' in a very cheery, affectionate way. Why else had his sister, for the last couple of years, gone about looking rather grumpy, as if a problem was lying heavily on her mind?

When Kevin looked, it *was* true, that at moments those two faces with their twins' common features had very different expressions: Miss Niven's dark and distracted, Mr Niven's quite sunny and relaxed.

'Maybe that old house is starting to get her down,' Mrs McIvor said to her husband. 'Or —' She dropped her voice, to sound theatrically cloak-and-dagger. ' — or it's their mutual friend out at Loch Bragar who's the reason why.'

Mrs Learmonth ventured into the hotel on another day, her very first time, to enquire of Kay McIvor if any guests – 'your regular visitors' – would be willing to sign a petition. 'About you-know-who,' she said, and nodded in an easterly direction, towards the Carnmor road.

'I'm sure they would be delighted to, Mrs Learmonth.'

When Jack McIvor was told, he objected. He objected very strongly.

'It's got damn all to do with the guests. And that busybody has got no business with any of *them*.'

More words ensued. And there was another early night for Kevin's mother. She must have been convinced her husband was trying to thwart her social advancement, because the discord started all over again in the morning.

'Mrs Learmonth would be a very useful connection for us to have, Jack.'

'How d'you work that one out?'

'She knows people.'

'So do we.'

'Well-to-do folk.'

'Well, *they're* not going to slum it in a private hotel, are they?'

'We're as good as any in Carnbeg, let me tell you.'

And so it went on.

Kevin heard Effie giggling when she came back from the shops, and he followed her down the kitchen corridor. She didn't see him – or if she did she wasn't caring – as she stopped at the open pantry door, leaned against it, and giggled again for Noreen's benefit.

She told her story. About being in the chemist's for milk of magnesia – to settle her stomach – and seeing Mr Niven there, and guess what *he* was buying and slipping into his pocket, comes in packets of six and one size fits all.

'Never!'

'Cross my heart.'

'Gee whizz! Isn't he a bit past it?'

'Men can do it till they're eighty. Well, *some* men.'

'Who's the lucky lady, then?'

'Won't be me.'

'You're not a lady, you mean?'

'Cheeky beggar, Noreen Greavie.'

'Won't be me neither.'

Their laughter went rippling shamelessly out of the window, across the downhill slope of side lawn to the high pavement, where the world as it passed might have heard but never guessed why.

'You'll be going to Loch Bragar?' Mrs McIvor asked the Nivens. 'As you always do?'

'Not this year,' Miss Niven replied.

'No?'

'Our friend's just set off on holiday.'

Mrs McIvor glanced at Mr Niven's face for a reaction. His opaque smile told her nothing.

'I expect,' he said, 'she'll go down to visit Patricia later on.'

'And you'll see her there?' Mrs McIvor asked. 'In Berwickshire?'

'Oh no, I don't think so.'

Mrs McIvor fidgeted with her reading glasses, couldn't think where she had been heading for with her reservations book, remembered to beam back at the Nivens but with her puzzlement written there all over her face.

Kevin didn't join his friends from the boys' school they attended as they took the longer way home, via the Carnmor road. It was so that they could see if *she* was having a lucky day or not, and to dare her to give a come-on to any of them.

Someone said the police could never get hold of her, she'd see the car and scarper.

Someone else said one of the Carnbeg polis was one of her regulars.

'Maybe it's to trap her?'

'If anyone's got trapped, it's him – by her!'

Senga made Kevin uneasy, with her mane of red hair and her narrow freckly face, one thin leg crooked at an angle to the other and her hand resting on hip. He was uncomfortable with the notion of someone living such a frankly physical life. He didn't like how she diverted their thoughts on to the subject of herself, and somehow managed to make the rest of them all feel guiltier than she clearly gave any evidence of being. She had no tact, no subtlety – God help her, no *class*.

'Have *you* been using my good soap?' Mrs McIvor asked Kevin.

'No,' he said. 'It wasn't me.'

The answer was an honest one, and his mother seemed to realise that.

'Well, there are nail marks on my buttermilk soap.'

Kevin thought she meant iron nails, until she showed him the cake of ivory-coloured soap with its crescent-shaped nicks.

Kevin held out his hands for inspection, backs uppermost. His fingernails were cut short because he had a fastidiousness about that. His mother knew that it couldn't have been him.

'When I got home yesterday,' she said, 'I noticed — '

She had been back to see her old schoolfriend Eunice down beyond Perth, at Gask.

'What's the *point* of having nice things?' she asked, with a crack in her voice.

All the McIvor gentility. Living – in the externals – like the traditional upper middle-class, although they weren't: living Kay McIvor's version of it, here in their private quarters. Silver napkin rings, EPNS photograph frames; Sanderson floral loose covers on the chairs, rugs instead of fitted carpets.

'Your father must know, then.'

Kevin's father had short nails too, bitten down, as she was very well aware. She did go

➼

through the formalities, though. She asked him, and he paused for a couple of seconds before replying, no, *he* couldn't explain how it had happened.

'One of the girls?' Kevin's mother suggested.

'They don't come beyond the door.'

She nodded, but she was unconvinced. Not about Noreen or Effie, rather that her husband didn't know *something*, which might be more than she wanted to know herself.

Although it was October, with no Indian summer for Scotland, Kevin noticed Mr Niven looking distinctly flushed two afternoons running.

He had to leave the hotel building for some air. The first time, Kevin saw his shirt tail hanging out from beneath his jacket; the next day his fly buttons were undone.

'Taking a little breather' was his explanation on both occasions, spoken to Kevin's mother who was at her post behind the front desk. He moved briskly past her, exuding a faint whiff of naphthalene from his herringbone tweed; his face was pink – Kevin supposed, from the all-inclusive convenience of heated radiator pipes with a control tap too stiff to turn. Kevin's mother smiled over-politely, but the smile faded as she watched his departure; a certain expression would settle on her face at times like this, whenever Mr Niven had his back to her and couldn't see it, a mixture of the sceptical and the worldly.

On both afternoons Mr Niven set out along Clune Road, not towards Haggs Loan which was three houses' distance away and the short-cut down into town, but off in the direction of the Carnmor road junction. The second time it happened, Kevin screwed up his eyes to focus on their guest veering undecidedly as he reached Senga's stand – did he go to left or right of the red-haired sentinel? And it was then that Kevin made the connection.

Kevin didn't actually *see* them together, Senga and Mr Niven, because he had homework, which he attended to in the hotel dining-room.

It was hard even to imagine what must be taking place: the where and the how, all the ins and outs.

On Saturday Kevin decided to get on with a geography home project. Which would allow him to keep an eye trained on activity out in the hall.

Sure enough there was an interlude before dinner when Mr Niven – pink in the face – came downstairs and went out, along the road. Upstairs his sister yet again locked herself in the big second-floor bathroom and ran enough hot water – as Kevin's mother in some alarm expressed herself – 'to make a Turkish steam room out of the place'.

When Mr Niven came back, after forty or fifty minutes, he had lost that high colouring. He was smoothing his hair down as he stamped out his cigarette and climbed the front steps. He looked at himself critically in the hall mirror, tidied the rumples in his shirt collar, straightened his tie, buttoned his jacket, even though he was due to change for dinner shortly. He kept glancing up the stairwell – nervously, Kevin thought – towards the second floor, where his sister would have vacated the bathroom and must now be putting on her gladrags, preparing to join him at their chosen table in the quietest, most private corner of the dining room.

Backtrack, rewind...

Kevin had been coming back from school during the last week of summer term, taking the quick way home by Haggs Loan. Suddenly she was only three or four yards away from him, Senga with her Celtic red hair and pale freckly face. He heard the clasp of her shoulder bag snapping shut; she was trailing a very strong perfume behind her. She must have spotted him out of the corner of her eye because she twisted her head away, but she was having enough trouble just keeping upright as she negotiated the lane's cobbles on her high heels. She reached one hand out for balance: an oddly shapely hand, with fingernails varnished bright orange.

The side gate hadn't been closed properly. (Kevin's mother would normally kick up a fuss about that; today, though, she was away visiting her old schoolfriend at Gask again. Kevin's father didn't appear to be listening when he mentioned the gate's having been left open, he just smiled vaguely.)

Kevin changed out of his school uniform, then he went into their bathroom. He had been overheating all day, so he filled the basin to the top with lukewarm water and submerged his face in it. He reached out for a towel, the nearest to hand, buried his face in the brushed cotton and smelt —

Perfume. Too much perfume.

He held out the towel and stared at it. His mother only used a little discreet eau-de-cologne now and then, as their most *comme il faut* guests knew to do.

In his mind Kevin was hearing again those peerie heels that had hurried past him in the back lane, squawking as they coped with the occupational hazard of rough cobblestones.

At the end of the Niven's week first Effie and then Noreen went down with gastric upsets. Mr McIvor sent them home for a day or two, to save the rest of them.

It fell to Kevin to help with some of their duties: 'the easier ones', his father said, those which could be done out of school hours. But it was difficult enough to dust or vacuum so that his mother was satisfied with the results.

Worse was carrying the loaded breakfast trays upstairs in the mornings. Room service wasn't considered economically viable by Mrs McIvor at the best of times – 'We give them special terms, what do they expect?' – but her husband's opinion was that they should respect the wishes of their regular guests even in an emergency like this one.

It so happened that on the Saturday night Kay McIvor went to bed feeling unwell. She was up in the small hours, Kevin later learned, and his father had to mop up after her.

Mr McIvor woke Kevin in the morning, and the boy hauled himself out of bed. His father looked tired, unslept, and for once was unshaven; in the kitchen he was in a muddle, all fingers and thumbs, wondering aloud about his wife but keeping an eye on the clock. Breakfast in the dining-room started later on a Sunday,

but the trays went up for the time they'd been requested.

'On your way now, Kevin!'

The Nivens took breakfast in their rooms. Kevin picked up Mr Niven's tray, since he was in the room that was closer. Mr McIvor clamped a hand on the boy's shoulder.

'For heaven's sake, son, ladies first!'

Off again.

Kevin concentrated hard. Up the first half-flight, then the second. On the first floor level he hitched the tray higher. Up the third half-flight, a dangerous wobble, and nothing stirring behind *his* door. Then the fourth half-flight.

He stopped outside Room 14, cocked his ear. He could hear sounds, a kind of moaning. Was she still asleep?

He tapped on the door. The sounds continued as before.

Again he tapped.

A cry, not a snore. Then a whelp, like someone in pain. What if Miss Niven wasn't well?

Kevin adjusted his right arm, laid the weight of the tray on top of it. In his left trouser pocket he found the pass keys, with '2nd' marked. He wasn't supposed to use them, but Noreen and Effie did to speed up the process.

He heard a groan. Then a second one, more urgent.

He got hold of the key, pushed it into the lock, flicked his wrist. He put the tray down on the floor, so that he could turn the handle and the key at the same time.

The door inched open.

Two figures were huddled on the bed in an embrace.

Miss Niven, with her hair down and nightdress open. Her brother, with as much as Kevin could see of him naked, his balding head bowed tenderly over his sister's neck.

Kevin backed away, round the door jamb. He stepped on to the edge of the tray and heard the contents go crashing, but what the hell.

He turned and he fled.

There was no complaint about Room 14's breakfast not having arrived. Mr McIvor presumed the tray had been put back outside with the food merely picked at, and someone else without the decency to own up had come along and trodden on it.

'Changed days. That would never have happened at one time, you know. Don't tell your mother, son.'

What the McIvors had forgotten in their haste to be up and about was that the clocks had gone back that morning, or ought to have done. Summer-time was officially over. Half-past eight was in fact half-past seven. The guests should have had another hour in bed before the tap on the door and the tray proffered, before the bell of St Saviour's Chapel nearby started to chime, at the double, sounding tinny and defensive in a town of presbyterian sonorities.

Mrs McIvor shook her head at them both, and looked cross, anticipating barbs and grumbles from the guests. In the event only old Mrs Craig said anything uncomplimentary to her, and Kevin's mother deflected her with a diplomatic infusion of charm. She was especially solicitous with the Nivens, because this was their final morning.

'Mission accomplished?' Mrs McIvor asked them, resorting to the Wrens' lingo of her War.

Reginald Niven hazarded a small enigmatic smile, and bowed his balding head, while his sister ostentatiously busied herself with her gloves and peered out of the hall window, scanning the sky for rain clouds.

'I hope your berths suited you both. I'm only sorry we couldn't keep to your usual arrangements. The connecting door, that is.'

Mr Niven held that faint smile in place as he completed his cheque to cover the charges on both rooms.

'Our special terms apply, Mr Niven. As per usual.'

His sister, with her hair neatly rolled up again and fixed with combs beneath her Tyrolean hat, stood plucking at trailing threads, real or imaginary, on her Inverness cape.

'And this is a minding for your staff,' Mr Niven said, removing a creased white envelope from his pocket.

Mrs McIvor received it from him without deigning to look.

'You're very kind.'

When their taxi had left for the station, Kevin's mother went searching for his father. Kevin noticed the baize door into their quarters sighing shut, which told him she wanted some moments alone with his father. He positioned himself outside, trying to hear what they were saying. He heard from his mother something about 'their old tricks', 'Gomorrah', and then his father laughing, telling her 'it takes all sorts'.

Kevin thought he was as shocked by that as by what he had witnessed earlier: that his parents should know, and that they both condoned what had been going on upstairs.

Later in the morning he was passing Room 14 and saw his mother standing by the bed which had been occupied. She had pulled back the blankets and top sheet; now she raised the lower sheet at one side, stretching it flat against the north light, at an angle which allowed her to examine it. When Kevin returned a few minutes afterwards she was going through the tallboy drawers, reaching into all the corners. In one hand she held something she must have found, a powder puff from a compact; when she'd pushed in the last drawer, she lifted the puff close to her nostrils and cautiously sniffed at it, for a reminder of Miss Niven's spinsterly, slightly pepperish, talcy fragrance.

By the middle of the afternoon it was raining. The Nivens would be well on their way to their separate destinations. More guests arrived, almost indistinguishable as they downed umbrellas and shook them out from the scores of other guests just like them whom the Abercrombie House received in the course of a year.

All this sober gentility, and suddenly Kevin wasn't at all sure about it any more. It was paying for his education, and the clothes on his back, and their annual Easter holiday on the continent, and his parents' periodic dinners over at Gleneagles Hotel where his mother liked to feast her eyes and ears and where they both lived grandly for an evening. Gentility too was a commodity, and Kevin's parents patently understood its value, for commerce (even on reduced tariff) and for their social cover.

Shortly afterwards Senga disappeared from the Carnmor road.

The McIvors' neighbours congratulated themselves that it must have been their doing. It wasn't anything of the sort. Two weeks later another girl was in place.

It was noted that some cars would circumnavigate the area, round and round, always decelerating when they reached the paved stretch of the Carnmor road. The canny drivers among the men held maps, so that they could be seen to have an excuse why they were stopping to ask for directions.

No booking came from the Nivens the following year.

Noreen caught sight of them while she was waiting for a pal to finish work, up at the Sgian Palace. She had looked into the hall and seen them collecting room keys.

'That'll cost them,' Mrs McIvor told her. 'They won't be getting special terms *there*.'

'Maybe it's a bit more... ' Impersonal, Noreen was meaning.

'Our guests come and go,' Kevin's mother said, rubbing out the question marks in pencil written against the Nivens' preferred rooms, with the communicating door between them.

It was a world, Kevin was learning, of surprise connections.

His mother got to her feet. At that same moment his father stuck his head round the end of the staircase banister and announced he was going out, to walk Mrs Dalrymple's pekinese for her.

'Where to?'

'Just along to the end of the road. To the junction.'

Kevin's mother banged the reservations book shut quite loudly.

'That's too far,' she said.

'"Too far"?'

'It's just a lapdog.'

'*I* need my exercise too.'

'All part of the service!' Noreen said, with an ironic lift in her voice.

Kevin's mother hesitated for a telling couple of seconds too long before she turned in the opposite direction, towards the wee side corridor and the baize door unambiguously marked 'Private'.

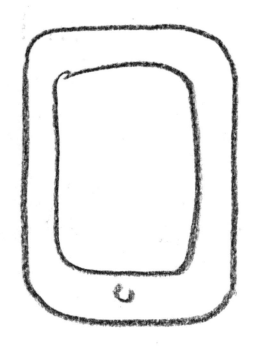

New Scottish book technology #4: The iTablet.
Like an iPad but with added sugar and condensed milk.

'Your sperm's in the gutter,
your love's in the sink.'

Jethro Tull

Extract from the novel *The Healing of Luther Grove*
Barry Gornell

THE UNUSED FLOWERS of the wild cherry fell like scented snow. Petals were dislodged, broken and dismembered by the breeze. They drifted against rows of earthed up potatoes, glittered the grass and flattened themselves against the hives in polkadot compensation for their inner night and to remind the bees they had been there.

Lifting the roof, Luther was faced with the true nature of the hive. There had been no change since yesterday; they had gone. In past years, late May had seen combs full or filling with pollen and honey and the brood area expanded down throughout the empty combs in the lower chamber as bee numbers increased and their activity became delirious. This year there was nothing. He was steadily losing his entire stock. His colonies had disappeared or died, though where he didn't know, for there was no sign of dead bees. He didn't believe they had swarmed; it was too early in the year. Survivors or stragglers wandered between the frames, distressed and aimless without a queen to service, cells to cap or young brood to tend. The emptiness was contagious. Luther replaced the roof.

Only three of his forty hives contained colonies capable of producing honey come harvest time, if they were still here. He felt betrayed. He had cared for these difficult creatures for almost thirty years, become immune to their stings and fed them through winters. His reward had been the solace he found in the continuity of their swarm and dance lifecycle when his had been out of control. He resented their absence; feared the chaos that would come without routine and the responsibility of caring. Their mutually beneficial need had been their contract, surely. How could they abandon him?

Standing in the decimated apiary, surrounded by pointless blossom, Luther could discern the individual buzz of each surviving worker that flew by. To his eyes, their flight paths were uncertain, lacking purpose. The fearless confidence embodied in the hum of communal foraging, that drilled through the summer like the drone of a bagpipe through its melody, had left the garden. He sighed and took his veil off. Unzipping his boiler suit, he went inside to piss some blood.

Drinking whisky on the back porch, Luther heard their voices getting closer, discussing him, without her. He reclined into the evening shade of his back verandah as they came into view, keen to observe. They stopped at the logs in the road and the other one started to shake his head as though in disbelief.

'He really didn't want you to get past did he?'

The man snorted in response. The other one stood on one of the tree trunks and began rolling it with his feet, walking as a circus performer would, arms extended for greater balance. The man tried three times to do the same but fell from his perch and gave up, affecting nonchalance. He stood with his hands deep in his pockets, his back to Luther, watching the other one show off.

'You've got no balance, never did. Remember the skateboard?'

'Yes, I remember the skateboard.'

'Broke it because you couldn't do it – wouldn't let anybody else have it.'

'It was mine.'

'I'd have liked it.'

'Too late.'

'I should've just taken it.'

'Too late.'

'Maybe,' said the other one as he began rolling the trunk underfoot, performing, pleased with himself. 'Anyway, who needs a skateboard?'

'There you go then,' said the man, 'no harm done.'

'Everything okay between you two, you know, since the thing?'

'Getting there. We'll be fine.'

'Fair play to you John, I wouldn't have taken her back.'

'That's all over, finished. It was a one off.'

'You don't know that.'

'I do. We all make mistakes.'

'What comes around goes around though, that's something.'

The man put his foot on the log, stopping its motion.

'Frank, what you saying?' The other one turned to him. 'You think she deserved it?'

'That's not what I said. Although you have to admit it does have a karmic kind of balance to it.'

The man kicked the log, almost toppling the other one.

'You are fucked Frank. You know that?'

'Hey, I'm sorry. I didn't mean anything by it, it just...'

'Just what?'

'Seemed obvious. I'm sorry.'

He rolled backwards and forwards in the silence between them.

'She's recovered though, from the attack?'

'Yeah, I would say so; seems fine to me. She doesn't really talk about it.'

'You've asked her though, about it?'

'She knows I'm here. She'll talk when she's ready.'

'You know her better than I do.'

The other one steadied himself and turned

to the man, squinting in the sun. Luther could see his face and the back of the man's head.

'She's looking good though, isn't she?'

Luther didn't like the way the other one grinned, or the length of time. It meant the man was grinning back.

'Yeah, she is,' the man said, 'she's looking good.'

The other one nodded, swatting a bee away. The angered bee came back, prompting more flapping, a loss of balance and a fall. He yelped as he hopped between the logs, one hand outstretched, this time for support instead of balance.

'Ah, fuck fuck fuck fuck, fucking logs.'

The man gripped him, taking his weight as he tried to stand on his twisted ankle, swearing at the logs, the bee.

'You want to go back? I'll tell Laura to give us a lift, she won't mind.'

'No, no, let's carry on, it'll walk off.'

He planted his foot.

'The alcohol will kill the pain on the way back at least.'

'Exactly, let's go see what Milton's got to offer as nightlife. Anyway, I want to see the "pooky" woods.'

'Wooooh.'

One hobbling, their arms around each other, they passed into the trees, giggling like schoolboys.

Luther smiled a smile of intent as he pushed the cork back into the whisky bottle.

The man was the first to get his breath back. Panting and holding on to each other, they stopped in a column of full moon night that fell through the canopy like the devil's spotlight. The single torch they had between them appeared to provide little comfort and they clung to the perceived safety of this new and vague illumination, as if merely finding this spot in the darkness was a victory of sorts. The other one continued to breathe heavily, hands on his knees for support, until he vomited, emptying his night's drinks onto the track.

'You okay?'

'Yeah, much better, can't even feel my

➡

ankle. Ah fuck.' He lifted his foot out of the puddle of lager and partially digested meat. 'Please, tell me we're almost out of here.'

'Can't be far now,' said the man, patting the other one on the back.

They were nearly home. From where Luther had concealed himself, he could see around the corner, the exit, his home, the sheen of copper strips along the top of the new house. He was enjoying himself. He'd paralleled their walk home through the trees, staying out of sight yet making no attempt to keep quiet, snapping branches, activating an ancient gin-trap, listening to them squeal at the fierce metallic clap of its jaws, their stumbling run that took them across his trip wire, falling into stagnant stench, scrambling to retrieve their torch. He wished he'd had more time.

'You think it's him, really?'

'I fucking know it,' said the man, 'he's got it in for me.'

'Hey, less of the victim, come on. What's your plan?'

'Beat him.'

'Fucking A.'

The man swung the torch around, too erratic and rushed to be of any real use as a searchlight but Luther crouched lower nonetheless.

'Where the fuck is he?'

The other one started laughing to himself, bent double, whilst coughing and spitting the last of his sick out.

'He's good though, isn't he? Look at us.'

'Well,' said the man, finding some humour in the situation, 'I think we did some of it to ourselves; can't blame the hillbilly for everything.'

'Hillbilly's fucking right. He's probably spent his life catching what he eats and fucks.'

'Or using whores.'

'True.'

'Probably has a favourite backwoods retard who obliges him.'

'Sucks her thumb and calls him daddy.'

'Touch of a good woman might civilise the cunt.'

Luther raised the air rifle and took aim.

The man unzipped, pissed where he stood, put it away, wiped his hands on his trousers and pulled the other one upright.

'Come on,' he said.

The pellet hit him in the thigh. The yelp was followed by a drunken dash for safety.

It was a matter of seconds before they snagged his second trip wire, two filaments of fishing twine stretched separately across their path. One was tied around the trigger of his loaded shotgun, its stock jammed into a nearby root system, the other around the makeshift peg securing a restrained lower bough. They screamed like children. The flash of orange had barely registered before the ear sucking explosion of both barrels woke every living creature they hadn't already disturbed. They were still screaming as the peg popped and the bough reasserted itself, sweeping through its dark kingdom at eye level like a medieval weapon, knocking them off their feet. The sounds of shock and fear faded as Luther skipped instinctively between the pines, through the bark of the fox and the clacking of the chickens, the squeal of pigs and the premature chorus of the birds, back to his home, to wait.

Luther was pleased with himself, having a fit of giggles as he slipped his shirt off in the dark; unable to remember the last time he had been audibly happy. The physical strangeness of the laugh and the realisation that it may have been his last one saddened him. He listened to the room in the hope a trace would remain, a reminder of what he had sounded like, but it was gone, just bare walls and the scuffing of his boot soles. The more he concentrated the more she came back and the memory of her joy brought him none. He dropped his shirt over the chair-back, covering Laura's cardigan, sat on his chair and undid his laces.

He was barefoot before the outrage began. Howls of abuse, threats and injustice thrown at his home, drink addled and vehement. A sly grin spread as Luther poured a bumper of whisky, swirling a mouthful around before scorching his gullet. Popping the button of his combats as he stood, he let them fall to the floor and stepped out of them, naked. One more mouthful; the flick of a switch, a grip on the handle, the straightening of his face, before he opened the door and stood framed with the light behind him.

'What's all the noise?'

The man stopped his shouting, scrunched his eyes to see.

'Don't be cute Luther, I know it was you.'

'What was me?'

'That stuff,' he said, flinging his hand out to point back to where they had been, 'the guns and booby traps, I fucking know it was you,' he jabbed a drunken hand at Luther, 'you won't win.'

Luther stepped off his front porch and walked down the path to the two men standing at his gate. As he came out of silhouette, the other one put his hands over his face to hide his laughter. The man was confused. He glanced at Luther's cock.

'Luther, you've got no clothes on.'

The other one's sniggering leaked between his fingers. Averting his gaze, the man used every muscle available to his face to stop himself doing the same.

'It's warm. I was in bed. It was your gun that woke me up.'

'My gun?' He found that serious form of sobriety that only the drunk can possess, turned to Luther and held firm eye contact. 'You know that's not the truth. Like I said, you won't win.'

'Look at me.' Luther held his arms out, vulnerable as Christ on the cross, insolent as a tormentor, egging his opponent to attack, to bring it on. 'I've got nothing to lose, so I can't.'

'Luther,' said the man, stepping closer, adopting a conciliatory tone, 'why can't we just be neighbours?'

'We are. That's the problem; your problem.'

Although they still stared at each other, the finality of this comment and the threat it contained ended the altercation. The other one sensed this and pulled the man away.

'Come on John. He's not listening.'

The man snatched his arm away.

'Fuck off Frank, I'll leave when I'm ready, me, not you, not him.'

The man hated him. He probably wouldn't remember the details in the morning but he would never let go of the hate that was in the black of his eyes at that moment. It looked to be the only thing keeping him upright. When the man decided he was ready he snorted and gave a toss of his head for some imagined victory.

'Arsehole.'

He slumped away, shoulders first until he collided with the other one who wrapped his arm around him with 'good for you' comfort and quickly made light of the situation in a conspiracy of cackling.

'Night then.'

Luther scratched his balls, pleased with his night's work.

Reflections
Carl MacDougall

BETWEEN DUNBRAE AND Kilrositer Andrew Robertson caught a flash of gold and in that moment knew what he had long suspected. The implications swept through him like a plough.

Trying to tell Margaret, his thoughts were rough. He could not describe the certainty, the rush of alphabet that formed no words. All he could see were the bits on the periphery, the edges that seemed not to matter, as if there was a gap between the moment and his conclusion.

He stood in the kitchen, his ruddy complexion and freckled, bald head moving awkwardly as he twisted his way towards the subject. It is, he said, difficult to describe an epiphany.

Margaret swirled butter round the pan, added milk to the scrambled eggs and turned to look at her husband. She hadn't seen him this animated for some time and expected him to pace the small kitchen. But he stood still, his head moving, as if he had found a solution, a kind of peace.

He was, he told her, on his way back from hospital where Mr Connor from the wee cottage at the back of Kilrositer Brae, overlooking the Rona Woods, asked, Will you pray with us? Will you pray for her? Please.

Andrew Robertson had gone into the small side room without knocking, thinking he could leave a tract by her bedside. Mrs Connor was sleeping, her body barely distinguishable beneath the covers. Mr Connor was standing by the window.

I don't know what I am going to do, he said. I don't know what I'll do without her. Thirty-seven years it's been.

And while Mrs Connor slept, Mr Connor closed his eyes and bowed his head while Andrew Robertson asked God to bless them, to give them His strength and help them pass through this difficult time.

Mr Connor shook his hand and thanked him.

Good luck, Andrew Robertson said. All the best.

And that was the turn, the start of it, the first infant kick.

What could I do? he said. Nothing. The woman was dying and all I could do was pray.

So what else happened? Margaret asked.

Nothing happened. Not there. Nothing happened there. It's just that I saw a wonderful, golden reflection, the sun on the water and wanted you to see it.

That's nice, she said, and smiled.

Andrew Robertson sat in the garden in the five minutes till tea was ready. He couldn't tell her. While he was talking he realised he could not conclude his discovery.

If it was true, if he had drawn the correct conclusion, his life and its work were pointless.

I'm a useless twister, a quack, a wastrel, he said aloud when Margaret called.

They came from the city where he had been an assistant minister for nine years. They came after Gemma died. Neither he nor Margaret could pass her school. Four months after the funeral, when they'd got back to talking, Margaret said she had booked a holiday, nothing much, just two or three days away in the car.

They stayed with Mrs McNulty at Craigdalton, sat in the garden and read, walked through Rona Woods and followed the path across the moor to a ring of standing stones that predated history. Then they found a cove and swam in the sea, danced at a ceilidh and on Sunday went to the morning service at Aberona, whose parish had been amalgamated with Craigdalton and Kilrositer.

He stood at the door and looked across the Craigdalton Sound while Margaret spoke to the minister's wife; and later in the kitchen she told them the drawbacks.

The manse was big and draughty, but it was a lovely charge with maybe as many as twenty folk coming to the alternate churches. The main church was Kilrositer, a lively wee community with a lot of incomers, mostly folk from England with their own ways of doing things, but they needed a minister like everyone else. There was always work to do at the cottage hospital which they were trying to save rather than have a round trip of more than eighty miles. All the churches were damp and cold, but very well kept by local committees.

What do you think? Margaret asked on the way back.

It'll do us fine, he said. He's not leaving till the spring and things will have changed by then. We could make a fresh start.

She nodded.

He preached his last sermon at the end of March and they had a reception where he introduced the new assistant, showed him round and received the parish's grateful thanks, cards, an album of photographs and a clock.

Things changed slowly over the next two years, windows were repaired, floorboards straightened and hinges mended. Cardinal red floor polish was applied to the entrance to Aberona parish church and a new porch light was fitted at Craigdalton. Margaret started a parish magazine and on 18th December Christmas tree lights were switched on outside every church.

He did 18 baptisms, 16 marriages and conducted 24 funerals, the last on the weekend after Easter Sunday when he buried Mrs

McNulty's granddaughter, who had meningitis. Her death had saved the cottage hospital, the sister said.

That night he watched Margaret lift the lid to see if the potatoes were done while shaking her head at the wickedness of the news on the radio.

He thought of the policeman who came to the door when Gemma died, the young man beside him obviously stricken with a sudden desire to laugh because of embarrassment. And he thought of the service, of watching the kirk elders carry his daughter's body and later standing by her plot in the kirkyard, when Willie Anderson, the church officer, handed him the earth and he heard it rattle on her coffin lid.

That was when he knew there was no God. Not any more, not for him. There may have been a God at one time, but not any more.

His last sermon was on the importance of finding your own God, the one that suits you. Never mind what anyone else thinks, no matter what they believe, you have to find your own God your own way, find a power that you can believe in. If you believe He made heaven and earth and all that in there is, and it sustains you, helps you, sees you from one day to another, that's fine. If you believe only in the miracle of creation you can witness, flowers in spring, birdsong, sunset, that's fine too.

Margaret spooned the peas and carrots on to the plate beside the stew and potatoes and they ate slowly, his mind on the girl who was maybe 19 or 20. He'd noticed her when she came out the Co-op and ran across the road in the rain, her white blouse wet; he thought of the way her breast tilted when she ran.

And on the Sunday coming back from Craigdalton he had seen the same girl raise her head towards a young man and smile, looking fully into his eyes.

She was the dead girl's sister, had cried throughout the service and later thanked him, asking if he was new to the parish.

I think I'm invisible, he said to Margaret.

She looked up and smiled, then put her

➥

plate on top of his, the knives and forks in her left hand.

I think I'm invisible and I don't believe in God.

I know.

I'm a fraud.

No you are not. You help other people who do believe in God, you guide them through the small ceremonies that are important to them and they like and admire you for it. So do I. Gemma's death has strengthened my faith.

I know. I can't see it that way. It isn't a burden. It's a loss. I saw something wonderful today. On my way back from the hospital, I saw the sun stretch itself across the sea and turn the water golden. The reflection caught me full in the face when I turned the corner and dazzled me, made me close my eyes and for a moment I thought I might lose the road, but, obviously, I didn't, even though I kept looking at the moving sheet of gold that rippled as though it was alive, moving like a bird's wing. It was wonderful, an obvious act of creation, but I looked at it and couldn't believe, not for the life of me.

Margaret pressed his head into her breast. She kissed his brow and stroked the top of his head.

Later, he went into the garden after rain and smelled the earth and the conflagration of roses and honeysuckle, the night stock narcotic in the moonlight. He stood on the path and listened to the wind in the trees, the sough of the sea and thought of the moment of calm on his dead daughter's face.

She's an angel, a woman behind him said.

'He set the rods which he had peeled in front of the flocks in the gutters, even in the watering troughs, where the flocks came to drink; and they mated when they came to drink.'

Genesis 30: 38

scottishreviewofbooks.org

Scottish Review of Books

VOL 6 · NUMBER 2 · 2010

ISSN 1745—5014

A View From the Edge —
Brian Morton's Election Reflections

ol 6 No 3:
UT 14/08/10

visit our website:
www.scottishreviewofbooks.org
tel: 01369 820229

The Cave
Jacqueline Thompson

Some say he was born down here,
that he's been submerged since birth.
Perhaps because his skin is white,
perhaps because his eyes are so large.

They say she gave birth behind the bar.
They say she wet the baby's head with whisky.
Now his eyes carry rings,
now his stomach hides his belt.

He traces a cloth over the wood,
polishing so hard the varnish fades.
It could be driftwood, this dry slab,
washed up from some broken ship.

He looks from under leaden lids,
surveys a young man counting coppers;
he is lining them up on the table,
little lights to reel her in,
stars reflected in a black sea.

The pursuit of thought
Graham Hardie

I think of her,
her tiny bones
and skeletal shins
and her voice,
so pale and so quiet;
and I think of her,
as a man thinks of love
and the pursuit of thought.

fragments from a european leg
Jim Ferguson

dublin.

behan had been there before us
in fact that cheeky bastard id been born there

of course we did neither of us (her and i) swear
and took great care to end our sentences

with the
proper grammatical clauses

where the english langwij
was concerned we were

of course — *snobs*
a shortsimple word, we've always approved of

sorry —
of which we have always approved...

...that tendency of behan's to indulge in the greek
so we therefore moderated our sweet glaswegian

classily class-strewn mellifluous brogues,
burst into a tune by the pogues

which was all about arses of course

fragments from a european leg
Jim Ferguson

dubrovnik.

sweating —
it was here I sat
removed my hat
let random raindrops
gather in my hair

watched
        crash
            after
                crash

of european history
seep in to my head

through my puny human
eyesockets — saw shells and rockets

i was ready for a dose
of everyday tv

ready to let bright lights drop out
into the ancient mystery

of a thousand years before

                        something

the centuries had now licked clean

                     just

the kind of thing that sensible tourists
travel to see,

horror so mercifully pure

The Poem WILD BOAR
Sally Evans

The Muse sent me the second half of a poem.
So, I asked her for a beginning.
She continued to refuse the beginning
because she knows I am seeking a major beginning,
after so many endings not so quick to see
in the water, flashing, a quick strong minnow
silver backed and patterned.
So, I roamed my hills and botched my poem
as poets will, to where she started:

The poem WILD BOAR has to contain
the words PLOD, BRISTLE and ACORN
or anyway OAK. The poem HERON
must have at least three words from PRIEST,
PATIENT, LECTERN, GRAVE, LIGHTNING
but a dig for remains of things
can never find a SHARD.
Is poetry a dig for remains? Not at all.
Is it a heron? Not entirely.
Is it a wild boar, glimpsed through woods
in a lifetime of clambering,
a frisson, this area dangerous
where the stag might shove,
birds attack or the black tick bore?
Is *this* poetry poetry?
Or not? 'We are sorry to say'
but, truly, guardians of the visible,
overground world, you are glad
to protect your gullible personnel
from lightning and risk from contamination
by those who have seen wild boar.
Boredom is your metier. As little
must happen and as slowly as possible.
Poetry is the impossible art.

Well now, Muse, you infuriating lesbian
and untameable arts administrator,
it's my turn to tell YOU something
as I wander home on my well-worn path
through the spring woods, primroses,
coming bluebells,
prostrate bracken,
about-to-disappear snowdrop leaves,
moss and stones and mud
down onto the tarmac.
I can finish this poem myself.

dachau-derry-knock
Donal McLaughlin

September 1979

University would be starting back soon n Liam was thinking about squeezing in one last trip. It had been a long packed summer but, his first working abroad, n part of him didn't feel like going to Ireland. Not so soon after his long journey home anyhow. And certainly not so soon after Mountbatten being killed n Warrenpoint. Aye, the Troubles were *bad* again getting.

When he said to his Da, Big Liam pleaded with him:

'I know it wasn't for definite. I know you said you *might* just. Your Granny's got her heart set on it but. She'll be wild disappointed if ye don't.'

Turned out: he could get a flight. From Glasgow, too! An uncle said he'd collect him.

Soon as it was definite, it was Pope-this, Pope-that. Folk wouldn't shut up about it. The Pope would be in Ireland when Liam was. Maybe his Gran n Bernie would take him? It would be a *great opportunity* if they did. *An honour.* Wasn't just the fact it was the first Polish Pope. Was the fact it was the *centenary* also: of the apparitions at Knock. 'You'll be representing us if you do go,' his Da, strangely solemn, stressed. 'Jays – I hope he comes to Scotland one day too!'

His Uncle Dermot picked him up. Liam. Not the Pope.

In the car back from Belfast, Dermot was desperate for *bars*. Liam felt awkward, not having any.

'How's yir Da?' Dermot said, to prod him.

Liam wished he knew, wished he'd summit to say. It was hard to talk about Dad but.

'And yir mammy?'

'Same as ever.'

'And the weans? Not that you're weans any more! Age are ye now, youngfella?'

'Eighteen there—'

'Which makes the girls seventeen, sixteen—'

'Aye—'

'Any boyfriends yet?'

'Not that we know about,' said Liam.

He kept *ßumm* about the German girl he'd met. 'How are things wi yous?' he asked instead.

'Jumpin!' said Dermot. 'Lookin forward to the Holy Father we are—'

'Ye goin?'

'To Galway, aye. The Youth Mass. I'm going down wi the young ones. Are you?'

'My Da was saying my Gran n Bernie might take me—'

'What, to Knock?'

'Aye—'

'Do *they* know that?'

'Don't know—'

'I'd take ye to Galway only the bus is full —'

There was a silence that felt kinda awkward.

'I've *never been* to Knock,' Liam said, to break it. Not that he'd ever been to Galway.

'Have ye not?' Dermot sounded amazed. 'Your Granda O'Donnell, God rest him, *loved* Knock.'

They arrived. His Gran saw them coming down

the path. She'd still her seat by the fire that she looked up the garden to the street from. Even watching the news she kept an eye out, shifting onto her hip to try n get comfortable.

The key was in the door so Dermot turned it – to get the usual welcome from Shep. The living-room door, as ever, was wide open.

'Yes, Liam!' the ones in chorused. 'Welcome home!'

Nine years the O'Donnells were over in Scotland. Derry was still called *home* but.

His Gran, in her favourite pinny, got up to hug him.

'It's good to see you, Liam, son—'

The 'How's yir Daddy? How's yir mammy? How's the rest of the weans?' routine followed. The 'How long are yis over in Scotland?' one too. And of course, 'Would yis never think of coming back?'

Liam *kept his counsél* on that one.

'Maybe one day,' he lied.

One day, *if he had his way*, he'd marry n settle in Germany.

'Can I phone to say I landed?' he asked once things calmed down.

'Go ahead, son, aye!'

Liam headed out to the hall, shut the door behind him.

When he dialled the number, his mum answered.

'So are ye goin?' She sounded all excited.

'I don't know. No-one's said—' he said. 'Dermot sounded surprised but when I mentioned it—'

'Put your Gran on!' his mum said. 'I'll get your Dad. You can't miss out on that!'

'Dad wants you, Gran,' Liam called over as he made his way back in.

His Gran was on for a good while before she came back. Then others went racing out to speak to his Da.

'Who's paying for this call?' was all they got out of Gran. 'Mind I'm paying when yis are quite finished!'

They were taking him to Knock! There might be a problem wi the BnB since he wasn't booked in, he could go wi them in the car but.

'Yir Aunt Bernie n Aunt Ita'll be sleepin in the car anyhow,' Gran said, 'so if the worst comes to the worst, ye can join them—'

Liam wasn't sure he fancied *that*.

'The actual Mass is on Sunday at the Shrine,' his Gran went on. 'We'll go down on Saturday but, n come back up on Monday.'

Ye could tell it couldn't come quick enough for her.

On the Saturday morning, the TV was already on when Liam went down for his breakfast.

'We can watch Phoenix Park before we go!' his Gran, realising, said.

Over a million people were goney be there, most of them there already, it looked lik. The camera focused on the giant cross backed by sixty banners. Sixty foot high they were.

Looking at the crowd in Dublin, Liam was minded of *The Tin Drum*, the film he'd seen in Germany. About a boy, Oscar, it was, who at the age of three decided to stop growing; to toddle around wi his drum just. There was this great scene where he hid beneath a stage Hitler was on, and here, the crowd picked up on his beat n started waltzing!

Liam tried to tell Bernie, his Gran interrupted but. 'What are ye tellin us that for? Are ye watchin this or not? It's once in a lifetime, mind!'

Stung, Liam forced himself to watch. It was a gorgeous morning, the commentator commented, and the *St Patrick* was on time. Soon, ye saw the Air Corps meeting it, to escort the Pope as he landed. They came in over Killiney n flew up the Liffey, over all the bridges. The Pope must've seen them all in the Park. Cat was out of the bag if it was meant to be a secret.

Finally, the plane landed n the Pope kissed Irish soil.

'Hope there isni any dogs about!' Liam nearly joked nearly.

In his own house, he would've. Not here but. He minded last year, sure, when John Paul I died: folk stressing how *only* Paddy could get away wi *that*; his joke about the difference between the Pope n a Rowntree's Fruit Gum.

➼

Gran n all her oul buddies had been in stitches. No-one was in any doubt but: anyone other than Paddy would be shown the door.

A wee girl of nine presented the Pope wi flowers.

He was walking in the footsteps of St Patrick, John Paul said.

'Wasn't that wild nice of him,' Gran commented, 'saying that.'

Next, all eyes were on the helicopter, red for some reason, that would take the Pope to the Park. The over-a-million had to be in there now.

The Mass itself dragged on. Nine cardinals, a hundred bishops n any number of priests were *concélebrating* it (the stress went on the *con*). The Pope gave his sermon, which people interpreted. John Paul didn't say as much, still wasn't having contraception but. Abortion n divorce were no-nos too.

Two thousand priests gave out Communion n soon it was time for the Popemobile. *He's Got The Whóle Wor-ld In His Hands* folk were suddenly singing. Swaying in unison they were. As if wee Oscar, a fellow Pole, was in among them, beating away at his drum.

The Pope was flying on to Drogheda. The three of them, Gran, Bernie, Liam, set off from Gran's house. Ita, they'd promised to collect.

'It's a pity we have to miss any coverage!' Gran was saying. 'A pity, in fact, Armagh was cancelled. A lot nearer it would've been—'

'We can listen to the wireless, sure, Mammy!' Bernie said. 'It's not as if ye'll miss anything!'

It was the first Liam had heard of Armagh. 'Why was it cancelled?' he asked.

'Did ye not hear about Lord Mountbatten?'

Alles klar, he thought.

'Drogheda's the nearest the Pope'll get to the North,' his Gran explained, leaving Liam half-wishing they were going *there*. It would be more *symbólic*. When Bernie said about loyalist paramilitaries but – the *very real fear* there'd be an attack – he changed his mind, pronto.

'D'ye need the toilet before we go?' Bernie asked. 'Cos no way am I stopping!'

Way she asked, Liam didn't know did she want him coming or was he only getting cos Gran said.

Gran, fortunately, had an answer for her. 'Ye'll stop surely at some point, weegirl? In fact, ye'll stop when I tell ye!'

'I meant *early on*, Mother!' Bernie clarified.

They picked up Ita, who was all smiles as she climbed into the back, then headed for the Carlisle roundabout.

Before they were over the Bridge even, Ita was asking how long they'd be?

'To Knock? Could be three or maybe *four* hours!' Bernie said. 'God only knows, wi all the traffic!'

Three or four hours was long enough, Liam reckoned. If nowt compared to his thirty back from Munich.

The signposts, at first, were for Omagh n Strabane. Places where his mum had connections. After Strabane, they headed for Lifford, another place he'd heard of. It was just before Lifford ye crossed the border.

The soldiers must've been scunnered, right enough. Sick to the back teeth of Papal colours. *Céad Míle Fáilte*: if they didn't know what it meant before, *boy*, they did so now.

A black boy hardly looked at them before he waved them through.

'And there was me thinkin the buggers would hold us up,' Ita said. 'That it would be just lik them to delay us—'

Liam, feeling nervous, changed the subject.

'This time last year I was in Berlin, and I visited Checkpoint Charlie, Ita!'

'Did ye? What was that lik?'

'A bit disappointing, to be honest. The checkpoints here are scarier—'

'You're just back from Germany, aren't ye?'

'Yeah—'

'Any girlfriends?'

Liam blushed.

'That mean there *is*? I think he's got a *Fräulein*, Mother! Have ye? A German sweetheart?'

Liam revealed nothing. Told them about Dachau instead. About getting a lift to Munich, a train back. About the hour's quick march through the mountains – pitch dark, trees either side – to get back to where he was working.

'Ye wouldn't catch me doing that!' Ita said.

Psycho was on, he explained, n they were all planning to watch it. That had been the reason for the rush.

He'd made it alright. Had even caught the end of what was on before.

'And wha d'ye think it was about?'

Ita wasn't for guessing.

'H-block!' Liam told her. 'The dirty protest—'

'Was it really?'

'Yeah. And it was weird seeing the two things within hours of each other. Dachau. And then H-Block on the telly—'

'I suppose it would be, aye—'

The wireless was playing n replaying the highlights of Phoenix Park. The bits about the Irish people's *faith*. Their *loyalty*. The warning not to rest on *past glories*. The dangers of *materialism*. And *affluence*.

'What's *affluence* when it's at home anyway?' Bernie asked.

Liam hated that kinda question. Ita, fortunately, who was doing evening classes, was able to answer.

Over n over again, the radio played the crowd singing. Ita n his Gran sang along. Oscar would've been proud of them.

'Join in, youngfella!' Ita would give it, nudging Liam. Liam but wouldn't but, was too shy.

The Drogheda coverage followed. *The nearest John Paul will get to the North*, the commentator constantly reminded them. He'd be asking the IRA to give up violence, it was rumoured.

'Quite right n all!' Gran said. 'And I hope they buckin listen!'

'Can't see it myself,' Ita answered.

Gran turned on her. 'Do ye want peace or not, daughter dear?'

'I do, aye.'

Was as if but Gran hadn't heard her: 'Ten years we've had of this! More than that! —What the hell d'ye want? Another ten?'

'Course I don't!'

'Well buckin start prayin then! Stead of sittin there sayin ye can't see it!'

There was an atmosphere until Mass began n Gran started praying.

Then came the homily, the bit they were waiting for: *I wish to speak to all men and women engaged in violence.*

Liam clocked the fact *women* were mentioned.

I appeal to you, in language of passionate pleading—

That was a *Pólish* expression. Had to be...

On my knees I beg you to turn away from the paths of violence and to return to the ways of peace—

'Isn't that fair enough, the way he put it?' Gran commented. 'How could the *boys* object to that, ay?'

A quarter of a million people, many from the North, were there to hear it. There were no boos but. Nor was there any mention of people walking out.

Those who resort to violence always claim that only violence brings about change. You must know there is a pólitical, peaceful way to justice—

'He's right enough!' Ita said. 'What do you think, Bernie?'

'I'm too busy driving, me, to think!' Bernie said.

Browned off, she sounded.

The signs were for Sligo now.

They'd been passing through the likes of Killygordon, Ballybofey, Ballintra n Ballyshannon. Names Liam knew from his mother n father talking. Names ye kinda remembered whether ye'd been there or not.

Once they hit Sligo, they took a pit-stop. Bernie pulled up behind a hotel.

The place they knew was across the bridge.

Bernie walked wi Liam. Out from behind

➼

the wheel, she was more friendly.

'Any other day, we'd be two-thirds of the way there now,' she told him. 'Don't be sayin to yir Granny: God knows what the roads'll be lik but, the closer we get to Knock—'

His Gran looked tired, a bit, as they sat drinking their cuppas. 'Ma stays are killin me!' she said, wriggling.

Ita-n-Bernie were beginning to tire n all.

'That's a lovely cuppa tay!' Ita said. For once but, the others weren't for saying much.

Galway, they were heading for next.

'But don't worry, Liam, we turn off for Knock before that!' Bernie said.

The place-names here meant nothing to him. Charlestown was the first to ring any kind of bell.

Thankfully, it was fifteen miles or so, only, to Knock now.

'Aye, n it could be the fifteen slowest!' Bernie warned.

'The Pope must be knackered, Godlove'im!' Gran said. She just came out wi it, suddenly. Liam nearly choked.

'What's he up to tonight?' Ita asked.

Way she said it, ye'd've thought he'd be out gallivanting.

'The ones from the other churches it is first,' Gran answered. 'Then he's meeting the Taoiseach n all the Cabinet—'

Ita winked at Liam. 'Listen to her! Your Granny has it all memorised. Isn't she terrific for a woman in her seventies?'

By the time they got to the BnB, it was dark. They were able to park in its grounds. Bernie went to the door to speak to the woman.

'She's only a blow-up mattress to offer Liam—' she told them when she came back.

'That's okay, sure!' his Gran piped up. 'It's only tonight n tomorrow!'

'She'll be wantin money for it—'

'Talk about buckin lousy!' his Gran gave off. 'He'll have to give it to her, I suppose, but! Tell her fine. Alright then.'

The next morning, Ita-n-Bernie were allowed in for breakfast. It was far from the full Irish.

Again there was a charge but.

'She's chargin ye that for a cuppa tay n toast? Yis have more money than sense!' Gran complained. 'I'd've waited, me!'

The wireless was on in the dining-area n the previous day's highlights kept being repeated. Footsteps of St Patrick, *The Whole Wor-ld In His Hands*, the Irish people's loyalty to their faith. Also, needless to say, John Paul pleading in passionate language: to turn away from violence.

Liam nipped to the toilet. The night before, the presenter was saying, journalists, *the world media*, inspired by John Paul, had suddenly burst into song. *For He's A Jolly Good Fellow*, they'd sung. Liam had to grin: ye had to hand it to Oscar n his drum! Some bloody nerve, the weeboy had.

The others filled him in when he got back.

Ita: 'Ye missed the bit about him meeting the other churches, Liam. It went well enough, cept he'd wanted to meet them standing up but was tired n had to sit down.'

Bernie: 'The Taoiseach gave him a statue of St Patrick!'

Gran: 'And he was up at the crack of dawn this morning to meet all the wee handicapped children! He's also met some Polish people. So it's next stop Clonmacnoise now, n then onto Galway before Knock.'

'Listen to her!' Ita said again. 'Ye'd think ye were his personal secretary, Mother!'

The question was: would they try to drive to the Shrine?

The BnB woman said they'd be better off walkin.

'I don't mind *now*. It's the gettin back afterwards!' Gran said.

Bernie decided to give it a go.

They'd hardly set off when they heard what awaited them: ten thousand cars descending on Knock.

There was no turning back n progress – even at that hour – was slow.

Bernie eventually conceded defeat n parked in someone's garden. 'It cost me an arm n a leg!' she complained. 'They're buckin at it!'

'That's the Free Staters for you!' his Gran said just. 'What do I always say? I swear to God – n this time *I mean it*: I'm never coming back!'

It had to be said: the Free Staters were making a mint. A hundred thousand welcomes, their arse. They were out to fleece ye! The BnB they were in was a brand-new bungalow n it was no wonder, the prices they were chargin. Houses selling *Cup-a-Soup* had the cheek to charge a pound for it n every garden or field was a temporary car-park. As for flags, posters, pennants n the lik: it only had to have the Pope on it, or CÉAD MÍLE FÁILTE, n they were charging through the nose.

'Themmins have me cursing so much, I'll need to go to Confession!' Gran said.

When they finally got to the Shrine, his Gran pointed out the new basilica.

'We'll maybe take ye tomorrow, Liam. Right now but, we need to find a spot—'

The Mass might've been hours away, the place was filling up but.

They chose their spot. A woman nearby had a wireless. The Pope was done in Clonmacnoise, she reported. He'd praised the early missions n was due to land in Galway any minute. There'd be live coverage from the Ballybrit racecourse where two hundred thousand were waiting for him.

That was in Galway. Even in Knock, ones were afraid to move in case they lost their place. Normally, they'd do the Stations of the Cross, perform the Fifteen Mysteries, Ita said. Not today but...

The Youth Mass in Galway was broadcast in full. Those wi radios or within earshot ye could hear praying along. His Gran-n-Bernie-n-Ita were saying all the responses. Sometimes Ita winked as if she was having him on.

The latest homily started n Liam tried to listen. The Pope *bĕlieved* in the youth of Ireland, he said. He loved them. The crowd in Galway went crazy. Soon *The Whŏle Wor-ld In His Hands* was being sung yet again. Jaysus, Oscar, gizza break! A joke's a joke, weeboy.

It was as if they'd sung too soon but. Next, it was *rĕligious and moral traditions* the Pope was on about. The very *soul* of Ireland. He mentioned *warped consciences*. Rhymed off a list starting wi *drugs, sex* n *drink*. It was hard to imagine the youth fancying this much. One remark it took but just, for all of that to evaporate:

Young people of Irĕland, I love you!

The crowd went wild.

The wireless couldn't get enough of it.

And it wasn't wee Oscar's doing this time.

Galway went on so long, the Pope was late for Knock.

People stood n stood n waited n waited in the grey n damp.

'It's Bishop bloody Casey's fault!' someone gave it.

'They seem to've conveniently forgot Knock's the reason he came—'

'I've been here since midnight, me!'

'It's them poor invalids down at the basilica I feel sorry for—'

Folk, Liam noticed, were eating fish n chips. His Gran spotted them too.

'Them fish n chips look gorgeous, Ita. Gaun ask the people where they bought them! I've not eaten since breakfast!'

When Ita found out, she was sent for some.

The Pope, needless to say, arrived before she got back n it was like a sin on Ita's soul, missing the start of Mass.

'I know *I* sent her,' Gran said. 'She shoulda made sure to get back but!'

If there was one thing you never were, it was late for Mass.

Gloomier n gloomier it had been getting. Now it started to drizzle. Their one consolation was: the chips would warm them up.

Ita arrived back in time for the sermon. To hear JP2 stressing Knock was *the goal of his journey*. The chips were so hot they burned their mouths off. They still tucked in but, half-catching, if that, the words they'd come to hear.

They weren't the only ones only half paying attention, Liam noticed. It had been too long a day.

'What d'ye mean I won't have fasted an

hour before Communion?' a woman's husband snapped at her. 'I've been fastin all bloody day!'

It was lik everyone's chips all froze between the bags n their lips somewhere.

'Your husband's right, missus!' an older man said. 'This Mass shoulda been over long before it started even. Wi the best will in the world, they can't expect us to fast all that time. Not when it's their faults—'

They all started to scoff again.

And when, finally, Communion was distributed, they all just received.

Eventually, the Mass was ended. They didn't go in peace but. The Pope had still to go round, sure, in his Popemobile. Ye could see the wee roof working its way, the bubble underneath. 'This is *hiʃtory*', a man kept repeating, 'and we are here!'

Desperate, the O'Donnells were, for the Pope to reach where they were. Others kept delaying him but. *The Whóle Wor-ld In His Hands*: Oscar, whoever seen him, was giving it laldy.

The Pope eventually got the closest he would get. It should've felt holy. Really holy. It was an anti-climax but. Pope or no Pope, he was *late*. The boy had kept them waiting. And now all ye saw of him was this.

To make things worse: the tour was cut short. Cos night was falling...

'We're the lucky ones,' Gran kept saying. 'There's parts of the crowd he didn't get anywhere near—'

Even she sounded wild let-down but.

Another morning, another breakfast.

Ita-n-Bernie popped in again.

'Yis'll never learn, will yis?' their mother said. 'I wouldn't give them the buckin money!'

The highlights were being repeated still. And the Pope's final day was being discussed. For the ones at the O'Donnell table but, it was as if it was over already.

Gran was still harping on about the day before's delays. The schedule should've been kept to. Bishop buckin Casey should've made sure.

'Here, I forgot to tell yis yesterday, wi all the excitement!' Ita was suddenly saying. 'Mind I went away for fish n chips? Well, at one point a Belfast woman I was speakin to overheard a local woman sayin the Pope had been held up. Wild shook up, your woman from Belfast was. *O Jesus, Mary an Saint Joseph!* she said, blissin herself. The woman from Knock looked at her just. *It's nót that bad, love*, she said. *He's juʃt a bit délayed.* Next thing, your woman from Belfast's blissin herself again. *O thanks be to God, missus*, says she. *When you said he was héld up, I thought the paramilitaries had gót him!*'

They all laughed. Gran got Ita to repeat it even, for the BnB woman.

'Where's the Pope today, Mother, anyway?' Ita pretended to ask. Ye could hear it was just for the sake of it. Gran could probably tell even.

She rhymed the answer off anyhow: 'Maynooth, Limerick, Shannon Airport, it is. And then on to America.'

'Rather him than me!' Ita said. 'Don't know about yous— for me right now but, Derry's far enough!'

Not even *Young people of Iréland*, the endless repeats n all the cheering n singing, was managing to gee them up. They were all just sitting there, shattered.

'Would ye say that rain's actually raining?' Ita, looking out, asked. 'Or is it just threatening just?'

'No, that's it on,' Bernie answered.

'Wouldn't it be great if we did get Peace?' Gran piped up. 'If the Pope's visit did bring it about? That's all I wish for now. I'd go to my grave happy even, if I thought he'd brought Peace.'

It was agreed they'd go to the Shrine before they headed home.

The rain, miraculously, had gone off again.

It wasn't just the Virgin Mary who'd appeared here, Liam now learned. Joseph n John the Evangelist had accompanied her.

'A hundred years ago this year—' his Gran stressed. 'Imagine!'

'Mind now n say a wee prayer for your Granda O'Donnell, Liam,' Ita whispered. 'He'd a great devotion to Knock. Raised a lot of money for Monsignor Horan—'

They got to where the Mass was held to find you could walk on the altar. Could even stand on the very spot where John Paul had stood.

Unusual thing was: no-one had thought to charge for it.

The carpet was indigo-ey blue.

The big cross was white.

You stood there n it was nearly as if the Pope'd not been at all lik.

All that excitement, already over.

Before they left, his Gran showed Liam where the Virgin had appeared. Where the Pope had knelt to pray the day before.

You couldn't see nothing.

They squared up at the BnB n headed back towards the border.

The coverage on the wireless was now on to Maynooth. Wee bloody Oscar had been at it again: *We want the Pope! We want the Pope!* young seminarians chanted. The official music had *no* chance, apparently. The chants n all the singing drownded it out.

This time, the Pope focused on priests breaking their vows. He'd a few words as well for ones not wearing their collars.

The O'Donnells listened to Limerick as they motored north again. The Pope's last address, here in Ireland. *Your country seems, in a sense, to be living again the temptations of Christ* was the quote picked up on this time.

DISCUSS, Liam thought. *1,000 words by Monday*.

Well seen Uni was starting back.

Will ye no come back again, the crowd sang this time. And *Come back to Éireann*.

Ye had to hand it to Oscar: he'd fairly extended his repertoire! And infiltrated the Band while he was at it!

A long way from Derry the O'Donnells were still when the Pope boarded his flight from Shannon to Boston. The President n Cardinal O'Fiaich were seeing him off.

A news bulletin followed on the hour. The IRA had issued a statement.

At the first mention of *evil British presence* Gran flipped: 'It's the same oul shite! Switch it off! I don't want to hear it!'

Force, the statement went on, was *by far* the only way to get rid of that presence.

'Turn it *off*, Bernie, I said!'

Once they'd succeeded, the IRA was claiming, the Church would have *no difficulty* in recognising them.

Gran had had enough: 'Trust themmins to spoil it all for everyone!'

She reached to switch the wireless off herself.

'*Excommunication's* too buckin good for them!'

Hearing her, and seeing her, Liam wanted to say something. Or *do* something. Not that he knew exactly what. Ita, seeming to realise, shook her head.

'Naw, don't be saying nothing, Liam!' she whispered, across the back seat. 'You're better off leaving it, sure. Not saying nothing.'

Honda's Tale

Extract from the novel *Dog Mountain*

Iain Maloney

A CHANGE WOULD do me good, so I accept a long-standing invitation and head round to Honda's. Man's apartment is tiny. He shares a kitchen and bathroom with the rest of the floor, so his apartment – room to be accurate – is, by design, for sleeping only. Honda however, being one of us whose social life happens in the safety of the internet, spends an inordinate amount of time there. The place is a clutter of the everyday radiating from his bulk like a web of junk. Visits are claustrophobic so we tend to meet in public, but tonight he insists on the interior.

Like him, the room is unique. He got hold of a vast piece of white linen which he tacked to the centre of the roof and at points halfway down the walls, creating a Bedouin tent. Furnished with various sized boxes, each draped with silks, cotton, more linen, a multitude of coloured fabrics, the floor covered with futon and cushions. The effect is one of patchwork chaos, beautiful.

I duck through tent flap, find him lotus position in a plain black yukata, for all the world in meditation, except for the top of the range Mac notebook open in his lap: a monk for the *Matrix* generation. I settle, cross-legged student, into a nest of cushions and wait for him to finish.

Honda took to computers like a politician to lying. Left the monk a luddite disciple and was writing code in a space of years. He makes the little cash he needs to survive by hiring himself out as Computerman to government and business. Most people, he explains, treat computers like magic boxes – you press the buttons and an answer appears. It never occurs to them to find out how the answer is reached. They trust, implicitly. If a computer told them 2+2=5 they'd accept it. Inside every box is a god, ready with info. Sometimes the god becomes displeased and descends into grumpy silence or spouts in tongues. The god must be placated by the priest-like Honda, a kind of inverse exorcist, goading the god into speaking his knowledge.

A flourish, the maestro concludes his concerto by hitting enter, bows to the screen, and slaps the laptop shut. He apologises profusely and formally for his previous rudeness but explains that he has just finished writing a new programme. It searches through his dream file – for he keeps such a thing – and correlates any recurring themes. Cool, all I can think to say.

—It was you that gave me the idea, he says.

I look, *huh?*

—Have you ever dreamt that you're walking along a bridge and all around you is black apart from a light above. There's a growling dog behind you. You have no recollection of starting, and no idea what is at the other end?

My look is enough.

—Often?

I nod.

—Ever since I was seven years old. It's dark, pitch dark, on a narrow bridge inside a hollow mountain. I know there are other bridges around me, all leading to the same central point, though I can't see them. I can't see anything. Behind me, somewhere in the black, but close, is a dog, growling, forcing me forward. Sometimes there's a light suspended above me, but usually not. Two or three times a week, from childhood until now, the same dream. I never dream of anything else. I never dreamt of stepping onto the bridge, and I never seem to be making any progress across it. A long bridge, to last nearly twenty years.

—Sake?

I nod, though he's already pouring my glass. I return the gesture, honouring the ritual, then knock it back in one.

—I'm going to tell you a story, he says, then I want you to phone your father. You see, you're not the only one to have had this dream.

Hokkaido, far in the north, suffers winter more than most. It rarely goes above zero and some parts are snow-bound for months. Cities are cities and are well looked after, but in the mountains, in the depths of the beautiful national parks, the fourth season storms unchecked by ploughs, salt and heaters. Here, high in the sharp white peaks lived a monk.

His home was a deep cave with a wooden shack built on the front. The cave was low but wide, and the strong stone walls kept the bitter wind at bay while the wooden front kept the rice stores dry. The view was unequalled but the bare ground allowed little growth and no farming, so once a year the monk climbed down to the nearest town to beg for rice. When generosity had filled the old stone jar he had made in his youth he carried it home on his back.

One year he passed a tree and, carefully lowering his stone jar to the ground, called up to the boy sitting amongst the highest branches.

'Is that apple the sweetest on the tree?'

'It's the only apple on the tree,' replied the boy.

The monk smiled and said, 'You look like a strong boy. Would you like to help me carry my load?'

Honda climbed down and, hoisting the jar onto his back, followed the monk towards the mountains.

Throughout the summer and autumn Honda chopped wood, collected fruit, roots and whatever other foods the valley thought to provide. Every morning he came from the peak and filled two buckets with river water, then carried them back up. He cooked for the monk. He kept the fire burning and the cave clean. In return he was taught how to make the paper upon which the monk wrote haiku. He copied his meditation and mastered sitting lotus for hours without discomfort. He asked the monk to teach him but the monk refused, telling him the story of Kakua, who studied Zen in China. Upon his return to Japan the Emperor asked him to teach Zen to him and his subjects. Kakua stood before the Emperor, removed the flute from within his robes, blew one short note, bowed and left.

The seasons moved on and winter fell hard on the mountains. Honda had to keep the fire burning all day and all night, and slowly the wood he had collected began to disappear. The monk gave Honda instructions. He planned a long meditation. Honda was to cook rice twice a day and place it beside him. He was not to slacken with his chores, regardless of the weather. He handed Honda a large block of cypress wood and bade him carve matryoshka dolls, the Russian dolls that fit inside each other.

For months Honda prepared the rice and kept the fire burning, carving the dolls. The monk never moved. Honda laid down the rice and chopsticks next to him, and later he'd wash the empty bowl, but in all that time he never saw the monk move.

The cave didn't hold any heat and even a few inches from the fire, Honda felt cold. On milder days he would venture out and bring back whatever wood he could find, drying it near the fire. Each time he had to venture further from the cave, wading through snowdrifts, braving the gales on plateaus and peaks, slipping and falling, returning exhausted and bleeding with only a few twigs to show for his effort. The monk never moved.

Gradually the loneliness eased and he got into a daily routine: rising at dawn, exercising, preparing rice, eating, stoking the fire, collecting wood, meditating, carving, preparing rice, washing, stoking the fire, reading, washing. He

➡

finished the dolls, seven in all, and was proud of his effort. They sat snugly, each hiding inside the next. He wished for paint that he might decorate them. He had carved the faces to resemble his family and realised one day that he had begun talking to them.

It was with relief and regret that he woke one morning to hear water dripping on the roof. He pushed the door back and looked out at the already shifting landscape. Life would be easier, he thought, now he could collect wood and water with less struggle. Only when he turned back to check the fire did he notice that the monk had gone.

Unsure what to do he stuck to his routine, only this time the rice went uneaten. At nightfall he climbed into bed and fell asleep with questions pounding his brain. Six bowls stood guard over the monk's place when he returned. Honda found him lying on his futon, thin legs covered in still-wet mud. He slept for the whole day and the next night as Honda went about his usual routine.

He woke to the smell of rice and cypress. It was dark yet the monk was crouched down by the fire, watching the rice pan. Rubbing his eyes, Honda saw the face of his mother-doll staring at him from the flames.

'You're back,' said Honda.

'Yes.'

Winter ended and the valley returned.

Spring, summer and autumn passed. They went and begged for rice. Honda began collecting wood earlier. He had lost a lot of weight, and his muscles were becoming defined. He was starting to look like a man. He asked again for the monk to teach him the secrets of Zen. You cannot teach a man to be tall, said the monk.

Snow began to fall. The rice jar was full and the logs were stacked.

'Is it to be the same?'

'Yes.'

And it was. Winter ran its course as it had the year before. This time Honda didn't think about it. He carved another set of dolls, each better than the last, his skill progressing. The monk disappeared, for longer this time, but returned, the same as before. Honda woke to find him burning his dolls.

'Why do you burn them?'

'Why do you carve idols of your family?'

'I miss them.'

'That is why I burn them.'

Spring came, cherry blossom. Rain, heat, typhoons. Leaves changed. Snow fell.

'Is it to be the same?'

'No.'

And it wasn't. Honda carved another set of dolls. Despite his intentions, they all still resembled his family. The monk disappeared and never returned. Spring, summer, autumn. No rice in the jars. No wood. Honda burned each doll himself. The smallest, the last doll, was of Honda. As the empty shell burned Honda walked to the city.

I look over Honda's shoulder at the row of Russian dolls, each unpainted, each in half, each with a completely blank face.

—What happened to the monk, I begin. The ...mud, disappearing... do you think that's what happened to me?

—It sounds like it, but I'm not sure. You're hardly a monk, are you? I mean, you're not even particularly spiritual.

Which is fair enough.

—What did the monk tell you about where he went?

—Nothing. Well, nothing directly. It was clearly his aim to disappear completely. That's why I left. I knew he wasn't coming back.

—Did he ever say why?

—No. The only time he ever referred to what happened, I didn't understand him.

—What did he say?

—I was pestering him to teach me something, anything, that might bring me closer to enlightenment. Some clue. He said 'I can't teach you. All knowledge comes from them. It is they who must teach you.'

—They?

—They. And, no, he never said anything else.

We fell silent. It couldn't be the same thing. Ok, the mud matches, but we don't know that I disappeared. How could I just disappear from my room? I was drunk and full of cheese flavour crisps, not deep in meditation high in the mountains. And anyway, even if it is the same thing, it doesn't answer anything. I still don't know where I went, what I did and why I came back covered in mud. I put this to Honda.

—Maybe.

—Maybe?

—I left Hokkaido and came here via many places, but I didn't forget. I've been doing some research.

He opened the laptop and handed it to me. The program he'd begun running when I'd arrived was complete.

—Look at the list of recurring themes.

—What am I looking for? There's a bunch of dreams about flying or falling, family, friends, Sapporo, the monk, Tokyo, fights, and sex gets a huge rating you dirty so-and-so.

—Any dogs? Any mountains?

—No, nothing.

—I thought so. When I lived with the monk I had one recurring dream, the one I mentioned earlier. The one about...

—The dogs inside the mountain, I finish for him.

—Yeah. The same one you have. Once the monk left the last time, so too did the dream. I've never had it since.

—I don't understand. What's the dream got to do with anything?

—I don't know, exactly.

—Exactly?

—I mean I have my suspicions, but I'm not sure of anything.

—Great, so we're no further along.

—Yes and no. I know someone who can answer these questions, but I can't ask him.

—Who? And why not?

—For one thing I'd never get anywhere near him. He's too well protected. But you could speak to him.

—Who?

—Your father.

It's too late to call or go, but I promise Honda I'll do it in the morning. Brains turned to tofu, we get bombed on sake and talk about anything but. He tells me stories of his life after the monk. All roads lead to Tokyo, and he wound up working as a bouncer in Shinjuku. Soul-drifting, caught up in the nightlife, the dark and the shadows. Years high in the highlands with only a monk for company, libido met Honda with open arms and wider legs in the narrow streets. He partook, dabbled, got stuck in. Late night noodles and early morning beers brought the weight back, and the strength got him noticed. Sleazy bars are owned by sleazy bar-owners, and lowlifes in high places need propping up and protecting from, so Honda got jobs, feet on the rungs, his bulk a boon on the greasy pole. Fate finds Honda behind the wheel, behind the tinted, bullet-proof glass of expensive imported cars. No Hondas for Honda, only top of the line Mercs. But.

You can take the boy out of the past, but you can't take the past out of the boy.

Fact: Honda is the only man in history to be laughed out of the yakuza.

While senior yakuza will never tire of telling junior thugs there is only one way to leave, in truth, there are two. Sure, for hardmen, raised by threats, educated by knuckles, death may seem the easier, but for Honda, raised in silence, educated by thought, laughter is nothing to fear.

Honda waits outside the pachinko parlour that is a front for more serious forms of fun, while Boss meets and greets a debtor. Judging by the Toolbox, this will be a long meeting with lots of friendly greeting, so Honda decides to spruce the car. Interior cleared and freshened, the outer is dusty thanks to an earlier off road drop off, but Honda lacks a suitable duster. But! What's this! He spies the parlour's cleaning trolley and finds onboard the very thing.

Just then another tinted import pulls up and the troops pile out with mischief uppermost in their minds. At the same time the parlour's back door opens and Boss plus entourage emerge. Rivals all, their eyes meet over the sparkling roof, but before violence can enliven the day, they catch sight of Honda, all umpteen suited kilos of him, polishing the bonnet of the Bosses chariot with an impressive pink feather duster. Laughter diffuses and defuses. Imports go their separate ways, but back at base Honda is let go. You can't kill someone for making you laugh, but nor can you have a clown driving you around town.

Realising the luck he's been dealt, Honda forswears the outlaw life, takes an evening class in computing and avoids tinted windows though not feather dusters.

—What would the monk think of your life since he left?

—He'd do what everyone else does: laugh.

Drunk, I doze off. The last thing I see before my eyes close is the row of seven Russian dolls, blank and empty, ranked like an illustration of evolution small to large; and after the seventh sits Honda, smiling at his past, happy.

A previous chapter of this novel was published in Gutter/01

More Death in Venice
Stuart Finlayson

I AM SITTING in the highest, quietest bar on the ferry, watching Britain sink into the waters excruciatingly slowly. Even global warming should be faster than this. Running away from home by coach and ferry is not the cleverest plan, but quick to leave means quick to return. No airport employee would strike long enough for the stay I require. I know I have to go back, just don't make it easy for me.

I'm still sober when we reach Zeebrugge. As the coach tour moves out of the low countries along the Rhine, I see that I am the youngest person on the tour. All the old men, peaceful, near death, I am not like them yet. Southern Germany is a succession of medieval villages penned by concrete and steel. If you looked through a small enough window you would find it pretty. One of these towns was home to Faust as he spun his potions, dreaming of industrial might and Elizabeth Taylor before she was fat.

I find myself being stalked by a woman in her late fifties called Nancy; fifteen years older than me, she is one of the younger travellers, and not unappealing. While she seems to have a husband (father? no) I imagine that if we got drunk enough I might sleep with her. That is the sort of thing they doubtless do in Germany. But the tour company does not allow drinking on the coach, and everyone would go to bed by 8.30 even if they did not take a moving slumber in the seats that are also our bunks.

We spin south, skirting the Alps, where the skiing season has already begun. I used to ski when I was younger, throwing myself down a mountain in brightly-coloured clothes,

feigning a flourish of skill in every ostentatious flick and turn, while loving death's closeness. Every bump ahead you hope will open out into a cliff-topped chasm. But skiing is not a viable pastime when you have young children, and I would not like to return to it and find myself useless.

Vienna, imperial city. Like most features on this trip, the Blue Danube appears to not exist. It is merely a creation of some fabulist waltzer. There are apparently lyrics: 'Viennese, be gay. Oh, why?' it begins. I do not want to see ponies or choirboys, so I utter a few words to Nancy and we head to the Egon Schiele museum. All modern art is a movement from decoration to pornography. Munch taunted himself with cunt he could not have; Manet was ironic; but Schiele is like a schoolboy scratching tits and pussies on a desk. His nudes are redundant; his self-portraits unconvincing; to his dreamy tortured image, I reply, 'Bullshit! You were slyly negotiating with porn dealers and trying to fuck underage girls. You're no more tortured than Ron Jeremy.'

I try to talk to Nancy about sex but she is principally enchanted by the colours and the tiny scribbles that form a face out of a village-map of lines. The real difference between art and pornography is that people look at art with their clothes on. As we wander back to the coach, through Hapsburg follies arrayed like the contents of a wedding magazine, I think about my wife. I have not seen her for around a year, except once briefly without words. In one

➡

of those clothes stores where you have to walk through the women's department to get out of menswear I glimpsed her holding a long grey skirt up against her hips in the mirror, and I thought about her legs.

When we reboard the coach we find Nancy's husband has not yet shown up, so she sits beside me for a moment to talk. She asks me why I am here. She suspects that I am on the run. I tell her that I killed a woman in a sado-masochistic game, just loudly enough for the people behind me to almost mishear. Eventually her other half struggles up on board, breathing heavily as if he were a car trying to start, collapsing up the front. She slides up to sit beside him like a snake over rocks. In fact, she is more like a carrier bag blowing through trees.

We come to Verona, a beautiful city shaped like a hernia in the foothills of the Alps. I try to find a horse-meat butcher and buy some horse-meat sausages. My son is a vegetarian and my daughter likes ponies. Children are much more virtuous than adults. Except when they're being shits. There would be no morality without children. Nancy is busy with her husband, talking in whispers as though they are in church. I read J M Coetzee's *Disgrace* to try and cheer myself up, although the rape is unsatisfying. I do not want to read about a place so far away and more primitive even than Lanarkshire. I brought so many books, but none of them seem right.

For instance, *Death in Venice* does not tell you how to kill anybody in any Italian city. Mann's novel is not even set on the main island; the protagonist von Aschenbach stays at a beach resort across the lagoon. My paperback edition is so thin and floppy it is like an old man's penis, which I assume is unintentional. It is also damp and slightly musty.

Arriving in Venice, you spill out into the Piazzale Roma, third-largest car park in Europe. Who counts these things? The city doesn't smell as bad as I expect. Probably rich Americans have taken some form of action. Perhaps they have a million photocopiers pumping out fresh sea smell.

Whatever the odour, I cannot take any more of the museum atmosphere. I am sick of history, culture, a world that doesn't do anything. Even Vienna had supermarkets and squat ugly office blocks, but nothing has been built in Venice since Napoleon was still at the age of snowball fights. I skip the churches and galleries and catch the ferrybus off the main island to wander the beaches near the Hotel Des Bains. Here they have cars, and the sea has waves. But it's out of season and most things are closed, including the hotel about which Mann wrote.

Between the beach-huts like birdhouses I look out to the Adriatic Sea. Perhaps I am hoping to find an illegal immigrant woman washed up on a lilo floated from some corner of the former Yugoslavia. However, toxic algal blooms have probably clogged her oars and pulled her down with the pearls and fragments of galleons. I am unsure if they still have pearls, but they are produced by foreign bodies in the oyster, so surely it is a boom-time.

I sit on the sand, which I have not done for a long time. Clouds are turning darker. Other people are walking up and down, though it is too cold for most beach pursuits. I think it is going to rain, and it does. I watch the rain splashing onto the sand, forming little hard discs like drawing pin heads. I do not notice that everyone else has left the beach until I look up and see a woman peering cautiously at me as though I might be drunk. She is dark haired, I guess a few years younger than me, a little too thin, wearing a long skirt and shawl of the sort that were fashionable a little while ago.

I say, 'Buona sera.' She does not open her mouth. I feel immensely irritated by the way she stands over me and I try to rise to my feet but slip again in the wet sand. She does not laugh, even. I brush off my trouserlegs and then wipe my hands on them. She cannot understand any of the languages I speak to her in – Italian, French, German, English, Czech. I cannot tell her, 'Suck my dick or I will call the immigrations secretariat.' I opt to remain seated on the beach as the rain continues, hoping my obstinacy will annoy her.

Without words or exactly touching we find

ourselves in a hotel room booked quickly in an off-season resort. Before I try to speak again I notice I am tied to the bed with strips of cloth torn from my shirt. I tell myself these are bonds I could surely break if I wanted to run. I feel like Samson in some part, at some stage in his history. Was he not chained to a pillar? I do not test my ties. I cannot delineate any one touch of her body on mine. All I know is that I feel it all together, as though what is inside is that which is outside, like being flayed. Except pleasurable, but who is to say that the pain of being close to death does not move into joy, just as exquisite agony does in closeness to orgasm?

When I return to the coach party I observe a commotion of up-pitched voices and flapping jackets. I hear that one of the American men has collapsed in a church before the grave of Titian. Nobody knows if he is dead, but his wife or widow, Nancy, is standing talking to the rep and has not followed his body. Here they empty the bins by gondola and the cemetery sits in the lagoon between tourist traps. We cannot leave yet. Venice is the sort of place that knows about detritus. They could shore up the sinking islets with skeletons and second-rate art and we would be taller than the Alps.

I do not speak to Nancy all evening, and there is confusion and babble everywhere. We must stay another night or two and the excursion to Rome and Pompeii may be cancelled; but because our rooms here are double-booked, at least we are upgraded to a drier establishment. As we are being led to our new beds in a mass of tired leisurewear, word seeps that Nancy's husband is dead. Although two or three people try to speak to me about the day's events I only want to bury my face in the pillow and yawn.

The following day I consider visiting one of the churches, just out of curiosity, but it seems inappropriate. Perhaps I fear that like Nancy's husband I too will be struck down by God. Instead I find myself once more on the noisy, packed waterbus sailing to von Aschenbach's island. I sit by the Lido boat halt. It looks so ugly all of a sudden, the dusty muddy roads, the square buildings, the crumbling walls, the stunted palm trees with their violently

protruding leaves. I wish the lagoon was full of cement. Cement sets under water.

Then I feel a hand over my mouth and I stop breathing. Airless, stillness, I close my eyes. Release comes and I look at her, still thinking of death. I want the hotel, not even to be tied up, just to wash in scalding water and listen to her not speaking. Yet we walk past them all, her just ahead of me across the island to the beach. As we stand on the sand I point up towards the tourist district, gesticulating, looking like an idiot. She doesn't reply or react to my pantomime. She sits on the beach and I kneel facing her.

Her hands reach out and touch my body through my shirt. She takes my wrists between her fingers and places them on her shoulders, the heels nudging into the softness of her breasts. People walk past us kicking up sand. The sky is clear. She moves my hands down over her. An old Italian couple are standing a little way along eating sandwiches. My palms run over her breasts, rubbing her nipples. Her eyes are narrowed, like against the sun, and dark. Our hands slide down to her lap.

A hundred greying tourists seem to stare like crows on a phone-line as she forces my finger against her cunt, her body rising up against my hand pressing into coarse, dark fabric. A muffled outline below is hinted to my touch like a shadow in the water. I feel it enveloping; she is hot volcanic mud I could pass my hand through, push it up inside her as the fabric parted like fog. Finally it's too much and my hand falls. Her mouth opens: 'Do you want me to say to you who I am?'

I nod. Then pause. She tells me in firm but stop-starting English, 'I was professor of the literature of South East Europe. And what use is that?' When I shrug she pushes me over and I remember her hands on my body. 'I throw you in the sea. You sail back to Shqiperia and do my job.'

I ask her who she studied and she tells me about the great novelist Ibrahim Ukaj and his classic *The Goat And The Machine Gun*. 'It is based on a folk tale,' she says. 'Back in the war of 1912, the soldiers of our country were under

➡

attack from very bigger Serbian army. Being desperate, our most clever general decided to deceive the enemy by dressing goats in army uniforms and putting guns around the necks of the goats. The trick worked and our men were able to escape. Our men were very happy and had a big party with much fermented milk. Then the goats ran off and joined the Serbian side. It is very moral fable.'

Later I will look up her author in the *Companion to World Literature*, and find no mention of him. Probably this is because he is not judged of international importance. 'Never give a firearm to a vegetarian,' I say, although I think her story is about us fighting our own wars: a tired message even with mountain-skipping mammals.

I tell her, 'Somebody died on the coach today. You could come back if you're prepared to be an elderly man, dead and risen.'

She is unenthusiastic. 'Ha. Sorry. I have come back much from being dead.'

I reply, 'I died for you yesterday, bound to the bed.' I look out over the lagoon, wondering what sickly fish live in its depths between the sewage and corpses, and tell her, 'Your wife is nice.'

We part as sensible adults. She will probably make it to Britain sometime; I will look out for her but she will still take me by surprise. The sun is setting over the lagoon, falling into milky fog so much paler than her skin. The red ball fades into whiteness long before it reaches the horizon, like an overexposed photograph. I disappear over the lagoon back to St Mark's Square and the land behind me vanishes.

At the new hotel, an old American gentleman wearing a fishing hat tells me we will leave tomorrow for France. He explains that he dislikes the French because of their indifference to good American beefsteak. I nod and eat rubbery veal; the thought of little dead calves mooing stupidly is no consolation. That night I dream of water and quicklime.

As we leave, I notice how many of the buildings are marked with graffiti. At Europe's third-largest car park we board the coach. I get on early and I watch Nancy on the steps deal awkwardly with the tour guide, rejecting sympathy and touches on the arm. I am surprised that Nancy chooses to sit beside me and I ask her, 'Where have you been all this time? With your husband's body?'

'No,' she says slowly. 'I went to the museums. This city was set up by a raggedy bunch of refugees on the run from the Vandals or Huns or Goths or… They ran to the faraway places they could get to, out in the marsh almost in the sea, and they built a city. Soon they ruled the seas – long before you folk. Their admirals beat the unbeatable Turkish fleet and saved Europe. Their armies challenged the Pope's armies. They stole bodies of saints from the Middle East to put in their churches, and metal horses. They funded great art and impossibly golden palaces. And slowly they declined, like the Romans.'

As the coach pulls away, Nancy continues, saying, 'Last night I thought I wanted to take hold of the steering wheel and pull the bus into the canals, yeah? Are we going anywhere near the canals? I guess not, jeez. In the olden days lots of people must have killed themselves in the canal. Merchants whose ships had sunk and who'd pawned all the rings on their fingers to bloodthirsty Shylocks. Women whose husbands had drowned, their fingernails chewed to the blood already. These waters have swallowed so many bodies, the boatmen fishing them out on the edge of the lagoon. And just thinking about all those people who've been and died here, it made me decide… Well, let's say for now, you're safe. If we can trust that fellow in the driving seat.' She smiles and I chuckle and the bus bounces like a kangaroo.

We will drive Nancy to Marco Polo airport and put her and her husband on the plane, her real husband, not a woman in disguise. I decide to go home as well, much as I decided to leave a little over two weeks ago. I will ride on to Milan and Nice and up to Paris and back to Britain where many things will happen that I am indifferent to, and perhaps in time some new city will rise out of the waters clad in both starfish and skeletons. In my mind I question her as to whether she loves her husband, then, now, ever. But I do not open my mouth.

'And David said on that day, Whosoever getteth up to the gutter, and smiteth the Jebusites, and the lame and the blind that are hated of David's soul, he shall be chief and captain. Wherefore they said, "The blind and the lame shall not come into the house".'

2 Samuel 5: 8

Sashimi
Martyn Murphy

THE WAITER BOWS and leaves as I wave away the knife and fork – the proffered presumption of Western incompetence. In the Land of the Rising Sun it's chopsticks or nothing, just like I promised myself. With my maiden manicure and straightened hair, it is time for change.

Clear chutes burble with water as they curve around the cool restaurant walls. There are few customers but in the centre a dark haired mother and son sit by a circular pool as the father stands slightly apart. The boy dips his rod in the water while the mother is at his side with words of encouragement and a yellow net – just in case. I gaze at them, unsure who to envy more; the child with devoted mother, or she maternally complete.

The waiter has already relieved me of my catch and removed it to the kitchen – a peachy little oval that could have graced any nature program swimming through golden waters. Within the swooping shoal it might have evaded its predators but here, alone, the fish was no match for my little rod. The thought that the small pool was designed to give the creature no chance makes me uneasy and I try to comfort myself that its life was already condemned regardless of my intrusion.

I am ignorant of the dish, but doubt Sashimi will involve a crust of batter and serving of chips like the suppers eaten on childhood trips to Ayr. In Marino's, my mother and sister would sit together, demolishing their fish, and chatter about jewellery and haircuts and clothes. I moved peas about the plate and gazed out the window, looking for the sea. I find that I'm tugging the ends of my hair towards my mouth but manage to alter the action and curl it round my ear. My mother had hated that I chewed on it. Why couldn't I be more like Emily?

Even in the fifth month of pregnancy she was perfect. At the graveside with Daniel by her, Emily had been striking in her grief, letting fall a single tear from beneath her veil. When the coffin had been lowered to the ground, bowed mourners passed me by to offer her their sympathies. Afterwards, Daniel surprised me by offering to take us for a meal. He drove us in the company car, but Emily claimed exhaustion and we stopped at the nearest pub. I realised then that the invitation had been a token gesture I hadn't been meant to accept.

She insisted on a table near the fire and as far as possible from the other patrons, some of whom, she whispered, were looking covetously at their labelled clothes. Daniel asked for the menus and ordered immediately. In the fifteen minutes it took for the meals to come their heads craned and peered like gulls', appraising the room for scavenge.

'This is disgusting. It's microwaved,' hissed Emily when the food arrived.

Daniel nodded but continued to chew. My burger wasn't half-eaten before they rested their cutlery.

'Why didn't you come more?' I asked.

They exchanged glances.

'This is just like you,' said Emily leaning over the table.

'What?'

'Always thinking about yourself. It never occurred to you that Daniel and I have lives of our own now. We are a married couple you know.'

She sat back and I followed her hand as she caressed the curve of her belly. When I looked up I saw she was watching me.

'You could still have visited,' I said.

'Daniel. I can't deal with this. I just can't. This is how she is. What I told you about.'

'Isn't it about time,' said Daniel, looking at me sternly, 'that you grew up a bit? You can't keep relying on Emily.'

'Daniel, it's not her fault. Not really,' she said, cutting him off before I could. 'She was spoiled. Always the favourite. She never learned. But, oh, how could you?' she said, turning to me. 'How could you? Just when I've buried my mother.'

She allowed her face to crumple, flapping her hand before it, feigning to ward off tears.

'Daniel, take me home. Please.'

He put a stiff arm around her, the only time I'd seen them touch, and glared at me as he led Emily away. That was the last we spoke.

A splash rouses me. By the little pool the woman claps as a fish wriggles on her son's line. He squints away from the spray and lofts the trophy before his father who acknowledges it with a nod. The waiter, who carries three dishes, bypasses the scene on route to my table. He places a bowl of Miso and a serving of rice before me.

'Domo arigato,' I say pleased to have remembered something from 'Japanese for Beginners' - the compensation I'd granted myself for sacrificing university. He puts down the last dish, bows again and leaves. I blink at it. The fish's flesh has been removed, sliced into diamond slivers and spread raw across one half of the plate. On the other side rests the body. Tail, fins, head, eyes and mouth are all completely intact, everything but the undercoat of meat.

I am repelled by the sight of it and look away; the obvious solution to devour the evidence, my pledge to embrace new experience a feeble retort. The cuts are so precise that, for a moment, I wonder if it would not be possible to piece them all together and set the fish back to swimming in its little pool. But my guilt cannot be so easily assuaged. I fumble for the chopsticks and return my attention to the creature that lies before me.

The mouth is moving.

It blows soft kisses at me.

Then comes the memory of my mother after the stroke. The sink overflows once more as she lies on pale-lit bathroom tiles; a film of water spread about her, strands of hair wavering like reeds.

My mask of composure crumbles. I wipe moisture from the corner of my eye and prepare to call back the waiter, but realise I lack the words. I need the knife and fork. It would be easier to finish the creature off, stabbing the skull or sawing away the head. Perhaps I should push a chopstick through its eye, surely that would do. I roll my tongue along the roof of my mouth to moisten it. I'm on my own again, in my mother's cramped flat, the place where I washed her and fed her and took her to the toilet. Just me and her, together.

Why couldn't I be more like Emily?

My arm is unreal. It trembles as I grip the chopsticks and confront the plate. The past comes in like a tide, empty as before, threatening to drag me under. I pinch my thigh, hard – pain the final buttress against despair. Still it lies there. Waiting.

Later, at night I exit onto the narrow street. It is dark, dotted with dim paper lanterns. The hotel is only a short way to the right. I go left. A bell chimes and I advance more quickly, racing my courage to the end of the road. The pulse of the city insinuates itself as a growing tremor of the air. Ahead the alley runs out below a red torii. Through the gate, a fusion of melting colour and boisterous sound begins to take shape. Heat wafts into my face. I walk on.

Passing through, there is an eruption of neon, with banners and J-Pop and posing Shinjuku girls clamouring for attention. Katakana figures stride through the air, entwined by moonlit Hiragana curls. Skyscrapers shower glitter and a red sun fires. I gasp at the uproar. A rogue-smiled rider meets my eye, rumbling

→

past at the head of a Yamaha convoy with bold flags flowing in its wake. The city drums roll. Taking the napkin from my pocket I hold it aloft, letting it unfold. Two small sticks fall out. I won't need them anymore.

Contributor Biographies

Dorothy Alexander is a writer and creative writing tutor who lives in the Scottish Borders. dorothyalexander.co.uk

Josh Byer is currently sleeping. A resident of Canada, he enjoys apologizing. His poetry can be read on shithouse walls.

Jen Campbell 23, graduated from Edinburgh University last summer and currently lives in London. Her work has appeared in *Poetry London, Flash: The International Short-Short Story Magazine, Short* FICTION and *The Times*. She's currently finishing her first book *The Aeroplane Girl & Other Stories*, which you can hear her talk about on BBC Radio Scotland. jen-campbell.blogspot.com

Elaine diRollo was born in Ormskirk, Lancashire. At school she was effortlessly mediocre, but somehow managed to get into Edinburgh University. She stayed there for 11 years and after a number of wrong turns eventually emerged with a PhD in the social history of medicine. These days she lectures in Marketing at Edinburgh Napier University. She has two children. Her debut novel *A Proper Education for Girls* was published in 2009.

John Douglas Millar is a poet and art writer based in London. He was born in Scotland in 1981, and studied Literature at the University of Glasgow. He is currently working on a book about the Dutch film-maker Renzo Martens.

Tracey Emerson began writing fiction after a career in theatre and community arts. In 2004 she was a runner up in the *Scotsman* and Orange Short Story Prize and has continued to have short stories published in magazines and anthologies. She's currently undertaking a PhD in Creative Writing and seeking representation for her first novel, *The End of The Habitable World*.

Sally Evans's books include *Bewick Walks to Scotland, The Honey Séller*, based round a group of Stirling Castle poems, and her long poem *The Bees*, illustrated by Reinhard Behrens. She is a gardener, beekeeper, bookseller, facebooker and editor, and she has lived in Scotland since 1979. She is delighted to be considered of suitable standard for The Gutter! desktopsallye.com poetryscotland.co.uk

Jenni Fagan's debut poetry collection *Urchin Bélle* sold out on Blackheath Books. The hardback is available from Kilmog Press in New Zealand. She is published in the UK, USA, Europe, India. Her new poetry collection *The Dead Queen of Bohemia* is due out soon. Jenni is writer in residence at Lewisham Hospital. She has just completed her novel *The Panopticon*.

Andrew C Ferguson is a writer and musician based in Fife. He performs regularly with Writers' Bloc, the Edinburgh spoken word collective. A chapbook of football stories, *The Secret of Scottish Football*, is available via writers-bloc.org.uk. A pamphlet of chess poetry co-written with Jane McKie, *Head to Head*, is available from knuckerpress.com. Like most poets he does Facebook, and can also be heard on myspace.com/andrewcferguson.

Andrew Elliott was born in 1961. His collection *Lung Soup* was published in 2009.

Jim Ferguson is a poet and prose writer based in Glasgow. Jim has been writing and publishing since 1986 and is presently tutor with Easterhouse Writers' Group in Glasgow's East End. His collection *the art of catching a bus and other poems* is published by AK Press, Edinburgh. He has a spoken word CD entitled *QUIRKY*.

Stuart Finlayson was born and raised in Edinburgh, and shows no sign of leaving. He studied at Edinburgh, Leeds, and Napier, and most recently creative writing with the Open University. He is currently writing a novel about white goods.

Ronald Frame's most recent novel is *Unwritten Secrets* (April, 2010). Many of his short stories have been broadcast on Radios 3 and 4. Several collections have been published, and stories appear regularly in newspapers and magazines here and in the USA and Australia. [He also writes drama for radio.] Read more at his website carnbeg.com

Hazel Frew's poems have been published widely in magazines and anthologies including *New Writing Scotland*, *Orbis* and *The Rialto*. Her poems have been translated into German, Arabic and Italian. Her chapbook *Clockwork Scorpion* was published by Rack Press in 2007 and *Seahorses*, her first full length collection, by Shearsman in 2008.

Graham Fulton lives in Paisley. His published collections include *Humouring the Iron Bar Man* (Polygon) *Knights of the Lower Floors* (Polygon) *This* (Rebel Inc) *Ritual Soup and other liquids* (Mariscat Press) and *twenty three umbrellas* (Controlled Explosion Press). New collections called *Open Plan* and *Upside Down Heart* are on the way from Smokestack Books and Controlled Explosion Press.

Ewan Gault has previously won The Fish Crime Writing Prize and had stories appear in *Gutter*, *NWS* and various other anthologies. He's just completed a novel set in a Kenyan athletic camp in the weeks before the violently disputed election of 2007. After living abroad for a few years he is thinking about coming home.

Barry Gornell was born in Liverpool and now lives on the West Coast of Scotland. He is a screenwriter and ex-fire-fighter, truck driver and book shop manager. His short films *Sonny's Pride* (1997) and *The Race* (2004) were both broadcast on Scottish Television. His short fiction has been published in *The Herald* newspaper and *Let's Pretend, 37 stories about (in)fidelity* (Freight, 2009). Barry graduated from the University of Glasgow's Creative Writing Masters programme in 2008 and was awarded a Scottish Book Trust New Writer's Bursary in 2009.

Graham Hardie's poetry has been in *Markings*, *The David Jones Journal*, *Weyfarers*, *Cutting Teeth*, *Cake*, *Nomad*, *The New Writer*, *The Coffee House* and online at nthposition.com. Later this summer five of his poems will be translated into Turkish and published online at soylesipoetrymagazine.com/about/ His first collection was published in 2007 by Ettrick Forest Press efpress.com. He is 38 and lives near Glasgow.

Aiko Harman is a Los Angeles native now living in Scotland where she completed an MSc in Creative Writing from the University of Edinburgh. Aiko's poetry is in *Anon*, *Fusélit* and *The Edinburgh Review*, among others. She won the 2009 Grierson Verse Prize and the William Hunter Sharpe memorial scholarship in creative writing. More about Aiko at: lionandsloth.com

Colin Herd lives in Edinburgh, where he co-edits *anything anymore anywhere* and reviews fiction for 3:AM magazine, poetry in the blog of *Chroma Journal* and exhibitions for *Aesthetica*. Recent poems have appeared in Shampoo, 3:AM, *Pop Serial* and *Vélvét Mafia*. colin-herd.com

Adam Hofbauer is a resident of San Francisco, where he attends San Francisco State University. His work has most recently appeared in *Decameron*, *Kaleidótrope* and *The Emerson Review*.

Brian Johnstone has published two collections and two pamphlets. His second collection is *The Book of Bélongings* (Arc, 2009). His work has appeared throughout Scotland and in the UK, America and various European countries. *Terra Incognita*, a collection of his poems in Italian translation, was published in 2009. He is the poet member of Trio Verso, presenting poetry and jazz.

Bridget Khursheed is a poet and geek based in the Scottish Borders. Published widely in magazines including *The Eildon Tree*, *Poétry Scótland*, *The Rialto*, *Trespass* and *The Shop*, her work also appears in *New Writing Scótland 27*.

Carl MacDougall has written three prize-winning novels, four pamphlets, three collections of short stories, two works of non-fiction and has edited four anthologies, including the best selling *The Devil and the Giro*. He has written and presented two television series and is currently working on too many things.

Rob A. Mackenzie is from Glasgow. His first full collection, *The Opposite of Cabbage,* was published by Salt in 2009. HappenStance Press published an earlier pamphlet collection, *The Clown of Natural Sorrow*, in 2005. He organises the monthly 'Poetry at the...GRV' reading series in Edinburgh, where he lives and works.

Micaela Maftei lives in Glasgow

Iain Maloney began life in Aberdeen, but is now a permanent feature of the Japanese landscape. He is a graduate of Glasgow University's Creative Writing MLitt. This is the second extract from his novel, *Dog Mountain*, to appear in *Gutter*. The novel, a magical realist thriller, deals with modern life, history and mythology through the experiences of two men. It features both dogs and mountains, sometimes together.

Richie McCaffery (born 1986) holds an MLitt in Scottish Literature. His poems have appeared, or are due to appear, in a range of places such as *Magma*, *Envoi* and *Horizon Review*. He is also the grateful recipient of a Scottish Arts Council Edwin Morgan Travel Bursary which he used to tour the Hebrides, writing along the way.

Marion McCready lives in the Clydeside town of Dunoon. She studied Classics, Politics and Philosophy at Glasgow University and has had poems published in various magazines including *Poétry Scótland*, *The Herald*, *The Edinburgh Review* and *Anon*. Calder Wood Press will be publishing a pamphlet of her poems early next year.

JoAnne McKay really was born to a family of slaughterers in Romford, Essex. Unexpected love has seen her living in a small village in Dumfriesshire for the past twelve years, where she combines motherhood and work with mixed success. Her first pamphlet, *The Fat Plant*, was published in 2009. She has read at The London Poetry and Wigtown Book Festivals.

Kirsten McKenzie was born in 1975 and worked as a Scottish Government press officer before completing at MLitt in Creative Writing at the University of St Andrews. Her first novel, *Chapel at the Edge of the World*, was shortlisted for the Saltire First Book of the Year award. Her second novel, *The Captain's Wife*, is published on 5 August 2010.

Donal McLaughlin is a Derry-born writer and translator and has lived in Scotland since 1970. His debut collection – *an allergic reaction to national anthems & other stories* – appeared last autumn. donalmclaughlin.wordpress.com

Hugh McMillan lives and works in Dumfries and Galloway. Last year his *Postcards from the Hedge* won the Callum MacDonald prize and this year *Devorgilla's Bridge* was shortlisted for the Michael Marks Award. Both these publications are by Roncadora Press. His latest full poetry collection, *The Lost Garden* (Roncadora Press) is an absolute stotter and everyone should buy it.

Martyn Murphy is a previously unpublished writer from Glasgow. He has studied at the University of Strathclyde and Glasgow Caledonian University. Martyn is currently working on his first novel.

Ewan Morrison is the author of *The Last Book You Read* (Chroma, 2005), *Swung* (Jonathan Cape, 2006) and *Distance* (Jonathan Cape, 2008). *Ménage*, his third novel, was published by Jonathan Cape in July 2009. He lives in Glasgow.

Donald S Murray comes from the Isle of Lewis but works in Shetland. His books include *The Guga Hunters* (Birlinn) and *Small Expectations* (Two Ravens Press). His next book is *And On This Rock; The Italian Chapel, Orkney* (Birlinn) will appear in October. He will be appearing at the Edinburgh Book Festival on 30th August 2010 with the celebrated writer, Will Self.

Stephen Nelson has recently appeared in *Chapman, Shadowtrain* & *Poetry Scotland*. His visual poetry chapbook is available from *this is visual poetry*. He sings in an unknown language & throws words & images on to a screen at afterlights.blogspot.com

Colette Paul's debut short-story collection was *Whoever You Choose to Love* (Phoenix, 2005). A specialist in short form, she won the Royal Society of Authors Short Story Prize 2005 and has had her work serialised on Radio 4. She teaches creative writing at Anglia Ruskin University and her academic work explores the framework of narratology.

Mary Paulson-Ellis's fiction has appeared in a number of anthologies including *New Writing Scotland*. She is a Hawthornden Fellow and has an MLitt in Creative Writing from the University of Glasgow. In 2009 she was shortlisted for the Sceptre Prize and won the inaugural Curtis Brown Prize. In 2010 she was Writer in Residence at the Royal High School, Edinburgh.

Chris Powici is a poet, teacher and recently appointed editor of *Northwords Now*. His poetry has appeared in various magazines and anthologies including BBC *Wildlife, New Writing Scotland, Albatross* and *Flashquake*. A collection of his poems, *Somehow This Earth*, was published by Diehard in 2009. He lives in Dunblane with the writer Helen Lamb.

Eveline Pye was widely published in poetry magazines in the nineties, mostly writing about the Zambian Copper Mines and her passion for all things numerate. She spent the intervening years in the hinterland – the Mathematics Department at Glasgow Caledonian University – but started writing poetry again last year and is now mentored by Liz Lochhead under the Clydebuilt Scheme.

➼

Elizabeth Reeder writes fiction (short, long, for radio) and lyrical essays. Her work has been published/broadcast by *Kenyon Review*, BBC *Radio4*, *Fodors*, PN *Review*. She teaches on the Creative Writing Programme at University of Glasgow. ekreeder.com

Elizabeth Rimmer is a poet, an occasional translator and writer on ecological issues and spirituality.

Mark Ryan Smith lives in Shetland with his wife and two young children. He works in the Shetland Archives and is a part-time PhD student at Glasgow University, studying the literature of his native isles. His writing has appeared in the *New Shetlander*, the *Glasgow Herald*, and PN *Review*. His pamphlet *Midnight and Tarantélla* was published in 2008.

Michael Stephenson lives in Bathgate. His poems have previously been published in *Poetry Scotland*, *Ironstone*, *The Red Wheelbarrow* and *New Writing Scotland*.

Zoë Strachan is an award-winning novelist. Her most recent piece of work is the libretto for a short opera, *Sublimation*, performed as part of Scottish Opera's Five:15 season in 2010. She lives in Glasgow where she is co-writing a stage play – *Panic Patterns* – with her partner, Louise Welsh. You can find out more at zoestrachan.com

E.P. Teagarden took writing seriously for several years, with mixed results. Since deciding to take writing less seriously, E.P.'s work is most definitely on the up.

Jacqueline Thompson was born in Arbroath and graduated from Dundee University in 2009 where she is now studying for an MLitt in Creative Writing. She has had her work in *New Writing Dundee*, *For A' That* (a Dundee University Press anthology celebrating Burns), and recently featured as 'Poem of the Month' in *The Scotsman*.

Kate Tough has a Scottish Arts Council bursary to complete her novel, *Critical Mass*. She's also writing a humorous, non-fiction book and has had many short stories and poems published. Since gaining a Masters in Creative Writing, Kate has taught writing in various professional and community settings. In 2009, she was writer-in-residence at the Wigtown Book Festival.

Maggie Wallis lives in the Highlands with her family. Her work as a speech and language therapist has developed her appreciation of sound and meaning. She has been published in *Northwords Now*, *Poetry Scotland*, the *Glasgow Herald*, *Pushing out the Boat* and *Quadrant*. Most of her poetry arises from her relationship with the natural world.

Louise Welsh's fourth novel is *Naming the Bones* (Canongate Books). Her play *Memory Cells* will be on at the Pleasance as part of this year's Edinburgh Fringe and *Panic Patterns* (written with Zoe Strachan) will be on at The Citizens Theatre, Glasgow, 19th – 30th October. Louise is the recipient of several awards and her work has been translated into twenty languages. louisewelsh.com

Kevin Williamson's first collection of poetry, *In A Room Darkened*, was published in 2007 by Two Ravens Press. Before that he laboured long and hard in nuclear power stations, late night bars, psychiatric hospitals, and small publishing houses (same things really). He would like to use his inclusion in *Gutter 03* to further world peace, abolish work, and improve the lives of needy children in Wester Hailes.

Lesley Wilson grew up in Aberdeen and now lives in Edinburgh. She has had one novel published, *Summer Fever* and a scattering of short stories and novel extracts. She endeavours to put the 'literary' back into erotica à la Anais Nin and Alexander Trocchi. Publishers, sadly, maintain their scepticism, she her optimism.